WHEN FOREVERENDS

BLOOD SISTERS
BOOK THREE

ROBERTA KAGAN

ISBN (eBook): 978-1-957207-31-5
ISBN (Paperback): 978-1-957207-32-2
ISBN (Hardcover): 978-1-957207-33-9
ISBN (Large Print): 978-1-957207-34-6

Title Production by The Book Whisperer

DISCLAIMER

This is a work of fiction. Names, characters, businesses, places, events, and incidents are either the products of the author's imagination or used in a fictitious manner. Any resemblance to actual persons, living or dead, or actual events is purely coincidental.

PROLOGUE

Wolfgang Fischer, known affectionately as Ulf by his friends and family, stretched his arms above his head. Then straightened his back as he walked through the cellar of the home he'd been given as a reward for his loyal devotion to the Nazi party. Quite satisfied with his work in the cellar, a smile broke across his young, handsome face. It took some work to clean and prepare the area. And he'd been busy with his official assignment with the nazi party. Still, he'd done the preparations after hours, and now he'd completed all that had been required. *It's finished, and I think it will be perfect. It's almost ready. All I need is the cage, and I can bring home my special little guest.* He climbed the stairs quickly, for he was an agile man. His long muscular legs were sturdy. Once upstairs, he entered the living room and picked up the telephone receiver. He let out a deep breath, then dialed the operator. "Connect me to the Gestapo headquarters, extension 238," he said.

"Right away, Herr Fischer," a young female operator answered. There was a brief silence, followed by a ringing sound. Then a woman's voice answered the call, "Herr Fischer's desk." It was Wolfgang's secretary.

"Pipi, it's me, Ulf," he said in a casual, friendly tone.

"Hello, Ulf. What can I do for you?" Pipi said. As soon as she heard his voice, her own voice became warm and welcoming.

"I was wondering if you could do me a favor."

"Of course. What do you need?" She was an excellent secretary, always pleasant, and willing to work. Ulf knew she had always had a secret crush on him. But she just wasn't his type. He thought about her. *It's a pity for Pipi that I just don't have any romantic interest in her. She'd make a good Aryan hausfrau. And, of course, she sees me as a good provider. A man with the potential to rise in the party. I suppose I am the kind of fellow the girls were told to look for when they attended their little bund meetings.* He smiled at the thought.

"Ulf? Are you there?" Pipi asked, and he realized he had been so lost in thought he'd been silent for several moments. "Yes, I'm here. Sorry. I think something was wrong with our connection. But I'm here now." Then he cleared his throat. "Pipi, can you please take a moment and go downstairs to the basement of the building? I need you to check if there are any dog cages available. I would like to borrow one for a little while." Then he cleared his throat, "And, Pipi, make sure it's a large cage."

"Sure. Can you hold on for a minute, or shall I call you back?"

"Call me back."

"All right, give me a few minutes, and I will telephone you right back."

Ulf placed the receiver back in its cradle. Then he went into the kitchen and sat down at the table where he cut himself a nice thick slice of white bread that he'd purchased at the bakery on his way home from work earlier that day. It was fresh and soft, with a light, flaky crust. White bread like this was a luxury that very few German citizens were privileged to enjoy. But he was a high-ranking official in the Nazi party, working for the Gestapo. He didn't need to eat that terrible brown bread that the regular population of German people was told they must eat if they were loyal to the party. *That brown bread is made with sawdust.* He thought as he shook his head in disgust. Then he slathered a thick mound of real butter on to his bread. Another luxury denied the general population. Good food was a luxury. And good German *hausfraus* were taught to prepare meals with inferior ingredients these days so that better-quality food could be given to the soldiers who fought for the fatherland.

Although, Ulf knew that the better food never made it that far. It usually ended up on the tables of the higher-ranking Nazis. Still, every good German family was told they must make these sacrifices for their country. For a mere second, Ulf felt a slight pang of guilt when he thought about the brown bread and the loyal Germans who served it to their children. But the guilt was soon fleeting, and he grew tired of caring about anything. Once, he'd been devoted to Hitler and the Nazi vision for the Fatherland, but as time passed, he saw the faults in the Nazi party. Hitler did not keep his promises to the German people. He was a liar. And Ulf could see through him. So, now, Ulf was devoted to no other than himself and was not about to give up any luxuries he could acquire.

He'd just taken a bite of bread when the phone rang. He swallowed quickly. Then, after wiping his hand on a kitchen towel, he picked up the receiver. "*Hallo.*"

"Ulf, it's Pipi. I have good news. We have plenty of dog cages. And I'm sure there will be no problem if you want to borrow one."

"That's good. Very good."

"I don't mean to pry, but I never knew you liked dogs," she said.

"Oh yes, I do. I've always liked dogs." He was telling the truth. He loved dogs. But that had nothing to do with his plan. In a cheerful voice, he continued, "I always wanted one, but I never had one as a boy. My stepmother refused to have any animals in the house. She said they were too dirty. She was afraid their fur would get all over her furniture."

"I love dogs too," Pipi said. "I wouldn't care about fur on my furniture if my husband wanted a dog. I would allow him to have one, and then I would just clean more."

Ulf laughed a little, but sometimes she made him uncomfortable. No matter what he said, Pipi always agreed with him. So, her reaction to his getting a dog was no surprise. And she was always trying to entice him to ask her out. He pretended not to be aware of her intentions toward him. It was easier than telling her that he found her boring.

"Yes, well, I am quite excited about getting the dog," Ulf said.

"What kind are you getting?"

"A German Shepherd, of course."

"A puppy?"

"Yes." He was getting tired of her questions, but she was talking fast. He knew she didn't want to hang up the phone. She desperately tried to keep the conversation going, hoping it would result in him asking her to go out for a cup of coffee or a beer.

"Are you getting the puppy through the party?"

"No, no. Actually, a friend of mine has a bitch who is having puppies. I am going to take one."

"Well, good for you. I would love to visit your house once you have the dog. I'd love to see her."

"Yes, of course," he said. Now he was really ready to get off the phone. The last thing he wanted was to have to think of an excuse for why Pipi must never come to his home. So, before she could say another word, he said, "Well, thanks so much. Someone is at the door. I have to run. I'll see you tomorrow morning."

"Shall I bring the cage upstairs and put it in your office?"

"Yes, that would be perfect. I'll come in early, before work, and put it in my car."

"Perhaps if you're here early, we might have a coffee together? I can prepare some coffee and pick up some pastries if you'd like. I mean, since you are coming in early anyway and might not have time for breakfast."

"No, it's not necessary. Don't go through the trouble."

"It's really no trouble," she said. Her voice was shaking. Ulf knew her ego was on the line, and he could hear the hope in her voice. But she was starting to get on his nerves.

"Like I said, please don't bother. I am sorry, but I have to go now. Someone is knocking on my door."

"I'll see you tomorrow then. Have a nice evening."

"Yes, you too," he said as he hung up the phone.

What a pain the neck she can be. But this is good news. A dog cage is available, and I am sure I will have no trouble borrowing it. Now that this is taken care of, I can begin to set things into motion. His heart was racing with excitement. *All I have to do is call my twin brothers and ask them if they would like to come to my house and spend a little time with me. I will tell them that I would like them to help me with an important mission. They'll be excited to be included as a part of my life. And, because of my position with the Nazi party, I won't have trouble taking them out of school for a while. However, I must be very careful to make sure they must never find out the truth about the mission we are going to embark upon together. I don't think they would turn on me no matter what I did, but it would take too much explanation, and I would rather keep them innocent. For now, at least. They are still young and have yet to be corrupted by the horror of war. And they are still too young to appreciate the exhilaration that comes with absolute power. Well, it shouldn't be difficult to handle them. They will believe whatever I tell them. I am their big brother, after all, and they adore me. They've always wanted to be like me. Everything is falling into place.*

Ulf closed his eyes. He felt a surge of excitement run through him as he imagined the dog cage with Anna locked inside. His penis grew hard, and he ran his hand over it as a smile came over his face. *She will never escape from me again.*

CHAPTER ONE

1942, Rome, Italy

The woman's screams seemed to shake the very foundation of the house. And with each loud wail, Mateo Leoni felt as if his heart was about to stop beating. He leaned against the wall and covered his eyes with his forearm. *This is all my fault.* He thought. The doctor had warned him. The doctor had been adamant when he said that Mateo's wife, his beautiful precious Aria, was not to attempt childbirth ever again. They had tried once before, and Aria had a terrible, life-threatening miscarriage, after which the doctor warned Mateo. He said that Aria could not carry a child full term, and if she attempted this again, there was a good possibility she would die. Mateo was ready to give up on having children. He had been afraid of losing her, but Aria was young and stubborn. She refused to give up on motherhood. Even after the horrible recovery she'd endured. His wife wanted a baby. Her need for motherhood was so strong that she was willing to risk her life to try again. He assumed it was because she had been orphaned very early. He didn't know how her parents had died, but he knew she was raised by her

7

grandmother, a cold and practical woman. Aria longed for a family of her own because of this.

Mateo had spent hours talking to her softly, holding her hands, and trying his best to discourage her, but she was unwilling to listen. And then, despite his efforts to protect her, she'd become pregnant again. He had to admit that even though he was terrified of losing her, her joy as she carried the child had been contagious. He'd indulged her every wish, and he'd even been excited when she called him and said, "Mateo, put your hand here on my belly. Can you feel the baby move? I think that's his little foot kicking me." She would laugh, and her laughter rang through the room like church bells. But when he was alone at night, after Aria had fallen asleep, Mateo prayed. He was terrified. His mother had been religious, and she'd made sure that he'd grown up in the Catholic church. Even though he was not religious, he returned to church every Sunday and donated generously. He would try to bargain with God to allow his wife and child to survive.

Mateo insisted Aria make an appointment to see the doctor. "Let's just go and make sure everything is alright," Mateo said.

"But I feel good," Aria insisted. "I don't need a doctor."

"Indulge me, please," Mateo begged.

She nodded and made the appointment. Mateo accompanied her on her visit. Aria was excited when she entered the doctor's office. "I feel so good. I never felt this good when I was pregnant before," she said. But the doctor looked at her with pity in his eyes.

"You should never have gotten pregnant. *Signora* Leoni," the doctor said. "I told you this before."

Aria's joy turned to sorrow, and she began to cry.

Seeing the tears spill down his beautiful wife's cheeks, Mateo became angry. He knew it was displaced anger. He was an important man, well known in Rome as one of Mussolini's top men. This doctor had some nerve. No one should have dared to speak to him as the doctor had. He looked at the kind old man who shook his head. There was pain in his eyes, and Mateo knew that even though he could have had the doctor executed, he wouldn't. And that was because he knew in his heart that the doctor was right. So, instead of taking his anger out on the old man, Mateo took his wife home and tried his best to put the fear rising in his throat to rest by continuing to pray. Then a few days later, he was at a restaurant in town having a cup of strong coffee and saw an old friend he had known since childhood. The man walked over to him. "Mateo, it's good to see you, my friend."

"Likewise," Mateo said.

"How are you? I heard you got married."

"Yes, my wife is going to have our first child."

"Congratulations are in order. Let me buy you a drink."

The man sat down and drank to his wife and the coming child. They spent the afternoon drinking. And by the time the sun was golden before it set in the sky, Mateo had shared his fears with his old friend. He told him what the doctor had said.

"Don't worry. I know a good midwife. She delivered my children and my brother's as well. I have seen this woman in action; she knows more than the doctors. You can trust her."

"You think she will be able to save the baby and my wife?" Mateo asked nervously.

"I know she will."

The following day, Mateo went to see the old midwife. He didn't bring his wife along with him. He wanted to meet her first by himself.

"A woman like me, who has been helping in childbirths since I was only fourteen, understands more than a medical doctor. I assume he is a man, and men don't know much about childbirth, even if they are doctors." The midwife, with a hump in her back and graying hair, assured Mateo, "I will take care of your wife. I promise you that she and your child will be all right. However, this is going to cost you more money than my usual fee, and that is because I may have to perform extra duties. Is that all right with you?"

Mateo nodded. He hated being forced to pay extra. She said it was because of extra duties, but he knew it was because of who he was. Everyone knew Mateo Leoni was a rich man. "Yes, I'll pay whatever you ask, so long as my wife and child survive this birth."

"You have no need to worry." The old woman smiled. He noticed she was missing a front tooth.

"Good. Then you'll come to my house to examine my wife this week?"

"Yes, of course, I will."

After he left, he went into his office. He'd asked several other husbands who worked with him if they had heard of this woman, this midwife. Several said that their wives had used her. This information gave him some comfort.

Then, when the midwife came three days later to examine his wife, she made him feel at ease. "Everything looks just fine. Her hips are a little slim. I have to admit. But I have confidence that this will all go very well."

After the midwife left, Aria was happy again. And Mateo tried his best to believe what the woman had promised. But as Aria's due date grew closer, Mateo grew nervous again. And then tonight, when Aria went into labor, her blood-curdling screams struck fear into his heart. He knew that giving birth was a painful process, but her cries were worse than he remembered from the first time when she'd lost the baby. *If she dies, I will never forgive myself.* He thought as another shriek came from the bedroom.

When the midwife arrived, she'd insisted that Mateo leave her and his wife alone in the bedroom. "Wait outside. I'll come and get you as soon as the baby is born," the old woman said.

And he had done as she told him to do. But hours had passed, and night turned to morning, with the screams ringing in his ears, and now Mateo couldn't bear it anymore. He had been as patient as he could be. This was his home, and no midwife was going to tell him he could not go into the bedroom to see his wife.

He stood up and straightened his back. But he hesitated for a moment. Then he marched up the stairs to the bedroom and opened the door. What he saw sent shock waves through his body. He trembled. The bed was covered in blood, fresh and bright red against the white sheet. His beautiful Aria was so pale that her face was as colorless as the white pillowcase. Tears ran from her eyes and covered her sweat-soaked cheeks. *She is going to die.* The thought made bile rise in his throat. Then he heard her whisper his name, "Mateo...." And he fell to his knees, covered his eyes, and wept.

CHAPTER TWO

M ateo knelt at his wife's bedside and took her hand in his. "Aria, I am sorry. This is all my fault. I should have listened to the doctor. I should have said no when you wanted to try again to have a child. I should have made you see how dangerous this was."

"It's not your fault," she said, barely above a whisper. "I begged you, remember?"

He nodded as he gently pushed her lovely blonde hair off her face. It was soaked in sweat. "I can't lose you," he said. "I can't." Then he bent his head and wept hard.

The midwife stood frozen with fear. She knew that Mateo Leoni was a member of Mussolini's elite. If his wife died in childbirth, he would probably blame her, even though it was not her fault. She had known that it was dangerous to take this case. But he paid so well that she had taken the risk. Then she'd done everything possible to bring the baby into the world. But the cord was tight around the child's neck. And not only that, it was not in the proper position to come through the birth canal. It was feet first. She had reached inside the young woman's body and tried to turn it. She had been unsuccessful. But that was how she knew that the cord had strangled the child. There was no doubt in her mind that the baby was gone. She said a prayer because Signore Leoni would blame her for the death of the child. He would be very angry. If his wife died, he would be inconsolable, and she knew he had the power to put her to death.

The old midwife cleared her throat. She wiped the blood from her hands on a towel by the bed. Her lazy eye twitched as she said, "Signore, I think you should hurry and get a doctor. Things went bad. I'm sorry. I'm very sorry. But this birth is too complicated for me."

His face turned crimson as he stood up and gathered himself to his full height. Mateo was six feet—tall for an Italian man. Glaring at the old woman, he slapped her across the face. Her nose spurted blood, and she began to shake. "I paid you well. I paid you very well. You promised me that you could do this. You said there would be no problems. You assured me that everything would be all right. And now you say to get a doctor. My wife is fading away. Go, run, bring back a doctor. Your life depends upon it, old witch."

The old woman left her medical bag behind and ran. She dashed through the streets, surprising herself that she could run so fast. But she was terrified. She'd seen what Mussolini's men could do to a person.

When she arrived at the closest doctor's office, she opened the door and saw it was full of sick people waiting for the only doctor available. It was the same doctor who had spoken with Aria and Mateo and told them it would be dangerous for her to have a child. He was an old man now and tired, but there were traces of the enthusiastic young man he had been when he was just starting out and was determined to save the world. The midwife brushed past the receptionist, who protested as she ran into the backroom where the doctor was examining a young woman.

"Please," she croaked. "Please, you must come with me. I am a midwife. I was trying to aid in a very complicated birth. But now the young woman is dying. She lost a lot of blood in childbirth. The baby is going to be stillborn. I am begging you. Please." The old woman began to cry.

The doctor looked at her face sympathetically. Then he glanced at her hands and dress, both stained with blood. He took a deep breath, shook his head, and said, "All right, I'll come."

CHAPTER THREE

When the doctor arrived, the first thing he did was order everyone to leave the room.

Mateo crouched on the floor right outside the bedroom, wringing his hands. Hot salty sweat stung as it dripped from his brow into his eyes. Several hours passed. But then the doctor came out of the room and looked at Mateo. "I told you not to do this," he scolded as he shook his head.

"Is she..." Mateo hesitated, "Is she dead?"

"She's lost a lot of blood. And she's very weak. But she's alive. The baby didn't make it. I'm sorry." He cleared his throat. "The next few hours will tell us a lot. I'm hoping she will pull through due to her age. However, you must know that she will not survive another attempt at childbirth. You must not try again. Do you understand me?"

Mateo nodded. Then, in a frantic but grateful voice, he said, "Yes, yes, I will never attempt this again. No matter how much she begs for a child. I promise. Please, I beg you. Save her life."

"If she makes it through the night, she'll be all right. There is nothing more I can do for her now. Stay close to her through the night. I'll be back in the morning."

Mateo nodded. Then he went into the room where Aria lay on the bed, took her hand in his, and kissed it. "You will be all right," he said repeatedly. She didn't answer.

CHAPTER FOUR

As Aria slept, Mateo closed his eyes and remembered how he and Aria had become husband and wife.

When Mateo married a woman twenty years his junior, he quickly found out that she longed to have children. He didn't care. He already had two grown children from his first wife, who had recently passed away, and that was enough for him. But it was Aria that he adored. And he would have done anything to have her. She was his dream girl, his Aria. And she made it clear that she wanted a baby. He remembered thinking she was so beautiful that whenever he looked into her crystal blue eyes, he couldn't say no. Not ever. He should have been stronger. He should have refused after the first attempt.

Now, she lay on blood-stained sheets, fighting for her life. He knew he must refuse her when she asked to try again. If he didn't, it would kill her. But what could he do to make this right? He repeatedly asked himself all night as he put his hand close to her nose to check on her and assure himself that she was breathing. At four in the morning, she awakened. He was so glad to hear her speak. "I'm thirsty," she said.

He ran to the kitchen, tripping down two stairs as he did. Mateo hurt his knee, but he ignored it. Quickly, he brought her water and some food. She drank but refused to eat. Then she turned and fell back to sleep. He sat beside her quietly. When the sun rose, Aria was still alive. And Mateo, who had been agonizing over it all night, finally had a solution to their problem. He would wait to discuss it with Aria until she was stronger. Even so, he was glad to have come up with a resolution. And now he went about looking into how to carry out his plan.

CHAPTER FIVE

Each day, Aria grew a little stronger. The doctor came and said she was recovering miraculously. Mateo picked flowers from their garden and put them in a vase in her room. She smiled at him and thanked him for the beautiful flowers. But he could see the sadness in her eyes. Patiently he brought her soup each day, and to make him happy, she ate a few spoonfuls, but not enough. She slept for hours at a time. It seemed she was hardly ever awake. One week later, he went into town and bought her a box of chocolates he had purchased on the black market, hoping they would cheer her. But when he looked at the box a few days later, he noticed she hadn't touched them.

"She's depressed," the doctor admitted.

"What can I do?" Mateo asked.

"Maybe take her to the sea?" the doctor suggested.

Mateo nodded. But he knew that a trip to the ocean would solve nothing.

Finally, he decided he must try to present her with his solution. He hoped she would accept it, or at least be willing to try. All night he thought about how he might present his idea to her.

Early the following morning, Mateo entered the room where Aria slept. Before he turned on the light, he checked to see if she was still asleep. She wasn't. She lay quietly in her bed with her eyes open. This frightened him even more than her continuous sleeping. "Would you like to go outside and get some fresh air? The doctor said it would be all right. The sun is just rising, and the sky is lovely."

"No, darling. I'm too tired," she answered.

He opened the drapes, allowing the pale light to filter in. Aria covered her eyes with her hand. *She's been lying here in darkness for too long.* He thought as he looked at her pale skin. "A little sunlight will do you good," he smiled.

She squinted as she tried to smile back. Then she said, "I suppose we can't try again. I suppose we will remain childless."

He took her cold hand in both hands and said, "We can't try again. This is true. The doctor has forbidden it."

She let out a sharp cry of pain. Then she put her hands on her chest as if she were feeling an arrow go through her heart.

"Shhh, my love. I know how much you want this. I've been agonizing over it. And I think I have an idea. Now please hear me out. I know this isn't exactly what you want. But it might just suffice. Please, will you listen?"

She nodded and dropped her eyes.

Gently, in a soft tone of voice, he began. "I went to the church where I spoke with Father Mariano about what we need. He told me that there is an orphanage located way up in the mountains filled with children who are desperately in need of loving families. Some are very young; they would never remember their birth parents. We would be everything to a child like that, just as if you had given birth to him or her. What do you think, darling? Perhaps as soon as you're feeling up to it, we could take a trip up there in the mountains, and maybe, just maybe, you might find a child you could love."

"I don't know." She shook her head. "It's not the same. The child won't be ours, Mateo."

"Of course, it will. It will be ours because we will love it and raise it to be ours. We have everything we could need, plenty of money, and a nice home. We are privileged, and we could give a child a beautiful life. I know you will be a wonderful mother," he said, pleading with her to accept his proposal.

She sat up in bed for the first time since the stillbirth. "All right." She nodded. "All right. Let's go up there and see how we feel. I can't promise that I will find a child that I can bring home with me. But I'll try."

"That's all I ask. Please, just try," he said, then added, "I'll have the doctor come by and check on you today to make sure you can travel. And if he says it's all right, we'll leave tomorrow. A few days up in the mountains might do you good. The air is fresh up there."

She smiled, and Mateo's heart swelled with love for her. Then he kissed her gently and left her room. Mateo dressed quickly, then walked out to his automobile. He didn't use his driver that day. Instead, he drove himself. Sometimes, he preferred to drive. It was relaxing for him. It gave him time to think. Besides, he had some personal business to attend to before he returned, and his driver need not know his every move.

On his way to the doctor's office, Mateo stopped by the midwife's house. She had failed him and his wife so badly. She had not kept her promise, and he was still angry with her. He knocked on the door, and she didn't answer. But hers was a poorly built apartment with a weak wooden door. He kicked it in. When he entered, the old woman was sitting on the sofa, holding her rosary beads and trembling. Two young children sat on the floor, playing with blocks. "Go to your room," the old woman told the children in a firm voice. They did not speak. The look on the old woman's face left no room for argument.

After the children left the room, Mateo shook his head. He was slender, and for his age, he was handsome. Some might have called him distinguished. "You idiot," he said to the old woman as he stormed through the woman's living room. When he got close to her, he grabbed the collar of her dress and pulled her towards him. She was so close that her hair moved with the force of his breath. "You greedy old woman, do you realize what could have happened? I almost lost my wife because of you."

"Yes, I know. And I'm sorry. I am truly sorry. But I promise you, I did everything possible. I tried everything." She was clearly nervous. Her body was trembling, and she was wringing her hands on the dirty apron she wore. "Please, I'm sorry. I am begging you. Take pity on me. My son and daughter-in-law died in an accident last year. I am the only living relative that my grandchildren have left. Please, if you kill me, what will become of them?"

He snorted. Mateo was disgusted by her. *She is old and ugly; how dare she lie to me? She made me promises she knew she could not keep. She wanted my money, so she told my wife what she wanted to hear. My dearest Aria almost died because of this woman's greed.* His face was the color of blood as he studied the old woman. *She's terrified of me. She knows she did something wrong, and she knows how powerful a man I am. This act of selfishness on her part will not go unpunished.* He pulled out his gun.

As soon as she saw the gun, she began to plead desperately. The two children must have heard her because they stood in the door-way. But Mateo was too angry to care. "Please, please have mercy on me," the old woman cried, and she fell to her knees.

"You deserve this. You old witch. I'll see to it that you never lie to anyone again," he said. Then he pulled the trigger, and her face exploded. The children began to scream. Mateo heard them wailing in high-pitched voices as he walked out the door and got into his car. He drove away and headed for the doctor's office.

CHAPTER SIX

As always, the doctor's office was overflowing with needy patients as Mateo opened the door. He walked inside but didn't go to the receptionist like the other patients. Instead, he ignored the receptionist and walked back to where the doctor was listening to the breathing of a young woman sitting at an examining table.

"You should not be in here, signore. Can't you see that I am with a patient?" the doctor said.

Mateo shrugged. He knew the doctor was no fool, and because of Mateo's position under Mussolini, the doctor would not dare to throw him out. But he also knew that the doctor was not afraid of him and that he knew Mateo needed him right now. So, carefully, Mateo apologized. "I am sorry to interrupt, doctor. But I need you to come and check on my wife again."

"Has anything changed with her?"

"It seems she's doing better. But, just to be sure, I want you to come again today and check to see if she's healthy enough to travel. Of course, I will pay you."

"I must finish with these other patients first. I will come right after I am done. I hope this will be acceptable."

"Of course," Mateo smiled. "Just make sure you come."

Everyone in town knew Mateo. The women found him handsome, even if he was known to be a little dangerous. That had always been part of his charm. And in contrast to his cruel side, he was also well known for being kind and generous to the poor. He often gave food or money to needy families and even awarded a small home to a poor man and his wife, who had done him a favor. However, everyone also knew Mateo's mood could change instantly, and Mateo was not to be crossed. Even the doctor knew this. So, no matter what time the doctor finished with his patients that day, no matter how tired he was, he would keep his promise and go to the home of Mateo Leoni to check on Mateo's pride and joy, his pretty, young wife.

Mateo left the doctor's office without closing the door to the examining room behind him. Then he walked outside. But before he got back into his shiny black automobile, he walked over to the florist, where he purchased a large bouquet for his wife.

As Mateo drove home, he thought about Aria. He remembered how they'd first met, how she had somehow enchanted him. It was at a dinner party he'd attended. A party to honor their leader, Mussolini. Aria was there. When he first saw her, he knew she was much younger than himself by at least twenty years; at the time, he had been fifty. He had been standing at the bar drinking with a man he worked with when she entered the room. His head turned as if he were attached to her by a magnetic pull. She wore her long blonde hair twisted into a knot on top of her head, with little tendrils of curls escaping on both sides to show off her long slender neck. Her bright blue eyes sparkled like gemstones as she laughed at something her escort said. Her legs and arms were long, willowy, and slim. And although she looked subtly sexy, she was elegant in her dark blue form-fitting dress with a matching bag and shoes. Mateo watched her as she floated into the room. His heart pounded because he found her exceedingly beautiful. At that moment, he decided she would be his sexual conquest that night. He always found a woman at these things who he brought back to his home to entertain his desires for a night. However, Aria had far different plans.

Mateo was well known to be a playboy. Behind his back, everyone in his crowd of friends said that he'd dated and bedded so many women that he must have lost count. But Mateo never lost count. He enjoyed each and every one of them, and they were not just any women, but beautiful women, some of them movie actresses and models, and then there were the daughters of important men. Whenever he heard the rumors about his reputation, they never bothered him. Although he liked these ladies well enough, Mateo disappeared from their lives as soon as they hinted at wanting more or even mentioned the word 'marriage.' He stopped calling on them and was cool whenever he happened to see them in public. Women, he believed, were not to be taken seriously. In his opinion, they were put on earth strictly to please men. Little more than toys. And when one stopped pleasing him, he found another. Most of the women he'd known had gone to his bed within a week of their first meeting. Some even on the first date. But not Aria.

In fact, when he found a reason to speak to her that night at the party, she gave him the impression that she was not interested in him at all. He was so surprised. This sort of thing never happened to Mateo. He was as charming as he could be as he tried to talk to her, but she was disinterested. Her eyes were busy glancing around the room at the other men, the younger men, at the party. Mateo was hurt and angry to have been snubbed like this. And so, he left the party early and furious. Over the next two weeks, he slept with at least one and often two women each day, trying to convince himself that he was still desirable. But the more he did this, the more frustrated he became because he couldn't get over the fact that Aria didn't seem to think much of him. His promiscuous behavior only made him want Aria even more. And soon, he lost interest in dating altogether. He stayed at home and brooded.

Then finally, almost a month after the party, he went back to the home of the host. He asked the man for contact information for Aria which, because he was a powerful man, he was given without question. Then Mateo set out on a plan to win Aria. He sent flowers to her home, the prettiest, most expensive red roses he could find. He sent candy. None of this worked. She still did not come to the phone when he called, so he sent a pair of large blue and white diamond earrings. Despite that, she did not answer the phone when he called her. Mateo was desperate. He went to her home, and with as much respect as he could muster, he asked her grandmother if he could speak with her. Aria's grandmother, afraid of Mateo because of his position in the government, forced her to come out of her room and talk with Mateo. Aria floated down the long hallway and walked into the living room where Mateo waited. When he saw her, his eyes lit up. She smiled serenely and told him it was good to see him again. But she looked puzzled why he'd come.

"I suppose you're wondering why I am here," he said, trying to sound as confident as possible.

"Yes, actually I am."

"Well, I was wondering if you would like to have dinner with me."

"Tonight?"

"Yes."

"Oh, that's a lovely offer. But I'm sorry. I have other plans," Aria said.

"How about next week?" He was losing confidence.

"I really can't. I'm just very busy these days, Signore Leoni," she said with a smile. "Perhaps sometime next month."

He left the house angry, telling himself she was nothing, just a worthless young girl. And he would forget about her. In fact, he told himself that he would never speak to her again. But on the first day of the following month, he found himself on the doorstep of her home. Mateo was not a man who was accustomed to hearing the word 'no.'

But once again, she told him she was just too busy to go out with him. And once again, he left angry and frustrated. The more she turned him down, the more obsessed with her he became. His friends brought women by his house to meet him, but he was not interested. He was depressed, and he'd lost interest in any other women. Instead, Mateo spent his days pining away for Aria.

And then a miracle happened. It wouldn't have been considered a miracle by anyone else's standards except Mateo's. Aria certainly would not have called it a miracle. She would have called it a nightmare because tragedy struck Aria's uncle. Her mother's brother, a small-time employee of Mussolini's fascist party, was killed. He had been in the marketplace shopping when he was shot dead in the street by someone who opposed Mussolini. The culprit was caught and punished, but that didn't make things better for Aria. She was distraught. Her mother and father had died when she was only five years old, and her uncle had helped her grandmother raise her. He was the only person in her family she felt close to. When she was a child, he'd taken her on outings. And when his work permitted, he spent as much time as he could with her. They were inseparable. And it was because Aria was alone and weak with grief she allowed Mateo to come into her life. When he heard about what happened to Aria's uncle, Mateo rushed to Aria's home. Then he made all the arrangements for the funeral. He brought her plenty of food and left money on her kitchen table. But most of all, he laid his heart on the line and pledged his undying love for her.

Aria had never married, refusing to leave her uncle, who had never married and had been like a father to her. He had been the backbone of her life, and now she was alone in the world. Mateo was her uncle's age, and so he, too, was like a father figure to her. He came each day and stayed until late at night, never trying to touch or do anything that might offend her. They had dinner together each evening and then played chess or cards. Mateo filled the loneliness, and Aria began to enjoy his company. He filled the gap losing her uncle had left in her life. So, after several months had passed, he asked her to be his wife, and she agreed.

Mateo and Aria were married on a sunny summer morning, when the sky was the same color as Aria's eyes. Bluebirds tweeted a wedding song outside the courthouse where the couple said their vows.

Although he never told anyone, Mateo had been afraid that his obsession with her might die once he slept with Aria. But he decided that if that happened, he would divorce her. However, he had been wrong. In fact, his desire for her had grown stronger. And he realized he was not just obsessed with her. He was truly in love. And this was why he had his secretary spend endless hours searching orphanages for a child with blonde hair and blue eyes like his wife's. A child she could adopt and make believe was her own. Once he'd found a little blonde boy at an orphanage up in the mountains, he'd made plans to take Aria there to see the child.

CHAPTER SEVEN

It had been two years since Viola had any word from Bernie. She had sent several letters, but they'd gone unanswered. With the state of the world, Viola feared Bernie might be dead. And the little boy, who she'd left in Viola's keeping, was growing up fast. He would turn four years old in a few months, and he was beginning to lose his baby fat. Older children were rarely adopted from the orphanage, and soon Theo would lose his desirability. Viola hid behind the door and watched the couple enter the room where the children were playing. She had been informed by the Mother Superior the night before that a very wealthy and important man and his wife were coming to see Theo. "If they adopt the child, they will provide him with a good life. It's better than having him grow up in an orphanage. We don't know if his mother will ever return. This is a good opportunity for him."

Viola nodded obediently, but she was worried. *Perhaps they won't take him.* She thought. Then the couple arrived. The woman was tall, blonde, and willowy. The man was distinguished and very handsome, although he was much older. And he seemed to be very in love with his wife. The Mother Superior was speaking to the couple, but

Viola could not hear what was said. She was standing too far away. The man seemed to be paying attention to what the Mother Superior was telling them, but the woman's eyes were on the children. Viola saw her walk away from her husband and go to where Theo was playing quietly. She smiled as she knelt beside him, but her eyes seemed glassy with tears. Aria and Theo played with something on the table for a few moments. Then Theo put his arms around her neck and embraced her. She closed her eyes, and at that moment, Viola knew this couple would adopt Bernie's friend's son. Viola was anxious. She'd promised Bernie that the boy would be safe at the orphanage. She had vowed that the child would be there waiting when his mother came to claim him. Now she knew she was going to be unable to keep that promise. All she could do was try to find out who these people were and as much information about them as possible, including what they planned to name the little boy. Viola planned to save all this information for Bernie and her friend, Elica Frey, the little boy's mother. She would give them the information if they ever came to pick Theo up from the orphanage. This was all she could do.

Viola bit her lower lip as she watched the couple fill out papers. Then she watched as they walked out the door with the little boy snuggled warmly in the woman's arms. *He must think that the woman is his mother. She looks so much like him. I wonder if that's what his mother looks like.* Viola thought as the smiling couple got into the back seat of a large black automobile. They had a driver who wore a lovely, well-made uniform. *At least these people who are adopting Theo have money. He won't want for anything while he is waiting for his birth mother to return. The Mother Superior is right. He will be better off than he would be here in this orphanage, where we have to make do with very little because there are so many children who need our help.*

That night, Viola trembled as she sneaked into the Mother Superior's office. She could be sent away from the nunnery for this. It was deceitful, and Viola knew it. Theo's files were right there on the top of a pile of papers on the desk. Viola opened the file. She felt a pang of guilt because the mother superior trusted her, and she knew she was breaking that trust. But she couldn't let Bernie down. She had to have this information. Quickly, she grabbed a pencil and paper and wrote down the names of Mateo and Aria Leoni. Then she read aloud from the paper. "They are going to call Theo 'Enzo.'"

Quickly, she scribbled the name on the bottom of the paper, folded it up, and put it into the pocket of her old robe. Then quickly, with her heart racing, she closed the file and hurried out of the office. When she returned to her room, she hid the paper in a drawer, lay on her bed, and tried to sleep. But she couldn't rest. Every time she closed her eyes, she saw the face of the child. The little blonde boy with his sweet smile. *I vowed to Bernie that the child would be here when his mother returned. But he won't. And I know nothing about the people who adopted him, only that the man works for Mussolini, a dark and terrible man. Where will that little boy end up? And most importantly, will Bernie forgive me for being unable to stop this?*

CHAPTER EIGHT

1940, The forests of Slovakia

The two Nazi officers stood under the star-lit sky. One of them lit a cigarette. Although it was a beautiful night, they hardly noticed. "I hate being so far away from home," Zigmund said to his companion. "I miss the fatherland terribly."

"Yes, me too," Ulf agreed. He had volunteered to be in charge of delivering supplies and an important letter to the head of a battalion stationed in the East. Upon his arrival, Zigmund, a young private, had immediately taken to him. He was a handsome, slender boy. And from his carefree demeanor, Ulf assumed he had not yet experienced battle. Well, I am sure that they are headed right for Russia. And soon enough, this boy, who is so childlike, will know the horrors of war.

"But since we're out here, do you want to have some fun?"

"Fun? What kind of fun?"

"You'll see. Come with me," Zigmund whispered to his companion. "No one will know that we went but us."

"Went where?"

"I know of a gypsy camp near here. Have you ever seen one?"

"Gypsies, Zigmund? If anyone important finds out that we went to look in on a Gypsy camp and didn't arrest them, we will be in serious trouble," Ulf answered. He didn't want to admit to his coworker that Gypsies had always scared him. They were dark, mysterious people who told fortunes and, he was certain, consorted with evil spirits.

"But no one will find out. How could they? All we are going to do is stand on the outskirts of the campfire and watch the women dance. I've done it before. It's something to see, I tell you. These women are like animals. They exude sex. You'll see. They dance in such a suggestive way. I promise you no good German girl would ever dance like that with men watching. And all of their men are sitting around the campfire watching. They sway their wide hips, and their shirts are cut so low that you can see the deep lines of their heavy breasts." Zigmund smiled suggestively. "And if we want to, we can scare one of the women into letting us have our way with her. Don't forget, they are terrified of us."

"I'm sure they are. But you seem to have forgotten that they are sub-humans. It's dangerous to have sexual intercourse with one of them. Who knows what kind of spell they could cast on you?" Ulf said firmly. He truly felt this way about Romany. However, although the party told him it was the same with the Jews, he never believed it. Not all, but many Jews he'd seen looked and dressed like Aryans. They didn't appear frightening like this. Especially Anna. Anna looked like any other German girl. If times had been different, she might have been his wife. But as it was, he would find her, and then she could never run away from him again. *Anna, my sweet Anna, will be my slave. And... I will be her master.*

"Yes, of course, they are subhuman. That's what makes them so exciting to watch. They are nothing like us. I wonder if they turn into bobcats when they are in your bed. I must admit, I would be willing to take the chance and find out."

"You wouldn't dare. You would be breaking the race laws.

Zigmund, I will go with you, but you must promise me that you will not have sex with any of them. They are dirty and will taint you forever."

"My friend, of course, I promise you this. We will only look, not touch. And, if one of the women should see us watching them, we will smile a friendly smile. Then, once we return to Berlin to report to headquarters, we can stop at one of the Lebensborn homes for the night. We will find a good German woman to take us to her bed there. Even now, she waits for the semen of an SS officer to impregnate her with a perfect Aryan child."

"That's rather brilliant."

"Yes, of course, it is. Now, come with me to the camp, and let's have fun as we watch these wild, untamed women."

Ulf followed Zigmund through the forest. He wasn't especially fond of this idea. It still frightened him. But he planned to stay hidden where the gypsies would not see him.

Zigmund knew exactly where the camp was located. It was in a small clearing. As they approached, they heard the haunting music of violins and the deep melodious sound of a man singing in a language Ulf didn't understand. He shivered even though it was a warm night. Zigmund pulled Ulf beside him, and they crouched behind thick bushes to watch the women dance. They wore colorful full skirts that swayed as they danced, and their long dark hair hung loose. Ulf thought they were beautiful, but something about them still scared him. His eyes scanned the crowd of gypsies, and he wished he were back in the safety of his own group. He and Zigmund had guns, but so did the Gypsy men. And there were far more of them. Ulf glanced over at Zigmund. Zigmund's face was shiny with sweat, and his eyes were on fire with passion. Ulf looked back at the campfire, wishing that Zigmund was ready to leave, when suddenly he saw her.

His breath caught in his throat. *Is this possible? Could that possibly be Anna? What is she doing here? How did she get here?* Anna was laughing and talking with another girl close to her age. A Gypsy girl.

She's happy here. She's not a prisoner. Ulf was puzzled. He watched Anna as two of the Gypsy men walked over to her and her friend. One of them handed Anna a cup of something. She drank from it. Ulf sucked in his breath. Then he realized something. *I have found her. Now, it's only a matter of how to get her alone, away from this group, so I can take her.* He was no longer paying any attention to the dancers. He was consumed with thoughts of Anna. *If only I could find a way to get rid of Zigmund, I could follow her. He's a foolish boy, and he talks too much. I can't trust him. Not that I believe he would tell on me out of malice or out of the hopes of receiving a promotion. He's too daft for that. But he is not a serious man; besides, he has a vile sexual attraction to these Gypsy pigs. The sooner I can get away from him, the better.*

His mind was racing. And he had a plan by the time they left to head back to their camp.

CHAPTER NINE

Ravensbrück was more terrible than Dagna Hofer had expected when she agreed to go there for her guard training. She'd applied for a desk job at Sobibor, but they had an opening for a guard instead, and the pay and benefits were better. She'd seen Sobibor when she went to the interview; it was also a terrible place. Ravensbrück was a women's only camp, but Sobibor was a concentration camp for both men and women. And somehow, when she was told she would be training at Ravensbrück, she believed it would be cleaner and more civilized because it was all women. She had arrived the previous evening, and although she had not seen the entire camp, from what she had seen, she knew it was not any better than Sobibor. It was a dirty, miserable place.

Dagna Hofer glanced into the mirror that hung over the dresser in the room she'd been assigned and tidied her hair. *This is a good opportunity.* She told herself. *The place is horrible. It smells, and it's filthy, but my room is clean, and there will be plenty of food. I'll only be staying here for a short time. Once I am done here, I will be qualified to be a guard at a camp instead of a secretary. Then I will earn a nice living, wear a smart uniform, and have plenty of power.* Dagna opened her suitcase and began to unpack her things. As she lifted a pretty blue dress in a small size out of her valise, she remembered how she had started out as a friendless, overweight, unattractive, and lonely girl. *I can't believe I have achieved so much. I've lost weight and bleached my hair. And it's all because of Elica.*

Not that Elica would have wanted to help me. She only cared about herself. But I wanted to be like her so badly that I changed myself to become everything she was. I still remember how I felt when I was eight and met Elica Frey. Elica was beautiful, popular, and carefree. She was the kind of girl everyone wanted to be friends with. But Elica had no interest in me at first. I tried to win her friendship, but she ignored me. However, that day when I happened upon Elica and her two girlfriends, Bernie and Anna, making a blood-sister pact in the park, I got an idea. First of all, I learned everything I could find out about Elica. I was like a bloodhound. She laughed out loud. *I was looking for some information that would force Elica to let me into her life. And then I found it. Elica's friend Anna was Jewish, and she also knew that Elica's mother was Anna's parents' maid. I knew I could use that as leverage to make those girls allow me to join the blood sisters. And once I became a part of the group, I was able to get close to Elica. So, I did what I had to do. I threatened Elica that I would tell her mother that she was sharing blood with a Jew if they didn't allow me to be a part of the club. It might have been underhanded, but this was how I became a blood sister.*

Glancing over, she looked at the second bed in her room. She wondered if she would be assigned a roommate or if she would have the luxury of having this space all to herself for the entire period of her training. A roommate could be an asset or a problem. Dagna knew this. After her friendship with Elica went sour, she wasn't as open to trusting anyone. *Well, hopefully, I won't need to share this room.*

Dagna had set her hair on pin curls the night before, hoping the set would make it look thicker. But after she combed it out, she shook her head and twisted it into a bun. Then she studied her reflection one last time before she left her room. Quietly, she closed the door and headed for the training area where she'd been instructed to meet the rest of her group.

As she left the dormitory and walked outside, she was slapped in the face by that terrible smell that permeated the entire camp. That same odor had made her gag when she'd first arrived, and she remembered that she'd had the same reaction when she smelled it at Sobibor when she went there for her initial interview. Dagna couldn't imagine what it was that could smell so bad. It was a sickening odor that made her stomach turn. She had to stop momentarily because she felt her gag reflex go off. *Breathe through your mouth.* She told herself.

The breakfast area was filled with new recruits, young German girls excited and talking loudly. Dagna knew there would be few men because this was a woman's only camp. This was a bit disappointing because since Dagna had begun to impersonate Elica, men had become her specialty. She enjoyed playing with their affections, like she'd watched Elica do so many years ago. She sighed. It didn't matter. She wasn't going to be here very long. Soon enough, she would be back at Sobibor, where she would have plenty of men to flirt with and plenty of prisoners to dominate.

The nasty odor of the camp lingered in Dagna's nostrils, making it impossible to enjoy the lovely food that had been provided.

After they had finished their breakfast, a group of women wearing black skirt uniforms stood up and went to the front of the room. Chairs had been placed there, and each of them sat down. All except one, who stepped forward. She had dark hair pulled back into a severe, tight bun. Her figure was slender. Dagna thought she appeared young, but her face looked strained and grave.

Everyone in the room stopped talking. There was a hush. It was almost as if the silence had a sound of its own.

"Heil Hitler," the woman said as she saluted.

"Heil Hitler," the new recruits stood up in unison and saluted.

"You may be seated," the woman said. The girls sat down. "My name is *SS-Helferin* Marie Mandl. I am the senior in charge here at

Ravensbrück." Then she indicated a stern-looking woman standing beside her. "At my right is *SS-Helferin* Hermine Braunsteiner. And this," she pointed at a petite and pretty blonde, "is Irma Grese." Irma looked up, batting her eyes. She smiled at *Helferin* Mandl. "And this lady over here is Herta Ehlert."

Then the woman who had introduced herself as *SS-Helferin* Mandl walked over to a woman with light hair and squinty eyes. The woman was tall, large in stature, and big-boned. On her belt, she wore a whip, and sitting at her feet was a large German Shepherd. "And this, ladies, is Theodora Binz. She is our chief wardress and training instructor. Fraüline Binz will be your main instructor. She is in charge of all the recruits. However, each one of the women who I have introduced you to today will teach you a different aspect of your job. But because she is the Chief Wardress, it is Fraüline Binz's responsibility to see to it that once you have finished your training here, you are qualified to honor the fatherland with your dedicated service. The valuable lessons you will learn here will qualify you to work at the women's divisions in any of the camps." Then she smiled, "Welcome to Ravensbrück, ladies. Now... once we have finished here, Fraüline Binz will lead you outside, where your training will begin."

Dagna eyed the German Shepherd, who sat calmly on the floor. She didn't trust him not to get up and attack. In fact, Dagna was terrified of dogs. And this one, although he seemed to be well trained, was no exception. Something had happened to her when she was a child that had left a mark on her mind and her arms. It had happened one afternoon when she'd played too rough with a dog that lived next door. He was a large black and brown dog. Dagna didn't know what breed he was. All she knew was that he was not a German Shepherd. And until that day, she'd noticed that he had always been friendly with her and the other children in the neighborhood. They often came around to play with him and bring him treats. But Dagna was an angry child, and she had something different in mind. Whenever she was frustrated, she took it out on that dog. So many times, when the owner left a food bowl out for the dog, Dagna had waited until he went back inside, and then she'd take the food away from the dog and tease it mercilessly. She did this several times until one day, she had not been quick enough to grab the bowl, and the dog bit her. The poor creature was tied to a tree. So, if she could find a tree branch long enough, she could beat it, and it could not reach her. She picked up a long stick and began to hit the dog. But to her dismay, it started growling and became so angry that it broke the rope that was restraining it. The dog pounced and bit her several times on her hands and arms. She was sure it would have killed her if its owner had not come outside and restrained the animal. "Now, maybe you are going to leave my dog alone?" he said. "Or next time, I will not be so quick to come out and help you."

Dagna was crying, but she nodded and ran home. She was bleeding and frightened as she cleaned her wounds. From that day forward, Dagna never got close enough to another dog to get bitten again. And as she looked at this one, sitting on the floor quietly eyeing the new recruits, she was hoping she would not be forced to have any contact with it.

Dagna was impressed by the power of all the women who had been introduced to her that day. All except for Herta Ehlert, who Dagna instantly hated. That was because Ehlert reminded Dagna of herself before she'd undergone the carefully orchestrated transformation to become more like Elica. Ehlert was overweight and clumsy and basically very unattractive. Fear of returning to that state of being made Dagna nervous. And because she was afraid of becoming like her former self, she couldn't bear to look at Ehlert.

"There are others here, guards, and so forth, but you won't have much to do with them. The ladies I introduced you to today are the women who will be teaching you," *Helferin* Mandl said. Then, without a smile, she continued, "While you are here, you will be given three meals a day. You will be given uniforms; most of you have already been assigned rooms and roommates. As you have already been told, and I am proud to repeat, Ravensbrück is the training ground for all female guards. Here you will learn everything that you will need to know. Remember, once you are trained, you will be judged either worthy or unworthy by your performance here. Those of you who are fearless and perform your work with the required devotion to our Fuhrer will be sent to their permanent positions. However, those who are too soft and weak will be sent home as failures."

Then, in a softer, more sympathetic voice, she said, "You see, this is a very important position. It is up to us to maintain control over the prisoners, and this must be done through fear and intimidation. As soon as these pigs detect even the slightest weakness in you, they will take advantage. You must never doubt that. And you must never allow them to think that you will be soft on them, or I promise they will walk all over you. And you will lose control. That's when you are in trouble." Then she turned to *Helferin* Braunsteiner and said, "Would you like to say a few words?"

"Yes, thank you," Braunsteiner said. "As you know, Ravensbrück is a woman's prison. And as our special guests, we have all sorts of female enemies of the Reich. We have political prisoners, filthy sex offenders, common criminals, gypsies, Jehovah's Witnesses, homosexuals, and others. Most importantly, we have our Jews. Our dangerous, sly, and treacherous Jews." She paused to let the importance of her words sink in. "Any of you who have had any dealings with Jews can testify that they are devious and manipulative. They will do anything to distract you from your job. They will try in every way to make you pity them. You must remember that they are manipulating you, and you must never allow yourself to feel pity for them, or they will destroy you. They will take power, and then all is lost."

"Thank you, Fraüline Braunsteiner. Now ladies, take a few moments to introduce yourselves, and then our training will begin."

For several minutes Dagna stood alone in the corner. She was feeling awkward, wondering if she'd made a mistake coming here, when a young woman with dark hair and a slim figure approached Dagna. "Hi, I'm Gretel. I'm from Berlin."

"Berlin is a beautiful city. I spent a summer there once. It's not far away from here. About how many miles would you say?" Dagna asked.

"I'm not sure exactly, but I think it's about ninety miles or so," Gretel smiled. "Where are you from?"

"Austria. Vienna. By the way, I'm Dagna Hoffer."

Their conversation had just begun when Braunsteiner pounded a heavy wooden stick on the desk to silence them. "All right, enough talking. Let's go. Get outside, all of you. Line up. I'm going to take attendance."

It was early December, and the wind blew straight through her like invisible knives made of ice, despite the warm coat she had been given to wear over her wool uniform.

Dagna followed the rest of the recruits outside and lined up. But there it was. Once again, she was slapped in the face by that terrible smell. Unable to control it, her gag reflex went off. Dagna covered her mouth with her hand to try and hide her gagging. But it was too late. Several girls had seen her and were now watching as she and Gretel stood in line. Gretel looked at Dagna as if Dagna were strange. Gretel stood ramrod straight, her head held high as the girls saluted. "Heil Hitler," they called out in loud, enthusiastic voices. Gretel didn't seem affected by the smell, and Dagna wondered how Gretel wasn't gagging.

After the roll call, the new recruits were told to follow Braunsteiner. Dagna joined the rest of the group as they were led through the camp. It was more than unpleasant; it was a miserable place. Although she'd only been there a single night, Dagna already wished her time at Ravensbrück was over. The girls walked past a wooden cart that was overflowing with the bodies of dead women. Among the dead lay the bodies of a few young children. The dead were not just dead, but had taken on a macabre look. They were little more than skeletons, and their chests and cheeks were concave. Thin skin covered with rashes and open sores hung from their bones. Arms and legs that seemed detached, not belonging to any of the bodies, dangled off the side of the carts. Flies congregated on the eyes and open mouths of the dead. *Open mouths.* Dagna shivered. *It's as if they died in silent screams.* Most of the bodies seemed to be looking up at the sky, questioning God, saying, "Why did this happen to me?" But one of the bodies seemed to be staring directly out at Dagna, who shivered when she saw the deep-set dark eyes fixed on her. Quickly Dagna looked away. The woman looked like a demon, but she reminded Dagna of Anna.

Gretel noticed Dagna looking at the dead bodies. She put her arm on Dagna's shoulder. "You haven't ever seen a death cart before?"

Dagna shook her head.

"You'll get used to it." Gretel smiled. "I was a secretary at Dachau before I came here for training to be a guard. It's a big promotion, you know."

"Yes, I know. Congratulations," Dagna managed. But she was still choked up by the memory of the dead woman's eyes.

"Well, working at Dachau, I've seen plenty of those carts. Before you know it, you won't even be affected by the sight of it anymore."

"It's the smell that is even worse than the sight. It's everywhere. There's no escaping it," Dagna said.

"I don't even smell it anymore. I am quite sure that soon you won't either. At first, all of this can be a bit overwhelming. But remind yourself that what we are doing, we are doing for our love of the fatherland."

Dagna nodded. "Did you see the size of that dog? It was huge. Do you think we are going to have to train with it? I don't like dogs."

"The dogs at these camps are very well trained. They are highly disciplined, and you needn't worry because they won't hurt you as long as their masters don't tell them to. They are here to keep the prisoners in line. The prisoners are afraid of them. And rightfully so. I've seen dogs tear a prisoner to pieces," she admitted as she nodded.

"Oh," Dagna said, feeling her stomach lurch in fear.

"Actually, they are very efficient killing machines. Watching them kill a prisoner is really quite fascinating. They can be sweet and loving but become vicious and incredibly powerful when commanded to kill. Once they've been set on someone, they will stop at nothing. They are merciless. I respect that. They have no weakness, none at all. No pity. Now that's a sign of true strength. And they can tear a prisoner up just like that prisoner was a rag doll."

"Sounds rather bloody and messy," Dagna winced.

"Don't be weak. Weakness is your worst enemy here. Admire the strength and power of the dogs. That's the way our superiors want us to be. Learn to turn off any disgust, fear, or emotions, and you will become truly powerful."

Dagna nodded. She wished she wasn't afraid of the dogs. But visions of the dog that had attacked her were still branded in her mind.

"You look like a frightened child," Gretel laughed at her. "Don't worry. You'll be just fine. For goodness' sake, Dagna, you must grab hold of yourself. You will appear to be weak. And if you are, they might send you home."

Dagna was ashamed. She hated to be laughed at. It brought back memories of when she'd been an overweight, unattractive child and had difficulties making friends. At that moment, she hated Gretel. But she didn't want Gretel to see the contempt in her eyes. So Dagna looked away and said nothing.

However, when *Helferin* Braunsteiner assigned Gretel to Dagna's room as her new roommate, Dagna was not happy. She hid her feelings well, pretending to like Gretel. But Gretel was thoughtless and unkind and just the sort of person who had teased Dagna when she was young, and she wasn't looking forward to getting to know her better.

CHAPTER TEN

Training began the following day, and it was intense.

The recruits were required to attend a roll call in which the prisoners were lined up and counted to ensure none had escaped. These roll calls took place outside twice each day. Dagna hated standing outside in the cold. The icy winds seeped through her warm coat and wool uniform. But she was shocked to see that the prisoners wore no coats over their thin uniforms, and many had no shoes. They stood upon the frozen, snow-covered ground barefoot. *I'm surprised they're not all dead.* She thought. *It's freezing out here.* The guards, who she and the other recruits were told to watch and learn from, were powerful women. They used brutal tactics to keep the prisoners in constant fear. Dagna was shocked and also enthralled. She'd never seen women in control like this, and she wanted to be like them. By the end of her first week of training, Dagna had witnessed plenty of brutalities, including beating a prisoner to death. This act of violence didn't frighten her, although it was messy. She didn't care for the sight of all that blood. But she'd seen many people beaten to death in the basement of the

Gestapo office. The entire time she and the other recruits watched the guard murder the young female prisoner, all Dagna could think about was, *I hope we won't be required to clean this up.* Because sometimes, at the Gestapo office, she'd been forced to clean up a nasty execution. But to her relief, the recruits weren't expected to clean anything. The guard, done with the prisoner, moved to the line of prisoners and pulled out two. Then she commanded them to clean up the bloody mess and get rid of the body.

As the group of trainees walked away, Dagna realized that the prisoners could be made to do whatever the guards wanted them to do. And, of course, the more vicious the guards were, the less likely the prisoners would resist. *As long as I don't have to clean up after these executions, I don't care what they do.* She remembered that day when the Gestapo agent had carved the Star of David into her friend Elica's face. Afterward, Dagna was required to clean up the blood. She closed her eyes for a single moment and thought she could hear Elica screaming. She tried to shake it off, but when she opened her eyes and glanced down at her hands, Dagna trembled because she thought she saw bloodstains on them.

The camp was filthy. Dagna had never been fastidious, but this was the dirtiest place she had ever been. She was appalled by the slop buckets in the barracks where the prisoners slept. They were always overflowing with human excrement, urine, and vomit. Almost all the prisoners had lice. They slept on dirty straw that was crawling with it. And their gray skin was covered in red pus-filled sores. The first time Dagna and the rest of the trainees were shown one of the barracks, Dagna ran outside and vomited. She wasn't the only one to vomit. But Gretel laughed so hard that all the rest of the recruits began to laugh too. They were laughing at Dagna, and this made her angry. She hated the sound of laughter, and she was growing more and more resentful of her roommate.

The recruits were shown around the camp hospital during the third week of training. They were introduced to the *Oberschwester*, or the head nurse, who introduced them to six young nurses who were on staff. The *Oberschwester* was a cold, compassionless woman. She was a large-boned woman who looked strong and capable. There were deep lines around her eyes and between her brows. She didn't smile often, and she spoke in an accusatory tone of voice. "You will find that this hospital is a difficult place to work," she told the recruits. "Some of these nurses you see here were sent to us at Ravensbrück as a punishment. For instance, that one..." she pointed to one of the nurses on staff, "she didn't want to be here, but she was foolish enough to let Göring catch her giving food to some Jew. He sent her here. She came as a stupid little fool, but we have since toughened her up. She can see where she went wrong. And now she no longer thinks of Jews as humans. I'm proud to say that we have stripped her of her weaknesses. We have shown her that she need not be compassionate, especially to Jews who are sub-human and never to be pitied. By the time your training here is complete, you should have learned the same things. That is, of course, if you don't already know."

Once Dagna learned the meanings of the colors of the triangles that the prisoners wore, it was easy to know the crimes they had each committed. Political prisoners wore red, and criminals wore green. Black was worn by prostitutes, lesbians, Aryan wives of Jews, and the disabled and mentally ill, who were done away with quickly, so there weren't many of them. But, of course, everyone knew that the yellow triangle was reserved for the Jews.

Dagna saw several prisoners who had once been Aryan women but had sacrificed that privilege to become wives of Jewish men. She looked at them with disdain, and she thought of Elica. She still resented her. But she decided that she was glad that Elica had not been sent here because she knew Elica would suffer more by living outside in the real world now that her face was scarred by the knife. *Poor Elica, she was once beautiful, but now, her face is the face of a monster. She is ugly enough to scare a child. And all this happened to her because she had to marry and try to protect her Jew lover, Daniel. And he's dead already, anyway. Stupid Elica. She could have had any man she wanted but chose that Jew, so she got what she deserved.*

"Ladies," the head nurse said loudly, commanding their attention, "this is Doctor Oberheuser."

Dagna was brought back to the present moment as a slender woman with her hair caught up in a twist at the nape of her neck nodded to the recruits. *A female doctor?* Dagna thought, impressed.

"Good afternoon," the doctor said. Then she turned to *Helferin* Braunsteiner and said, "You may go. I'll take our new trainees from here and show them around the hospital."

"All right," Braunsteiner agreed.

"Follow me. First of all, I would like to show you my rabbits," the doctor said as they walked through the halls.

"Rabbits?" one of the recruits asked. "You have rabbits here?"

"They are not real rabbits. I just like to call them that," the doctor smiled. "They are a group of Polish women I am using to test the effectiveness of sulfonamide drugs on healing infections."

Dr. Braunsteiner opened the door to a large room, and a nauseating smell filled the air. It was a new odor. It was so strong it made some of the recruits gag. Young women, who were referred to as 'the rabbits,' were scattered around the room. Looking at them, Dagna could see they had once been pretty. But now they were all painfully thin, just like all the prisoners Dagna had encountered. Some of the women had large sores on their legs that were oozing pus and blood. Red lines of infection traveled from their wounds to their thighs. She saw that at least two of the women's sores and the flesh around the sores had turned a sickly shade of green. And then there were others who were missing limbs.

"I create wounds on their legs, as you can see, and then fill them with glass or sawdust. Once the infection sets in, I can test the effectiveness of sulfonamide drugs on healing," the doctor said with her head held high. She sounded proud of her work.

The rabbits looked down at the ground. Not one of them would meet Dagna's gaze.

"Do they sometimes die from the infections?" one of the recruits asked the doctor earnestly.

"Of course. But it's no matter." The doctor smiled. "There are plenty more."

CHAPTER ELEVEN

That evening, when Dagna and Gretel retired to their room, Dagna was brushing her hair. Gretel said, "I heard something interesting today."

"Oh?"

"I heard from one of the nurses that Dr. Oberheuser knows that the sulfonamide drugs don't work to heal infection, but she enjoys torturing the prisoners. She gets some kind of sadistic pleasure from it."

"Really?" Dagna said, but she wasn't surprised. "Well, I don't give a damn about those women rabbits, but the smell and the wounds make me want to puke."

Gretel laughed. "I think she likes the power." Then Gretel said, "Have you ever had complete power over another human being? Real power, I mean."

"Actually, no. I haven't," Dagna admitted.

"I haven't either, but I can't wait to see just how that might feel. I mean, imagine that you are so powerful that another person's life depends on your whims."

"Hmmm." Dagna contemplated the idea. She thought of all the

people she hated and how she would like to have power over them. Dagna remembered how she'd been glad to see Elica finally receive punishment for how she treated her. "I can see where that could be addicting in a way."

"Yes, my feelings exactly," Gretel said. "I mean, when I was living at home, my father was the boss. I had to do whatever he told me to do. And in school, the teachers were in control of my every move. It seems like here, at Ravensbrück, the power belongs to the guards, and almost all of them are women. I like the idea. I hope when I go to work at my job, it will give me power like this. I could get used to it."

"Yes, so could I," Dagna admitted.

Dagna washed her face and got ready for bed. The lights-out bell rang, and both she and Gretel said goodnight. Although Dagna was exhausted, she couldn't sleep.

Her mind was on the blood sisters. How they'd grown from children to teenagers. Dagna had done everything in her power to make Elica like her. And for a while, she believed that she'd won Elica's friendship. She shoplifted clothing and cosmetics for herself and for Elica. And she studied Elica's every move and imitated it as best she could. She spent hours attempting to copy Elica's hairstyle. But Elica's hair was soft, thick, and blonde, while Dagna's was thin and mousy brown. Later, Dagna bleached her hair and kept it in a twist to hide how thin it was. She tried to speak like Elica, laugh like Elica, and be just like Elica. Elica loved the gifts that Dagna stole for her, so she allowed Dagna to trail behind her like a puppy. But then, when Elica became pregnant, her parents threw her out. *I remember how she refused to tell me who the father of her unborn baby was. But even though she didn't trust me, I wanted to help her. I was that devoted to her. I was such a fool. I remember how we dropped out of school, so we could get jobs. I did that just to help her afford to rent a flat. And I have to admit, those were the best days of my life. It was just me and my best friend facing the world together. But then, Daniel came back to Elica. That was when I learned that he was the father of her unborn child. Daniel, a Jew. I was appalled, but even then, I would have accepted all of it if Elica had turned away from him and stayed with me. But she was such a fool. When he proposed, Elica turned on me like a snake. She left me in the flat we rented. But of course, I didn't have enough money to pay the bills without the contribution of her salary. Elica knew that, but as always, she was selfish, and she didn't care about me. I didn't know what to do. I couldn't go back home. My parents warned me they would disown me if I dropped out of school. So, I had no choice but to get a second job. Dagna sighed aloud. It was so hard trying to make ends meet. Some nights I went without a meal because I didn't have enough money for the rent. But I wanted a better life. So, I went back to school to learn to type and take shorthand. It was very hard to go to school and work two jobs, but I forced myself to continue. And it paid off.*

Dagna hated Jews. She had grown up hating them, so when Hitler called them dangerous monsters, she'd readily agreed. However, after Elica left her and moved in with Daniel, she hated Elica too. She finally saw the girl she'd always admired as nothing but a selfish, stupid brat. Still, over the years when she and Elica had been friends, she had learned a lot. Now the friendship was over, and she was moving away from her childhood home to a new job in a new country. She planned to use that knowledge. *I will become Elica. And once I do, no one will ever again treat me like the ugly, unpopular girl.*

The hardest part of her transformation had been to lose the excess weight. However, each time she wanted to overeat, she remembered Elica's figure and the dresses Elica wore, and she stopped herself. After working at the police station, she finally earned enough money to go to a salon where her hair was professionally bleached. It was still stringy and thin, but when she wore it up, she thought it looked pretty. Dagna became popular at the police station where she worked. She flirted with the Gestapo officers, who returned her flirtations. They told her about the arrests they'd made of Jews, and she congratulated them on their contributions to the party. But she knew she could attribute her newfound popularity to having been clever enough to follow the Nazi party when it began to rise.

I am no longer the pathetic little girl who once hung on Elica's heels. I am a powerful Aryan woman. An attractive woman. And although Hitler doesn't allow women to join the SS, I will be a guard over Jews and other inferiors at my new job.

Dagna was proud of how far she'd come in her life. But she was most proud of the day when Elica had come to her begging for help. Dagna had been working at the Gestapo headquarters in Vienna when Elica came, begging her to help find Daniel, Elica's Jewish husband. After all that Elica had put Dagna through by leaving her with all the bills and running away with Daniel, Dagna was pleased to tell Elica that Daniel was dead. It was true; he was dead. He'd been murdered at the Gestapo headquarters. Dagna had witnessed his death with pleasure. The Gestapo officers were certain that Elica had other Jewish friends. Friends who were in hiding. Elica denied this, but they were determined to make her tell them where her friends were, so they locked her in a cell in the basement of the police station. They tortured her daily. Elica begged for mercy. Dagna was pleased to hear Elica beg. *It was about time she was on her knees.* And then, one afternoon, Elica gave in. She was exhausted and weak, and she gave the Gestapo the location of the hiding place where they could find Anna and her family. Dagna knew it was because she wanted to be released. But Dagna had no intentions of intervening on Elica's behalf. And she wasn't surprised to discover that Bernie and her mother were hiding Anna and her family. Dagna hated Bernie, too, because Bernie always stood up to her. Bernie was loyal and a true friend to Anna. Dagna knew that Bernie would suffer for this, and she was glad. But that still wasn't enough for Dagna. She talked a few Gestapo agents into keeping Elica a while longer so she could go down into the basement and torment Elica. However, she still could not bear to look at Elica's face. It was too exquisite. Far too perfect.

And a constant reminder that she, Dagna, was a fake. She was not really beautiful. She was, in fact, still ugly. This angered her, and so she knew if she were ever to feel beautiful, she must destroy Elica's beauty. Dagna decided that she must see that Elica's face was ruined. But she didn't have the nerve to cut Elica herself, so she asked one of the Gestapo agents to do it for her. He obliged and carved a star of David into Elica's face. It had been a nauseating mess of blood and torn skin, but once Elica's cheek was cut, leaving her scarred for life, Dagna could rest.

Dagna thought of the day Elica's cheek was carved and went to sleep with a smile.

CHAPTER TWELVE

The following day Dagna was taken to see the kitchen where the prisoners prepared their meals. And once she saw what the prisoners were given to eat, she knew why there were always more dead prisoners on carts around the camp. They were not only dying of disease, but they were also hardly given any food and dying of starvation. There was a large cauldron filled with water. In it, the prisoners added spoiled potatoes, rotting carrots, heads of cabbage that were turning brown, and large vats of potato peelings. The peelings were garbage from the regular kitchen, where the potatoes were peeled for the guards' meals.

Gretel leaned over and looked into the soup pot. Then she grabbed the sleeve of Dagna's uniform and pulled her over. "Look in the pot," she said.

Dagna glanced into the pot and saw several dead insects floating among the spoiled vegetables. She had gotten her period that morning, and her stomach was extremely sensitive. When she saw the dead insects, she couldn't help herself. She gagged again. Gretel laughed heartily, "Poor Dagna, you're always ready to vomit. It seems to me that you're weak like a Jew."

Dagna resented Gretel and her teasing more each day.

Dagna wasn't feeling well when the recruits were served sausages for lunch that day. Her menstruation sometimes affected her like this. She was wracked with cramps, and she couldn't eat. Her stomach ached, and she was afraid she might vomit if she tried.

Gretel watched Dagna, "Don't tell me that the kitchen this morning made you sick like this."

"Actually, no. I have my period. And, sometimes, it's like this."

"You get sick like this from your period? My, my, you really are weak."

Dagna glared at Gretel. She was sorry she'd told her about how she was feeling. She hated having Gretel around. *This girl is not a friend. She's a mean person just waiting to see me fall. In fact, I hate to admit it, but being around her makes me miss my real friends. I never knew how good they were to me. She closed her eyes and saw their faces: Bernie, Elica, and even Anna.*

After lunch, *Helferin* Braunsteiner gathered the recruits and led them outside to an open area. In the center of this field stood a prisoner, a young girl. Her body trembled from the cold, and she was bent at the waist, weeping softly. Beside her was a guard, a skinny woman with big dark eyes and thin dark hair. Her small lips were pursed.

"Ladies," Braunsteiner said, "I would like you to meet Juana Bormann. She's known by all of us here at Ravensbrück as the woman with the dogs.

The small skinny guard with deep-set dark eyes stepped forward, a wicked-looking half smile spread across her lips. Dagna trembled. *Woman with the dogs.* She thought.

"Good afternoon," Bormann said. Then she turned to Braunsteiner, "And thank you for the introduction."

Braunsteiner nodded.

"This afternoon, I would like to introduce you to my dogs. Dogs, I find, are a very powerful weapon against weak prisoners. They are terrified of them, and therefore they will not misbehave when faced with the threat of being attacked by dogs." She sighed. "Before I began working here at Ravensbrück, I was a guard at a mental hospital. Most of our patients were incorrigible. They refused to follow instructions from the staff. However, after they witnessed a few of their peers being torn to shreds by the dogs, they no longer resisted. Therefore, I find that every so often, each week, or every other week, depending upon what other chores I must complete, I do a demonstration. I gather all the prisoners in this field and then choose one unlucky one to use as an example." She smiled. "Today, it happens to be this one." She pointed to the young girl, who was visibly trembling and still weeping. Without another word, Bormann walked away. Several moments passed. No one said a word. The prisoner was shaking so hard that Dagna thought she might fall over. But then Bormann yelled, "Run." The prisoner began to run. Dagna was sure that Braunsteiner would shoot her, but she didn't. Instead, five large German shepherds came rushing out from behind the building. Bormann was at their heels, yelling, "Get her! Get her."

The dogs didn't take long to catch up with the prisoner. They attacked the young girl, jumping on top of her. She let out a scream of fear and pain. Dagna was trembling. The dogs bit into their victim's legs and arms. Then another bit into her face. The snow grew red with blood. One of the dogs had bitten off a finger and was now eating it. Dagna was transported back to the incident with her neighbor's dog. She fell to her knees and cried out, "Stop this! Please, stop this."

Braunsteiner nudged Bormann, and the two of them began laughing. Then the rest of the recruits started laughing, too. "You're too weak to be an Aryan." Then, turning to Braunsteiner, Bormann added, "She might be a Jew."

"She acts like one." Braunsteiner agreed.

"I'm sorry." Dagna croaked, "I was attacked by a dog when I was a little girl. I'm afraid of dogs because of it."

"You're pathetic," Braunsteiner said. "But nothing to worry about. We'll get that fear and weakness out of you. You will spend the next two days training with Bormann and her hounds." Braunsteiner smiled wickedly. "She will teach you everything you need to know about dogs."

"Oh no, please. Anything but that."

Braunsteiner shook her head. "This is what you need. So, starting tomorrow, you'll train with Bormann."

Bormann gave Dagna a vicious smile that sent a chill up her spine.

CHAPTER THIRTEEN

For the next two weeks, because Dagna was in training with Bormann, every day began with a demonstration by Bormann. It was always the same. A prisoner was selected by Bormann, and Dagna was forced to watch the dogs tear that prisoner to pieces. Then she was made to watch as another prisoner cleaned up the mess, dragging the dead body and putting it on one of the carts leaving blood on the snow. Instead of making Dagna stronger and less fearful, it only made her more scared. Bormann tried to force Dagna into the dog's kennel to feed them, but she refused to go. In fact, she couldn't even make herself do it. Her feet would not move. At first, Bormann laughed at her, but as time passed, Bormann lost patience and grew angry that Dagna was not becoming any stronger. "You are much too weak to work with us," she said in a loud, guttural voice. "You had better get a hold of yourself. The dogs can smell your weakness, your fear. If I let them out, they would tear you up, the same way they do those prisoners because of it."

To make matters worse, Dagna had become known amongst the other recruits as pathetic and incapable of doing this job. They made fun of her every chance they got. Meals became miserable. No one sat with her, and she began overeating again the way she had when she was young, and the other children teased her. She could see she was gaining weight but couldn't stop herself. Gretel requested a move, and the following day she was moved out of the room she shared with Dagna. Gretel was then settled into a room with another recruit. After that, Gretel became the ringleader of the girls when they were teasing Dagna. It was terrible. Every day at Ravensbrück was terrible for Dagna. Although she hardly noticed the smell anymore, she hated the prisoners, the guards, and the other recruits. But then, one day, Bormann sent Dagna to her office to retrieve Bormann's overcoat. And then, while she was in Bormann's office, she decided to look at Bormann's desk. *Perhaps I can find out something about her, anything I can hold over her. I hate her. I would love to destroy her.* Dagna thought as she rummaged through Bormann's desk.

She looked through everything but found nothing unusual. Dagna continued to search until she found several chocolate bars. One of them was open. The thought of eating a little chocolate was soothing to her. She carefully broke off a piece and shoved it into her mouth. For a few moments, she savored the sweet flavor. But then, something happened. Something she was hardly expecting.

Dagna felt lightheaded, excited, and filled with energy. Her face flushed, and she was no longer afraid. Not even of the dogs. *I feel like I could conquer the world. What's in this chocolate?* Dagna knew the chocolate was more than just candy. However, she couldn't ask Bormann about it because she wasn't supposed to be rifling around her superior's desk. Dagna had heard of the candy that had Pervitin in it. She'd read about *Fliegerschokolade*, flyers chocolate, and *Panzerschokolade*, the tanker's chocolate, both of which were chocolate bars given to the troops to help them become courageous and strong. Could this be the same chocolate? She certainly felt invincible, and it was a wonderful feeling. Dagna took a bar of candy and boldly stuffed it into her uniform pocket. *If I get caught, Bormann will be furious. But hopefully, I won't be found out. And, if she should realize it's missing and ask me if I saw her candy, I'll say I never saw it. I'll blame it on a prisoner.* And at that moment, Dagna had an idea. She was ready to find a special prisoner who she could use for her own ends.

CHAPTER FOURTEEN

F rom the moment Aria and Mateo brought the little boy home, he'd become the light of their lives. They renamed him Enzo, and he looked so much like Aria that most people who saw them had no doubt that she was his birth mother. A few months after Enzo's arrival, he turned four years old. Aria was excited. She wanted to make this day a special one for this child, who she believed had never been anything more than another orphan. So, she told Mateo that she wanted to see Enzo's eyes light up, so to make her happy, Mateo gave a party. Everyone of importance in Mussolini's regime was invited. And they brought their wives and children and lovely expensive gifts, which Aria helped unwrap. Most of the gifts were clothes or jewelry. There were wool sweaters, fancy little suits, and tiny gold pendants that Aria knew Enzo would probably never wear. However, she thanked each of the guests for their thoughtfulness.

A few of them brought toys, and each toy made Enzo laugh and smile with excitement. The finest baker in Rome was commissioned to prepare a birthday cake that would rival the wedding cakes ordered by most common people. Any outsider who viewed this birthday party would have been in awe of the opulence. In fact, they might have even believed that a fascist government was not so bad and that the Italian people thrived under Mussolini. However, they would have been wrong. The average working family in Italy under Duce, as Mussolini was called, endured a life of strict governmental control and poverty. However, no Italian citizen dared to speak out against the dictator. Mussolini put laws in place firmly forbidding it. And should anyone even think of breaking this law, they knew that they would be subjected to torture and violence at the hands of Mussolini's black shirts. These were henchmen who watched and waited readily at all times to use violence against anyone who opposed the dictator.

Aria had hired a band to entertain the adults and clown for the children. Enzo was sitting between his parents when the clown entered the ballroom in the Leonis home. Enzo trembled and dropped his fork. He was clearly afraid of this costumed man with a face full of grotesque makeup. The little boy slipped from the bottom of his chair and hid behind his mother. Aria laughed. Her laughter rang like church bells through the room. She gathered him up into her arms and held him. She smiled at her husband. He returned her smile, knowing she thought the child's fear was sweet and endearing. "Don't be afraid. Nothing will ever harm you as long as I am with you," she whispered to Enzo. He cuddled closer to her, and her chest swelled with love for him as he did.

After the guests left, Mateo told Aria and Enzo to wait in the living room because he had a special surprise. "Now it's time for my gifts, Enzo," he said.

Enzo clapped his hands together. Mateo laughed and left the room.

Aria held the little boy in her arms. He lay his head on her breast and sucked his thumb as they waited. A few minutes later, Mateo came out of the bedroom carrying two large packages wrapped in brown paper with blue ribbons and bows. "These are for you, son," he said to Enzo. "Go on. Unwrap them. They are for you."

Enzo climbed down onto the floor. But then he just stared at the gifts. It seemed that he did not know what to do with the packages, as he'd never unwrapped a gift before. He looked up at Aria, puzzled. He seemed afraid to touch the gifts as if he might be punished. Aria smiled at him and then got down on the floor beside him. She still wore the elegant pink dress she'd purchased for this party. "It's all right. Don't be afraid. I'll help you unwrap your gifts."

"Mama," he said lovingly.

She kissed his chubby cheek, and he plopped down on her lap. She glanced up at Mateo and saw the love shining in his eyes. "Come on, I can hardly wait to see your excitement. Hurry, open the gifts," Mateo said, smiling.

The first package contained a large toy rifle and a handmade tiny military uniform that would fit Enzo perfectly. The uniform was an exact match for the one Mateo wore. Enzo picked up one of the toy guns and held it for a moment. Aria's face grew dark. Seeing her son holding a weapon seemed like a prediction to her, and it made her nervous. She smiled at Enzo, gently took the gun away, and laid it on the floor. "Let's open the other one," she said cheerfully.

Enzo giggled and hugged his mother. Aria opened the second gift. Inside was a large, well-made puppet. It was almost the size of Enzo. "And what's this?" she asked Mateo.

"Watch," Mateo winked. Then he picked up the puppet. It wasn't just any puppet, but a special puppet made for a ventriloquist. The puppet took on the form of a young boy with rosy cheeks and bright orange hair that stood up straight. He had bright blue eyes and a wide mouth that moved as Mateo began to speak without moving his lips. It was obvious to Aria that Mateo had practiced this because he was quite good, and Enzo loved it. He clapped his chubby hands and spoke directly to the puppet in his broken child's speech. And for over a full half hour, Mateo entertained his son. Aria giggled. But finally, Mateo sighed and said, "Well, I have some work I must complete by the end of the day. So, I can't play anymore right now." Then he hugged Enzo. "But, I promise you, we'll play again tomorrow, alright?"

"I love you, papa," Enzo said, nodding.

Aria got up from the floor and kissed Mateo on the lips. "Thank you," she said.

"I love both of you," Mateo said, but he was looking directly at Aria, who was smiling broadly.

CHAPTER FIFTEEN

L ife at Ravensbrück was hard at best, and friendships were often the only thing that stood between hope and giving up. When Moriah's closest friend, Bernie, died, Moriah fell into a deep depression. Ravensbrück was hell; she was ready to let go, stop fighting, and stop clinging to life. She was ready to die, and she would have if it had not been for the promise she'd made to Bernie. Bernie was insistent that if the war ever ended and Moriah managed to survive, she should make every effort to search for Elica Frey or Anna Levinstein. She must tell them the secret Bernie had shared about the address she had left in the blood sister's tin box. This was the address of the orphanage where Bernie had left Elica's son, Theo. Bernie had also told her to remember the name Dagna Hofer. She warned Moriah that Dagna might try to find her because she might be looking for the little boy. Bernie explained how Dagna had been involved with Bernie, Elica, and Anna. "Dagna is a dangerous woman. If you run into her while searching for Elica and Anna, be careful. Beware of Dagna Hofer," Bernie said.

At the time, these names meant nothing to Moriah. But that was before the new guard had come into her block and introduced herself as Dagna Hofer. Moriah was shocked and instantly terrified by Dagna. She'd expected her to be terrible, but she hadn't expected to meet up with her here in Ravensbrück.

After Bernie died and Moriah was lost, a middle-aged prostitute named Heidi took Moriah under her wing. "I like Jews," she'd said to Moriah. "I'm not Jewish, of course. But the Jewish men who came to visit me were always generous."

Of course, it was obvious to Heidi that Moriah was Jewish because she wore the yellow triangle.

Needing a friend desperately, Moriah clung to Heidi, who was protective in a motherly way. And in turn, Moriah often stole bits of bread from the kitchen where she worked and shared them with Heidi. They talked about their lives before Ravensbrück. Although Moriah had been sheltered by her parents and she'd never met a prostitute before, she didn't judge Heidi. Heidi explained how difficult life had been for her. "I had two young children. I had to feed them after my husband left us. I had no skills and no education. All I had to my name was my body. It was the only thing I could use to earn money. But it doesn't matter anymore. These bastard Nazis killed my children. Both of them. I had a boy and a girl. They were the light of my life. Now, my life is dark. I don't care what happens to me. I'm old. But you're young. You still could have a good life after this is over."

"Who says this will ever be over?" Moriah asked.

"Everything comes to an end. Whether it's good or bad. Everything ends. Everything changes eventually. However, my children are dead, and there is nothing I can do to bring them back. So, although this will end, I will never find light in my life again."

Moriah understood. She just nodded her head. "It's all right," she said. "It's all right."

When Dagna came into the block where Heidi and Moriah slept, along with another recruit, and introduced herself, Moriah could hardly contain her fear. She didn't look directly at the woman called Dagna Hoffer, but when Dagna turned around to leave, she looked up at her and saw a blonde with big shoulders. Dagna's eyes were bloodshot, her face was beet red, and she looked fierce. But then again, all the guards looked that way to Moriah. Since she came to Ravensbrück, Moriah learned it didn't matter how the Nazi guards looked on the outside. They could be ugly like Bormann, who used dogs to murder, or beautiful like Ilse Grese, a sexual sadist responsible for the torture and murder of many young women. They were all horrible. Every single one of them was vicious.

After Dagna and the other recruit left, Moriah whispered to Heidi, telling her what Bernie had said about Dagna.

"Bernie knew her?"

"Yes, apparently she did. I don't know much more than that. But yes, she knew her," Moriah said. Then Moriah went on to tell Heidi the entire story about the promise she'd made to Bernie. "You see," Moriah explained, "when Bernie was a child, she made a pact with two other girls. One's name was Elica Frey, and the other was Anna Levinstein. The pact was that they were blood sisters and would stand by each other forever. Well, from what I understood, Dagna was also a part of the group. She forced her way in somehow. Bernie never explained how. But apparently, when they grew up, Bernie hid Anna and her family in the attic of Bernie's home because Anna was Jewish. But one night, Elica came to see Bernie and asked her to watch her son, Theo, who was a baby. Elica needed Bernie to watch Theo because she had to go to the police station to search for her husband, who was a Jew, and he'd been arrested by the Gestapo. Elica was afraid to take the child with her because the boy was half-Jewish, and she feared the Gestapo would take him away from her. So, she left the child with Bernie. When Elica didn't return after several days, Bernie decided she couldn't risk keeping him at her home. So, to keep the little boy safe, she had to hide him somewhere. She would not tell me where she took him because she said that if I was ever tortured for some reason, it would be better if I didn't know all the details. I didn't care. At the time, it didn't matter to me at all. So, I promised Bernie that if this ever ended, I would do my best to find Anna and Elica, and if I found them, I would tell them to look in the tin box."

"The tin box?"

"Yes. When these girls were children, they had a tin box and hid it somewhere. Bernie wouldn't tell me where they hid it. But she said they would know as soon as I mentioned it. Apparently, Anna was arrested while Bernie was away, taking the child to his hiding place. Bernie had no idea what had happened to her. And she never saw Elica again after Elica left to go to the police station. Bernie said she wasn't sure that any of these girls were even alive. But what's interesting and terrifying is that Dagna Hoffer was part of this group, and Bernie warned me to be careful of her. Now, Dagna is here at Ravensbrück."

"What a frightening story. I wonder how she got here as a guard in training if she was once part of a blood sister group with a Jewish girl."

"I don't know. But what I know is that we might just have something on her. And we might be able to use that information."

"We might. But that knowledge is dangerous. It could cost us our lives. I don't suggest you tell anyone else but me," Heidi said.

CHAPTER SIXTEEN

The following day, the prisoners were lined up for evening roll call. Moriah shot a glance at Heidi. The group of trainees gathered around a heavy-set woman. Her dark blonde hair was twisted into a knot at the back. However, she'd rolled the front of her hair into large sausage-like rolls.

"Who's that one with the hair rolled like sausages? Is she new?" Moriah asked Heidi.

"No, I've seen her before. Her name is Herta Ehlert. They call her the whip master," Heidi whispered to Moriah as they entered the line. "Watch your eyes. Don't draw any attention to yourself. Make sure you don't look directly at her. She's looking for a prisoner to make an example. Keep your eyes down on the ground."

Moriah felt a chill run down her spine. *Whip master.* She thought. *Will these people never cease to find ways to torture us? If it weren't for my promise to Bernie, I would quit and just let them kill me. I'm tired. I'm worn out by misery and pain.*

"For those of you who have not met her, this is Herta Ehlert. She will be in charge of your lesson today," *Helferin* Braunsteiner said to the recruits.

Herta Ehlert was a big-boned, thick-faced ox of a woman. Her eyes were small, beady, and cruel. In a holster by her side, she wore a whip. This whip, due to the unbelievable cruelty shown to the prisoners with its use, became her signature trademark.

Moriah stood, looking at the ground and listening to the thumping of her heart in her ears. Something terrible was about to happen. She knew it as she cast her eyes up for a moment to steal a glimpse at Dagna. *She is so terribly ugly.* Moriah thought. Dagna was flushed, just as she was the day before. Her face was turned to stare at Braunsteiner, and she listened intently to everything Braunsteiner was saying. Even in the mere second, when Moriah looked at Dagna Hoffer, she saw that Dagna was shifting her feet. It seemed she could not stand still. Quickly, before anyone took notice, Moriah looked back down at the ground. *I wish I had listened more when Bernie talked to me about her. I can't remember what she said except that she told me to beware of her. And, of course, now I can see why.*

The whip master walked in front of the prisoners, snapping her whip on the ground. If fear had a sound or smell, it would have been overflowing from the prisoners. Those who, like Moriah, had not yet met Ehlert would soon learn that she was as close to a demon as a human being could be.

Ehlert enjoyed her work. It was written all over her face. This woman was a pure sadist; as promised, Ehlert was a master with her whip. Walking back and forth as she cracked the whip in front of the prisoners, she looked like a predator, keen on finding the perfect victim. An animal that would sniff out the woman who feared her the most. Slowly, ever so slowly, Ehlert continued to saunter back and forth in front of the terrified prisoners. Then she returned her whip to its holster, and there was a sigh of relief. A few moments passed. It seemed that Ehlert was not going to choose a victim today. But then she stopped, pulled the whip out quickly, and cracked it hard on the floor. At the sound of the cracking whip, several prisoners jumped.

Ehlert stopped walking and laughed. Then she began to pace

again, and a half smile crossed her face. Then, for no apparent reason, she pulled a young girl with a yellow triangle out of the line. *A Jewish girl.* Moriah gasped. The guards were the hardest on the Jews. And this young girl couldn't have been more than fifteen years old. She was scared. Anyone could see that. She did her best to pull away from Ehlert, who was far bigger and stronger. Ehlert pushed the girl down, and she fell to her knees. That was when she began to beg. It was no use. The harder she pleaded, the more Ehlert smiled. "Take off your uniform," Ehlert said.

"No, please, no," the young girl answered. "I've done nothing wrong."

Moriah looked at the prisoner with pity. Her fate was sealed, and Moriah knew it. This girl would die today, no matter what she said or did. Moriah shivered. She didn't know this young woman personally. Still, she began to think about what the girl's life might have been like before she'd been arrested and brought to Ravensbrück. She'd been someone's daughter, perhaps a sister or friend. Was her mother still alive? Wherever her mother was, could she feel something was wrong with her child? Moriah felt tears coming to her eyes. But she knew she must not cry. This would draw the attention of the sadistic guards, and instead of evoking pity, they would go after her blood. She tried to look away from the young teen but couldn't. Ehlert had taken a knife and made a cut in the girl's uniform, then she tore it away. Instinctively, the girl covered her naked breasts with her hands. Her body was shaking hard, and she was weeping.

The poor thing. Moriah was both sick with pity and terrified, and she felt like she might vomit. Then Ehlert lifted her whip and lashed the girl across the back. The prisoner let out a scream and urinated. A stream of urine began to pool on the ground. The girl was panicked. She tried to get up and run, but Ehlert was faster, and another crack of the whip fell upon the girl's back. Fueled by the sight of blood, Ehlert began to circle the young girl, wielding her whip and lashing the girl's face and shoulders. Then she noticed the urine. "*Juden-schwein*. Jew pig. You pissed on the ground," Ehlert said. Then she lashed the girl again. She did not stop until the young Jewish prisoner lay dead in a pool of blood.

CHAPTER SEVENTEEN

After Herta Ehlert's demonstration with her whip, the new recruits were sent to the main dining room for their evening meal. Dagna had seen plenty of violence in her life. But nothing compared to the disgusting, horrible things she'd witnessed since her arrival at Ravensbrück. She didn't care about the Jews, but she was disgusted by all the blood, the smells, the bodily fluids, the lice, the disease, and the death carts. However, the chocolate candy she'd discovered was like magic. It gave her energy, and when she ate it, nothing bothered her. In fact, she felt invincible. With the candy, she had even learned to be less fearful of the dogs, although she stayed away from them.

However, she knew that without the special chocolate, she wouldn't be able to get through this training. The other recruits and the instructors noticed the change in her. The other recruits no longer teased her. In fact, they began to invite her on picnics and hikes on their off days. The only problem was getting her hands on more of this chocolate. She realized that not only would she need it here at Ravensbrück, but she would also probably need it once she started working at Sobibor. She had to have the chocolate, so in desperation, she'd stolen a bar from Bormann's desk. She had eaten it very sparingly. However, now it was almost gone. And soon, she would need another. Dagna was afraid of getting caught. She'd witnessed the insane cruelty and viciousness of Bormann. *Who knows what she would do if she found out I stole from her? She might turn her dogs loose on me.* The thought made Dagna shiver. *No matter what, I must never get caught rummaging through her desk. But... I can get the chocolate if I use one of the prisoners to steal it.*

CHAPTER EIGHTEEN

Ilse Grese was known to be a sexual pervert who loved to control not only the prisoners but her fellow guards as well. Especially those who ranked below her. She had curly, light blonde hair and pure Aryan features. Ilse was slender and would have been considered both beautiful and heartless—a terrifying combination.

Dagna attended a picnic with several other recruits on her day off. It was there that she met Ilse Grese. Dagna had always admired and emulated beautiful women, and because of this, she was immediately drawn to Ilse. Because beauty had always eluded her, Dagna had hung on to Elica Frey, who was everything she'd wanted to be at the time. After she had watched as the Gestapo destroyed Elica's face, she tried her best to become the woman Elica had once been. Dagna had lost weight, bleached her hair blonde, and imitated every gesture of Elica's that she could remember. However, as hard as she tried, Dagna knew that she was never really beautiful.

And to make matters worse, since she had begun training at Ravensbrück, she'd started gaining back the weight she had lost. So, when Ilse introduced herself to her, Dagna was awestruck by Ilse's natural beauty. She was filled with admiration. After all this time without Elica, she'd finally found a new woman to befriend and mimic. "Hello, you probably already know who I am?"

"Of course, you're Ilse Grese," Dagna said. "Everyone knows who you are. You're the prettiest guard at Ravensbrück. Everyone says so."

Ilse laughed. "Is that what they say?" She tried to appear humble, but Dagna could see that Ilse was very confident. She knew she was beautiful.

"Yes, that's what everyone says. And I agree."

"Well, isn't that nice? Thank you. I'm quite flattered."

Dagna smiled, but then she noticed a strange-looking girl standing alone behind a bunch of bushes. The girl had orange-yellow hair and was very heavyset. She was watching Ilse with an odd expression on her face. Dagna found this girl to be very off-putting. "Who's that?" Dagna asked.

"Oh, that's just Hilde. She's rather strange. Don't pay her any attention."

That day, as they were having the picnic in the park, Ilse was attentive and friendly to Dagna. What Dagna liked most about her was that Ilse treated her like an equal. It made Dagna feel like they were both gorgeous Aryan women. There was little talk of the camp that day. Mostly, Dagna and Ilse discussed the latest fashions and how to use cosmetics. And at the end of the long, sweet afternoon, when they returned to Ravensbrück, tired from a day in the sun, Dagna was happy. She had a new friend. Ilse was the kind of girl Dagna could be proud to be seen with.

At first, Ilse invited Dagna to her room, where they had a few glasses of schnapps. They talked and giggled, and Ilse even permitted Dagna to try on her lipsticks and mascara. Dagna was elated. However, Ilse's true nature had not yet surfaced. Dagna had heard that Ilse was sadistic towards the prisoners but assumed it would never occur in their friendship. However, after Dagna and Ilse had been meeting in the evenings for a week or so, something strange happened.

When Dagna arrived at Ilse's room, Ilse was sitting on her sofa wearing a silk robe with high heel shoes. Her curly blonde hair fell loose about her shoulders. A bottle of schnapps sat on the table with two glasses. All of this was not unusual. However, a young female prisoner was kneeling on the floor this time. She was naked. But she was not crying. In fact, her face was still, but her eyes were defiant.

"We're going to have some fun tonight," Ilse told Dagna.

Dagna had not needed to eat the chocolate on the nights she visited with Ilse. However, as she looked around at the naked girl on the floor, she wished she'd eaten it tonight.

"Oh?" Dagna asked cautiously. "What kind of fun?"

"Lots of fun. We are going to have a good time. And the best part of it all is that there are no consequences. None. We can do exactly as we please," Ilse giggled.

"All right," Dagna agreed, but she was not enthusiastic about what was to come. She would have much preferred to go on talking about fashions.

Ilse forced the prisoner to crawl on all fours across the floor. The girl didn't move, so Ilse kicked her in the ribs, and Dagna noted that the girl's rib cage jutted out from her flesh as she finally followed the instructions.

"You're too slow," Ilse said, then she kicked the prisoner again. "I should have worn my boots," she said to Dagna. "These shoes don't make much of an impact." Ilse took off one of her shoes and hit the prisoner across her naked back with the high heel. The prisoner let out a scream. Then Ilse handed the shoe to Dagna. "Hit her," she said. "She's a Jew. You hate Jews, don't you? Hit her, punish her for all the terrible things every Jew ever did to you."

Dagna took the shoe. She thought of Anna. She thought of how Anna had stolen the place that should have been hers amongst her blood sisters. She was certain Bernie and Elica had always liked Anna better than her. Dagna took the high heel and hit the prisoner. The heel cut into the girl's flesh, and she began to bleed. But this time, the prisoner did not cry out. She winced but remained silent.

"Good job," Ilse said, smiling. Then she turned to the prisoner. "Stand up."

The young girl was weak and had trouble getting to her feet.

"Move a little faster. You move like an old woman," Ilse laughed a wicked laugh. The girl stood up. She was obviously uncomfortable being naked. She covered her breasts with one hand and her vagina with the other. "Now move your hands," Ilse said.

"No," the girl said defiantly.

"I said do it," Ilse said, brandishing the high heel.

The girl dropped her hands and glared at Ilse.

"Look at those tiny nubs she has for breasts," Ilse said. Then she stood up and took something out of a drawer. She clamped the prisoner's nipples. The prisoner stifled a scream.

"Your turn." Ilse smiled at Dagna.

Dagna thought of Anna and slapped the prisoner across the face as hard as she could. It felt good to take out her hatred of Jews on this young woman. It made her feel strong and in control. She thought of all the times that she'd been teased by other girls, and suddenly she wanted to make all of them pay by torturing this prisoner—this young, vulnerable, and innocent girl.

The torture continued for several hours. Ilse knocked the prisoner down again. It was easy to push her over. She hardly weighed anything at all. "I don't think we will kill her," Ilse said. "I've enjoyed her too much. Perhaps we'll bring her back here on another night. What do you think?" She asked Dagna.

Dagna nodded. "Sure, why not?" In Dagna's mind, the young female prisoner had become Anna, Elica, and every girl who had ever teased and laughed at her. Dagna looked down at the heap in the corner. "She looks half dead already. She might die before morning," Dagna said to Ilse.

"So, what if she does?" Ilse smiled. "It's no concern of ours. There are plenty more of them that we can use in the future. But I would prefer she dies in her own block rather than in my room. Let the rest of the Jews carry her filthy body to one of the carts. I don't want to be responsible."

"Get up, Jew pig," Dagna said as she kicked the young prisoner in the ribs. She was enjoying the power far more than she ever realized she would. It made her feel good to punish one of the prisoners, especially a pretty one. Especially one who had so much more going for her than Dagna did. She thought about how good she felt when the Gestapo agent carved that Jewish star into Elica's beautiful cheek. All the years she'd spent in Elica's shadow came back to her. Boys never showed Dagna any attention until recently. Everything had always been all about Elica at the beginning of her life. But now, even though she had started to gain weight again, Dagna was in charge of these weaker pathetic women. Dagna was no longer someone to be teased or ignored. She was powerful, and soon she would be at work as an official guard in Sobibor. Then she could do what Ilse did, take a prisoner at night like this, and torture her. The feeling of power ran like a bolt of lightning through her veins, filling her with energy and excitement. *I would love to do this while eating the chocolate.* Dagna let out a laugh as she kicked the girl again. Then she turned to Ilse, who seemed bored with the whole thing.

Ilse turned to the prisoner. "Get up, Jew whore, and put your uniform back on. You're lucky I've decided to let you live another day. So go and get out of here before I change my mind. Go now. Return to your block. Don't get caught being out at night, or you'll be severely punished."

The prisoner, still bleeding, slipped her clothes on as fast as she could and ran out of the room.

CHAPTER NINETEEN

When Moriah returned to her block, Heidi was awake and waiting. She'd been there when Ilse had chosen Moriah as her victim for the night. "Psssst," Heidi said, "come here. Get in bed already."

Moriah, in pain, walked over to Heidi and climbed onto the dirty straw beside her friend.

"Poor girl. Poor little girl. What happened?"

Moriah told Heidi everything that had happened that night. When she'd finished, she said, "And Dagna was there. Do you remember me telling you about what Bernie said about Dagna? She was horrible, just like Bernie said she was. I am so afraid the two of them will come for me again."

"Ilse probably won't bother with you again. She likes variety in the women she chooses for her sadistic pleasures," Heidi said sarcastically.

"But what about Dagna? I'm afraid she will want to bring me back there again. Her cruelty was far worse than Ilse's, if you can believe it."

"I don't want to imagine it," Heidi said, running her hand over

Moriah's hair like a mother trying to comfort a child. "Shhh... don't think about it right now. Get some sleep. You'll need it. We have to work hard so that they have a reason to keep us around. And it's almost dawn. We're going to have to get up soon."

"I'd like to kill them both," Moriah said. She was crying softly.

Heidi began to sing a lullaby softly in Yiddish.

"How do you know Yiddish?" Moriah asked. "You're not Jewish, are you?"

"No, I'm not. However, I had a few Jewish clients when I was a working girl. Nice men. They paid me well. One of them taught me this lullaby. It gave him some comfort for me to sing it to him."

"Was prostitution terrible?" Moriah asked, "You don't have to answer if you don't want to."

"Sometimes it was. But other times, it wasn't. However, even at the worst times, it was never as bad as this place is," Heidi admitted.

"I can't sleep. I'm in too much pain," Moriah said.

"All right, then I'll stay up with you. Why don't you tell me more about Bernie and the little boy called Theo? Tell me how Dagna, this Nazi guard recruit, could be involved."

"You really want to know?"

"I do. I mean, you've told me some of it, but I know there is more, and I need to hear a story. Something to distract me from our reality right now."

"I'll tell you everything. I'll tell you all about Bernie and her blood sisters, Anna and Elica. And I'll tell you about Theo and the hidden tin box that holds all the secrets."

They lay together on the dirty straw, cuddled up for warmth, as Moriah began the story.

"As you know, I didn't know Bernie on the outside. Bernie and I became best friends here in this place...."

CHAPTER TWENTY

When Moriah heard the click of boots on the pavement outside her block, she glanced out the window. It was Ilse. Moriah was tiny. She easily fit between the cots and the wall. Quickly, she ducked between them, hiding from Ilse's view. But she needn't have worried because Heidi was right. When Ilse entered their block, she was searching for a new victim. She had already lost interest in Moriah. Moriah was grateful as Ilse pulled a pretty young girl by the arm and led her away. But Moriah felt sick the following morning when she saw the naked corpse of Ilse's latest victim lying on top of a pile of dead bodies. *That could have been me.* She thought. *Maybe I would be better off if it was me.* She thought, but then she remembered her promise to Bernie. She'd promised Bernie that she would do whatever she had to do to survive. Bernie had been her best friend; she'd stood by Moriah even while the other prisoners shunned her because she'd been chosen by one of the male kitchen guards to be his lover. *That was a terrible time for me. I was constantly humiliated. And I suffered humiliation again the other night when Ilse and Dagna took me. But Bernie never looked down on me. She helped me cope with my strange feelings about the kitchen guard. She wanted me to survive not only for myself but also so I could help that little boy, Theo, find his mother again. I wish I had asked her more about her friends, especially Dagna. However, at the time, I never thought Dagna would come here to Ravensbrück as one of the guard trainees. I didn't think I would ever meet her unless it was in the outside world after the war. That is, if it's ever over. But now that I've met her and suffered at her hands. I can see why Bernie said she was vicious, and I truly hate her. Maybe even more than the other guards, because I think she may have done things to hurt Bernie before Bernie was arrested.*

CHAPTER TWENTY-ONE

Italy

Mateo awoke early one morning. He stretched in bed, then turned over to watch his precious wife sleep. This was a pastime of his. Even though they'd been married for years, he was still crazy about her. He found that even if they spent the night before making love until the wee hours, he wanted her again by sunrise. Mateo had been indifferent about the child when they'd first adopted Enzo. He'd adopted to make Aria happy. But as the weeks passed, Mateo found that he had grown to care deeply for the little boy. Part of it, he knew, was because the child had fulfilled Aria's need for a baby. She was no longer depressed. And Mateo found that the more he was able to do for the child, the happier it made his wife. And so, one afternoon, he took off early from work. Then he had his driver drive the three of them out to a farm in the country. He'd already contacted the farmer and made arrangements for Enzo to go for a pony ride and attempt to milk a cow. Enzo loved the farm, with its fresh vegetables and animals everywhere. Mateo found it endearing as the little boy ran around chasing the chickens while Aria watched with the eyes of an adoring mother. Mateo smiled. Aria was enchanted by the child, and he, Mateo, was enchanted by his wife.

Mateo was brought back to the present moment as Aria stirred in bed beside him. She saw him watching her and smiled. "Good morning," she said in the husky morning voice she had that drove him crazy with desire for her.

"How did you sleep?" he asked, taking the hair out of her eyes.

"Well, I would say I slept well... but the truth is, someone kept me up all night... making love. Can you just imagine?" She giggled.

"And you didn't like it?" he asked coyly.

"No, I didn't."

His face dropped. He was offended and suddenly worried. But then Aria added, "I loved it, silly." And she got up on her elbow and began tickling him. He was much stronger than she and turned her onto her back. Then he leaned over her and kissed her. Passion rose in him. She sighed. Then he took her into his arms, and they made love again.

Once it was over, Mateo stood up. He was naked, and his body was in excellent shape for a man his age. He attributed this to his time in the military as a young man. It was there that he formed the habit of exercising each morning. And, even after all these years, he still kept up with that routine. He walked over to his jacket, which hung in the closet, and pulled out a small box. Then he sat down on the edge of the bed, facing his wife. "Remember last week when I went to Florence for the day? Well, I got you a little something. I've been meaning to give it to you, but I was waiting for the right time."

"For me?" she asked.

"Of course, for you. You are my one and only true love, aren't you?"

She smiled. "I hope so." She giggled.

"Believe me, you are."

"And you are mine," she said.

He handed her a white box tied with a red ribbon. She looked into his eyes. "What is this for? It's not my birthday."

"Let's call it a 'just because I love you' gift."

She opened the box. Inside, she found a large single diamond drop necklace. The diamond caught the light from the window and sent a rainbow of colored light across the wall. "Oh!" she gasped, "it's beautiful."

"I saw it, and I couldn't resist. I had to get it for you."

"Oh, Mateo, you are so good to me!"

He took her in his arms, and they made love again. Then they lay wrapped up in each other until they heard Enzo's voice. "Mama," he called out from his room. "Mama."

Aria smiled at Mateo. Then she stood up and kissed Mateo one more time. "You should probably get dressed and come downstairs for breakfast," she said.

"Yes, you're right, I should. I must get to the office. But I'd rather spend the entire day in bed with you."

After Mateo left for work, Aria planned her day with her precious son. She loved to take him into her room, where they would lie in her bed as she read to him. And somehow, he seemed to understand everything she read. He would listen quietly and watch her eyes. She adored him. Sometimes she sang to him, singing songs she remembered from her childhood, which would put him to sleep. He had moments of fussiness, but he was an easy baby most of the time. Aria gave him a bath each day in a large tub she set up in the middle of her bedroom. He played in the tub for as long as she would allow him to. "I think you're secretly half fish," she told him. And he giggled. *I don't know if he understood what I said or if he just liked my tone of voice.* But regardless of why, it made him chuckle. Aria loved the sound of his childish laughter. And between her little boy and her loving husband, she was fulfilled.

CHAPTER TWENTY-TWO

I t took Dagna nearly two weeks to find the strength to go to one of the blocks by herself to find a prisoner to do her bidding. She knew she wasn't supposed to do this, but she was all out of chocolate bars, and without them, she felt so tired and let down.

Dagna entered the block where she and Ilse had taken the prisoner they'd tortured together. It was getting late, close to the time for lights out. Dagna glanced around to see if any of the guards were watching her. But they weren't. She hurried because she wanted to find the same girl that she and Ilse had taken that night. She knew that one was already afraid of her, and because of that, she would not need too much prodding to do her bidding. Besides all of that, there was something about that one that especially annoyed Dagna. Unlike Dagna, who was a very large woman, that girl was tiny and had that dark beauty that Dagna had seen some Jewish women have. It was the same kind of delicate beauty that Anna had. *Yes, I have to admit to myself that there is beauty in some of those Jews. Some men would want to protect one like that with her small bones and those big dark eyes. She looks a bit like Anna. Yes, I must find her again. She's the one who I will send to Bormann's office to steal for me.*

Dagna didn't care much about the sexual aspect of humiliation. She preferred to inflict pain; in her mind, sex had little to do with it. Her eyes darted around the room like the tongue of a snake.

When Moriah looked up from the card game she was playing with Heidi and saw Dagna walk into the block, she tried to hide. Still, like a crocodile, Dagna spotted her prey immediately. "You," she said, pointing to Moriah, "come with me."

Moriah didn't want to go, but she knew Dagna might shoot her on the spot if she didn't. She stood up. Her knees were weak. Her small shoulders were aching even more than usual that day.

"Come on, Jew pig. I don't have time to wait for you."

Moriah began to follow Dagna out of the room. She looked back for just a second and saw Heidi watching her with an expression of horror on her face.

Moriah caught Heidi's expression and tried to be courageous by giving her friend a smile of confidence. A smile that said, "Please don't worry, I'll be all right." But her lips trembled, and she was too terrified to muster a smile. Instead, she just held back the tears.

Outside, the snow was falling hard and fast. As a child, Moriah loved the snowflakes. She'd always been one to see the beauty in everything. But that was before this nightmare had begun. Before her family had been murdered for no reason, and she'd been arrested and sent to this hell.

Dagna hurriedly led Moriah to a secluded space behind one of the office buildings. "You're in luck." Dagna smiled, then winked. "We won't be playing any special games tonight," she said. "Instead, I have a special job for you. And you had better do exactly as I say. Now listen, and I will tell you what you are to do. You must go into the office building and follow the corridor to the right. The third door down belongs to the office of Juana Bormann. You will go into that office. There is a desk by the window. You must quickly look through the desk until you find a chocolate bar. Bring that chocolate bar to me."

Moriah knew of Bormann. Everyone in the camp knew of

Bormann and her vicious dogs. "I'm afraid I'll get caught," she murmured, thinking of the demonstrations of Bormann's dogs tearing prisoners to pieces.

Dagna slapped Moriah's face. "Don't even think of defying me. And you had better make certain you don't get caught. If you do, you will be killed. However, if you are dumb enough to mention my name, I will see to it that you suffer a terrible death. And not only will you die, but that friend of yours who I always see you with will die too," Dagna hissed. "Do you understand me?"

Moriah nodded, staring down at the ground. She knew she had no choice but to do as she was told.

"The lights will be out for the night in just a few minutes. Once the camp is dark, wait a few more minutes and then go in. Take the chocolate back to your block and make sure it doesn't get stolen by another Jew pig or one of the other worthless prisoners. I will find you on your way to roll call in the morning. Make sure you have the chocolate with you. I will take it from you then."

Until recently, Moriah had not attended roll call because she worked in the kitchen and had to be there early to begin cooking for the morning meal. But a few months ago, Heinrich Himmler changed things when he visited the camp. He'd insisted that every prisoner be accounted for each morning and each evening at roll call. So, Moriah would be outside early tomorrow morning, wading through the snow. *Hopefully, I will be carrying a chocolate bar that will save my life.*

CHAPTER TWENTY-THREE

Being alone in the building in the dark was unnerving. Moriah stayed close to the wall as she made her way to Bormann's office. Her hands trembled as she carefully went through the desk. It was difficult to see anything, but she finally found a chocolate bar. Her heart was in her throat as she grabbed the candy and stuck it into her pocket. Then she quickly left the building. Her head ached as she made her way back to her block. She slid in beside Heidi, who had fallen asleep. Careful to be quiet and not wake her friend, Moriah lay on her side and tried to sleep.

CHAPTER TWENTY-FOUR

The roll call was faster than usual the following day because it was exceptionally cold, and the guards didn't want to stand outside any longer than was necessary.

As she promised, Dagna was waiting for Moriah as she made her way to her job in the kitchen.

"Give it to me," Dagna demanded in a harsh whisper.

Moriah reached into the pocket of her uniform and took out a bar of chocolate, which she handed to Dagna. The wrapper was missing.

"This is disgusting. You ate some of this?"

"No, no," Moriah insisted.

"Then why is it open?"

"I don't know. I tried to find a fresh one, but this was the only candy bar in the drawer." Moriah insisted. She was shivering from the cold mixed with fear.

"Hmmm..." Dagna grunted. "All right." She stuffed the candy bar into her pocket. *Good thing it's freezing out here. At least this thing won't melt all over my uniform.* Then, under her breath, she added, "I'm sure Bormann will get more. Then I'll send you again. Now go to work."

Moriah ran all the way back to her job, slipping and falling on the ice two times on the way.

The following evening Moriah was forced to work extra time. She had accidentally spilled some soup. Wiping it up quickly was not satisfactory for the angry kitchen guard. She demanded that Moriah stay after everyone else had left and wash the floor on her hands and knees. Moriah missed the evening meal because of this. It was very late when she returned to her block.

Heidi was awake when Moriah returned. "Are you alright? You didn't wake me up last night when you got back."

"Yes, I know you were asleep, and I didn't have the heart to wake you."

"What happened? Did she hurt you?"

"No. But she sent me on a mission for her."

"A mission?"

"Yes, I had to go into the office and steal something from Bormann's desk."

"How did you get in? Wasn't it locked?"

"Dagna had a key."

"What did you steal?"

"A candy bar."

"Are you serious? A candy bar?"

"Yes, it was very important to her. She wanted it badly. I don't know why. But she said she plans to send me back again to take another one for her. I was so afraid. If I got caught, the guards would have killed me."

Heidi nodded her head, "Of course, they would have." Then she thought for a moment. "I think I know why she wanted that candy so badly. I'll bet it is the candy the Wehrmacht gives the fliers and tankers. It's made with a drug that gives them courage. I know about it because when I was a working girl, I had a few customers who had taken it."

"You had men in the German army who were customers?"

"I had men of all kinds who came to see me," Heidi said. Then they were silent for several moments before Heidi added, "I have an idea."

"Tell me."

CHAPTER TWENTY-FIVE

Dagna was glad to have the candy, even though only half of an open candy bar was left. The very idea that this candy had been in the pocket of a prisoner's dirty uniform would have sickened her in the past. She wouldn't have eaten it. However, this candy was magical; once she had it, it changed her life. So, she would eat it regardless of the condition. *What happened to the stack of candy bars on Bormann's desk? She couldn't have eaten all of it that fast. Maybe she shares it with the others.* Dagna put the candy up to her face and smelled the chocolate. She anticipated the sweet taste of sugar and the wonderful feeling it would bring. *I shouldn't eat this until morning. It will keep me up all night, but I can't wait. It's been almost a week since I had any, and I've sorely missed it. Maybe I'll have just a tiny bit now.*

She broke off a piece and laid it on her tongue. A smile came over her face. *Ecstasy.* She thought, closing her eyes. But then she remembered. *I only have two more weeks here at Ravensbrück, and my training will be finished. Where am I going to get this candy after I leave here?* The thought made her anxious as she felt the blood rush to her face. Her body grew warm all over as the drugs entered her bloodstream. *I'll wait a few days, then send that little Jew bitch to check Bormann's desk again. By then, hopefully, she'll have a new supply.*

CHAPTER TWENTY-SIX

Moriah collected tiny amounts of rat poison each day, which Heidi told her she could find under the sink in the kitchen. "How do you know there's rat poison under the sink?"

"I saw one of the guards take it out one day," Heidi said, smiling. "Of course, she used to poison a prisoner, poor soul. But now, we shall get a bit of revenge, right? And no one will know who's responsible."

"I'm a little scared," Moriah admitted.

"Me too. But it certainly will be nice to see one of them die at our hands for a change, won't it?"

Moriah nodded.

CHAPTER TWENTY-SEVEN

A few days later, Moriah was lying on the straw beside Heidi at the end of a very long and tedious day. It was a very cold night, and the women huddled together to stay warm. Then as they lay there, almost falling asleep, Dagna walked into the block. Moriah had yet to close her eyes, so she saw Dagna immediately. Moriah grabbed Heidi's hand and squeezed it.

"Don't do it tonight. I'm afraid. It's too dangerous," Heidi whispered. She was shivering. Moriah didn't know if it was from the cold, nerves, or maybe both.

"I have to. It's the reason we've been collecting the poison. Might as well get it over with," Moriah said as Dagna walked over to where they lay.

"Get up. Now! Follow me," Dagna said to Moriah. Moriah shivered as she looked at Dagan's warm coat. This might have made Moriah hate Dagna even more.

Heidi squeezed Moriah's hand one more time.

Moriah got up, followed Dagna out of the block, and walked behind her to the office. She knew what Dagna wanted. She wanted Moriah to steal more chocolate from Bormann's desk. But this time, when Moriah went inside and searched through the desk, she found a pile of chocolate bars in the top drawer. *Look at all of these. I'm sure that bitch Dagna would want me to take several.* However, Moriah only took one, and with trembling hands, she stood in the darkness and opened it. Her heart raced as she looked around to see if any guards had discovered her.

There's no one here. I'm alone, and I need to do this as fast as I can. Moriah's knees were weak, and she was afraid she would freeze and be unable to complete the task she'd set for herself. Moriah eyed the chocolate. Then tore off the entire wrapper and broke off a piece to make it look like someone had eaten some of the chocolate. The same way it had been done only a few days ago when she'd given Dagna the half-eaten chocolate. Quickly, she took the piece of fabric in which she'd wrapped the rat poison from the pocket of her uniform and opened it. Then she said a prayer in Yiddish. An apology to God for committing murder. *After all, thou shalt not kill was one of his commandments. But did this woman not deserve to die? Did they all not deserve to die? God forgive me.* She whispered as she sprinkled the rat poison on the chocolate. She thought the poison would blend into the chocolate, but it didn't. It stood out. Moriah hadn't counted on the white power being so visible, so she rubbed it into the chocolate with her fingers until it was undetectable by the naked eye. Every sound, no matter how common, a night bird's crow, a rustle of the leaves of a tree in the wind, made Moriah jump. Quickly she put the candy bar in the pocket of her uniform, and then carefully, almost hugging the walls of the building, she made her way back outside.

This time Dagna was waiting for her. She wanted the chocolate now, not in the morning. "What the hell took you so long? It's cold out here."

Moriah didn't answer. She handed the open chocolate bar to Dagna.

"Another half-eaten one? Weren't there more than this?"

"This was all there was," Moriah lied. She wanted to be sure Dagna ate the chocolate with the poison on it.

"Shit, I don't have much more time here at Ravensbrück, but I'll send for you again in a few days. This is unsatisfactory," Dagna said, shaking her head. "Now go back to your block, and don't get caught."

CHAPTER TWENTY-EIGHT

"Did you do it?" Heidi's voice was shaking.

"Yes."

"She'll be dead in the morning?"

"Yes, she should."

"No one will know it was you. How could they? They don't know that she sent you to steal for her."

"I don't think anyone will know?"

"What if she tells them?"

"Tonight? I don't think she will. I am hoping she will go back to her room and eat the candy. Then boom, that's it. It's over. I've avenged Bernie," Moriah said.

"I'm nervous. I can't help it," Heidi admitted.

"I know. Me too. It's not like I commit murder every day," Moriah said, swallowing hard.

CHAPTER TWENTY-NINE

Dagna walked quickly to her room. She was glad she didn't have a roommate. It had been weeks since Gretel had abandoned her and moved into another room. She entered and locked the door. Taking the chocolate bar out of her coat pocket, she laid it down on the night table. Then she quickly stripped off her clothes. It was late, and she knew she wouldn't sleep if she ate the chocolate now. But it had been several days since she'd had a dose of it, and she craved it again. *Don't eat it until morning. Last time you were awake all night.* She told herself even as she broke off a small piece and put it in her mouth. *I wish that little Jew had been able to get me more. Now I am going to have to send her in there again before my training is over. How will I ever get my hands on more of this once I leave here?*

Dagna was anxious. Sometimes the chocolate made her more anxious and nervous. She started sweating. Her breathing became shallow and rapid. This had all happened before, so she was not alarmed. But then something happened that had never happened before. She felt her throat close. Dagna could hardly breathe and began gasping for breath. Her body twisted, then shuddered hard.

Something is wrong. Something is terribly wrong. She would have screamed for help, but she couldn't speak. It was as if someone or something had closed her throat, and she could not get any air into her lungs. Dagna was drowning, but there was no water. Her eyes rolled back, and her hands shook. Still, she gripped the chocolate bar. It was melting now in her hot, clenched fist. She was burning up. It felt like her lungs had caught fire. Then her grip loosened as the light of life faded out of her.

CHAPTER THIRTY

A light snow had begun to fall as the trainees clustered in a circle outside, whispering among themselves. When the morning bell rang, Heidi and Moriah lined up for roll call. Moriah's quick eyes scanned the group of recruits. "She's not here. I think it worked. I wish I could kill them all like that."

"Be quiet. God forbid someone should hear you," Heidi snapped at her in a whisper.

Bormann conducted the roll call, and nothing unusual happened except that it went quicker than usual. The prisoner's numbers were called, and they responded. Then everyone excused and sent to their jobs. No one had mentioned Dagna that morning, and Moriah foolishly thought that somehow it was over. *If she is actually dead, then they must think that she overdosed.* However, when nightfall came and the prisoners lined up their final roll call, *Helferin* Braunsteiner stood taping a whip as she walked before the group. Her mouth was twisted, and her face was red with deep lines burrowed between her brows. She called out each number in a loud, angry voice.

After the prisoners were accounted for, Braunsteiner stopped walking and stood in front of the lineup. It was growing dark, but her breath was white in the cold air.

"I'm sorry to inform you that one of our recruits was found dead this morning. It seems that she was poisoned. A sad state of affairs, don't you think?"

There was a moment of silence. If fear could be heard in the wind, it would have been as loud as an orchestra that night. Then Braunsteiner took a breath and continued, "I have a feeling that someone here knows something about this. You will not do yourself or your fellow prisoners any favors by keeping silent. I promise you this. So, if you want to save yourself and your fellow prisoners plenty of pain and suffering, I suggest you speak now."

No one spoke. Moriah felt as if she might faint, and her heart was pounding so hard and fast. *What more could they possibly do to us? We are already freezing as we try to sleep in a pile of insect-infested hay without blankets. We are starving; we never had enough to eat. And they work us until we feel like we are going to drop. They murder and torture us whenever they feel like it.* Her eyes darted across the group of women prisoners. They looked exhausted from working all day. But even so, there was still fear in their eyes. *The other prisoners don't know it was me. Or I am sure they would turn me in. I can't blame them. They live in fear of what this Nazi will do to them.*

Braunsteiner was even more enraged now. Moriah thought she could see the guard shaking with rage, but now she was no longer yelling. Her voice was quiet and filled with foreboding. "All right, have it your way. Don't speak. Go on and protect your fellow prisoners. This is all very noble of you." It dripped with sarcasm. "So, since this is your choice, instead of one person paying for this crime... all of you will pay." She hesitated for a moment. "It's a very cold night, isn't it? Well... then... all of you... get down on your stomachs and start doing pushups."

The ground was freezing. It was miserably cold during the day but always colder at night when the sun went down. There were patches of ice and snow on the ground as the prisoners began to do the pushups. Moriah was sick with guilt. She knew she was the reason the others were being forced to suffer.

Herta Ehlert walked through the group of prisoners, whipping their backs and slicing through their thin uniforms. The blood pooled around them in the snow as the prisoners began to bleed. It appeared black rather than red in the moonlight. There was no evening meal that night. A half-hour later, the prisoners were still on the ground attempting the pushups when Ilse Grese walked over to them carrying a large hose. She began to douse the women with ice-cold water. Their teeth were chattering. Heidi glanced over at Moriah. Moriah was crying. "Keep your mouth shut. Don't be a hero. It won't help anything. Don't you dare tell them," Heidi whispered, her voice barely audible. "These bastards won't stop this. But they will kill you. Keep your mouth shut."

"No talking!" One of the guards hit Heidi across the back with a club.

Heidi fell forward. A terrible pain shot through her shoulders.

"Get up and do your pushups, you lazy sow. Get up, or I'll shoot you," the guard, a young woman no more than nineteen, held the club in her hand. She was a pretty slender blonde who should have been working in an office somewhere, perhaps newly married or maybe raising a child. But instead of being a normal young woman, she was a monster, a product of Hitler's vision for his new Germany. A vicious sadist. And she was not the only one.

Heidi could hardly move her arms, yet she knew if she wanted to go on living, she must get up off her belly and do the exercise. Her body ached, but she forced herself to continue.

The night went on. And still, the women were outside, wet and freezing, doing pushups in the light of a full moon. Moriah heard one of the guards yelling at a prisoner. "Get up, you lazy pig. Get up." Then there was a gunshot. Moriah let out a moan.

"All right. All of you. Stand up. Get on your feet. You've been on your bellies all night. Now, you'll stand, and you'll stay standing," Braunsteiner said.

The women stood. In the darkness, Moriah could see their shadows. Some of them were bent over at the waist. Others were waving like flowers in a windstorm.

Hours passed. Braunsteiner left, and another guard took over. Then Grese returned with the hose and doused the prisoners again. One woman fell forward. The guard walked over to her. "Get up!"

"I can't."

"I'll shoot you. I swear it."

The prisoner lay where she'd fallen, but the guard didn't shoot. Grese dropped the hose and walked over to the woman lying on the ground. She kicked her hard in the ribs. The woman let out a groan, but she didn't move. "Stupid bitch. Get up." But the prisoner lay on the ground. Grese took her gun out and held it to the woman's head. Someone gasped. Then Grese pulled the trigger. "Now you can't get up even if you try," Grese said, then she laughed.

Moriah glanced at Heidi. "Be strong," Heidi whispered.

It was close to dawn, but still, the prisoners were forced at gunpoint to stand outside in the cold, wet, and exhausted. Ice formed on their thin uniforms. Moriah's tears froze on her eyelashes. By the time the sun rose, eight women lay dead on the frozen earth. Moriah wished she were among them, but somehow, she and Heidi had survived the night.

"Let this be a lesson. Keep an eye on your fellow prisoners. If you see someone doing something they should not be doing, tell a guard. It could save you from another night like this," the guard in charge said. Then she added, "Now, all of you, get in line for roll call. It's time to go to work."

CHAPTER THIRTY-ONE

The next day was even worse than any typical day at the camp. The prisoners had been up all night. Moriah was beyond exhausted. But she was glad that at least she worked inside the kitchen, where it was warmer than it was for the women who worked out on the roads like Heidi. All day long, Moriah was worried about Heidi. She had been sent out to work, still cold, wet, and exhausted. When Moriah saw Heidi was still alive that night, she was relieved. They both lined up to receive their soup for the night. Then, as they ate, they spoke to each other in whispers.

"I was worried about you today."

"I'm all right," Heidi lied. She was trembling.

No one in the camp, except Heidi, knew that Moriah had poisoned Dagna Hofer. It was remarkable that no one saw Moriah take the poison out from under the sink. But even though no one had seen or heard anything, Moriah did not feel good about what she'd done. She hated Dagna, who had represented all the Nazis to her. She felt no remorse for killing Dagna, but guilt still consumed her for all the women who had died during that night of punishment. A punishment she was responsible for. *I will carry the burden of this for the rest of my life.* She and Heidi vowed to each other that they would never speak of what Moriah had done. They couldn't risk having anyone overhear them.

CHAPTER THIRTY-TWO

Elica returned from her terrible visit to the office of the Gestapo, defeated. Her face, where the Gestapo agent had carved the Star of David, was healing. And at least it had not become infected. But she'd lost everything. Her beauty and Daniel, her Jewish husband, were dead, murdered by the nazis. She had no idea where her child might be or how to begin looking for him. And she wasn't sure she wanted him to grow up with her now that she had this scar on her face. Elica knew that she could not hide her sins. They were right there for all the world to see. And the girls who had once been dear friends, her blood sisters, were all gone. Dagna had betrayed her. She'd been the reason that the Gestapo had cut Elica's face. Bernie was gone. Elica had no idea what had happened to her. She'd taken Theo, Elica's son, wherever she went. But Elica knew that Bernie could not return to her home in Austria because Bernie had been hiding Anna. And to protect herself, Elica gave Anna up to the Gestapo. *How do I live with this?* She had no one left in the world but her mother. So, she moved back into her childhood home.

"You can sleep in your old room. You will be comfortable in there," her mother told her. "I kept it as you left it."

Elica nodded.

"Do you want some tea?" Frau Frey, Elica's mother, asked.

"I'd love some."

"Come, I'll make tea."

They sat down and drank the hot liquid. "I'm sorry, but of course, there's no sugar," Frau Frey said.

"I know. It's all right," Elica said.

There was silence for several moments. Then Elica said, "*Mutti*, can I ask you something?"

"How did *Vater* die? What happened?" Elica asked.

"Oh, Elica, I hate to have to tell you this. But you know, your father was a heavy drinker. And as he grew older, he started drinking even more. After a while, he started drinking first thing in the morning. I got up early one day to find him already drunk. We fought. I told him that he spent every penny he earned on alcohol. So he stormed out of the house. I guess he went to work. He shouldn't have been working on the machines in that condition. He wasn't steady enough. And the machine he worked on was dangerous. He had an accident and was killed. I blame myself. But anyway, it was as simple as that. I'm sorry, Elica."

"I'm sorry too, *mutti*. I feel guilty for not being here. I have been so caught up with my own life. And I've made so many mistakes," Elica began to cry.

"Yes, well, we all do. I did when I was young, too," her mother said. Then they were quiet for a while.

"*Mutti*, are you working? How have you been getting by? I know I should have come here and checked on you when Daniel and his parents were still alive, and I still had plenty of money. I could have helped you." She hesitated. "I should have."

"Yes, perhaps you should have, Elica. But I am working as a maid for a family who lives a few miles from here. At least I have a job. But since I am gone all day, it would help if you could keep the house up until you can find some work."

Elica nodded. "*Mutti*," she looked at her mother pleadingly. "I hope you can forgive me because I lied to you. I told you that my baby died. He didn't die. I gave birth to a son. I named him Theo. He is a beautiful boy, and now I must find him. I am sick with worry about Theo. I am going to look for him in the morning."

"Your son. Yes, I knew you lied when you told me your baby died. I heard from the women in town that you had a child, a boy. I wish you would have brought him to see me. But I knew you didn't want any part of your father or me. You were trying so hard to fit into that family of rich Jews you lived with: your husband and his parents. I just assumed you were ashamed of us. You didn't want your little boy to see that you came from a mother who was a maid and a father who was a drunken factory worker. That's right, isn't it?"

Elica didn't answer. She looked down at the floor. Then she looked up at her mother. "Growing up, I always wanted to be like Anna. But you knew that, didn't you?"

"Of course, I knew. That was the hardest part of working for Anna's family. I was the maid, and you were nothing but the maid's daughter. And yet you and Anna were the closest of friends. I was always afraid you were going to get hurt. Then when you met Daniel, and he was Anna's boyfriend, and you got pregnant by him, I was so afraid of what Anna's father might do."

"But Anna's parents were kind to you. They were always kind to both of us. I didn't think you would be afraid of Herr Levinstein. I thought you liked the Levinsteins," Elica said. "Anna always liked you."

"Yes, they were kind. And Anna was always a good girl. She never gave me any trouble when I worked for them. However, I was always aware of the class divide between us. Not only that, but they were Jews, and we are Gentiles. And that alone makes us different. Do you remember that incident with the doll when you were about eight or ten, something like that? Oh, Elica, you wanted that doll so badly, and I felt terrible because I couldn't afford to buy it for you. Then, at Anna's birthday party, her parents gave it to her as her present. Do you remember? I felt so bad."

"Yes, I remember."

"The look on your face, when you saw them give that doll to her, tore my heart out."

"I never knew you cared so much."

"Of course, I cared. I always cared. I am your mother. Then a few weeks later, when Anna came to your birthday party and gave you the doll as a gift, I wanted to let you keep it. But I was afraid that if Anna's father found out, he would fire me. I couldn't afford to lose that job. Your father was always losing his job. Most of the time, he was out of work. Everything depended on me, Elica."

"I never realized it. I never thought about how you felt. Only about my own feelings," Elica admitted. "I wanted to be like Anna. I wanted to live in a big, beautiful home with a wealthy family. She had such pretty clothes and nice things. I'm sorry, *mutti*. I hurt you. I know I did."

There was a long silence. Then her mother said, "Well... it doesn't matter. No matter what happened in the past, I am your mother, and I love you. I won't throw you out. You may come back home and live here with me."

"Thank you, *mutti*. I am sorry for everything I did. I am truly sorry."

"Yes, well, but I know you, Elica, and if you had the chance, you would do it all again. You are hurt right now. This scar on your face has broken your confidence. I can see that. But I also know that you've always been a very selfish girl. And that doesn't just go away. I'm afraid that you still are. People don't change. A mother always knows the truth about her own child. She knows their good qualities, and she knows their faults. I know yours."

Her mother's words made Elica feel dreadful because she knew they were true. She promised herself she would change; she would become a good person. If not for herself, then for her mother and her little boy.

The following day, Elica got dressed and went out in search of her son, Theo. Since the last place she'd seen him was with Bernie, she went to Bernie's house. Just like Daniel's old house, Bernie's house had been given to another family by the government—a young German family. There was no trace of Bernie or her mother. They were gone. And with them, so was Theo. In a panic, Elica knocked on the door of the neighbor's house next door. An old woman answered. She could hardly hide the horror in her eyes when she looked at the scar on Elica's face.

"What do you want?" the old woman asked.

"The woman and her daughter who used to live next door to you, Bernie Ebner. Her mother's name was Inge Ebner. Do you know what happened to them?"

"Those two? I heard that the Gestapo took them away for hiding Jews."

Elica's heart began to pound heavily in her chest. "Please, can I have some water?"

"No, you can't come in. Go away."

"Wait. Please, wait. Did you see them get arrested? Was there a small boy with them? Did you see a child?"

"I didn't see them get arrested. I only heard about it from someone in the neighborhood. Please, go away. I don't know who you are or who did that to your face. But I am an old woman. I am helpless and alone. I can't have the Gestapo coming around here. I don't want any trouble. Just go."

"But the child?" Elica croaked. "The little boy. He is helpless too. Please, if you have any information, anything at all. Please, I am begging you to help me."

The old woman closed the door and left Elica standing outside without any idea of what to do next or where to go. She sat down on the stoop and put her head in her hands. There was nothing left for her but to pray. She was ashamed before God for all the terrible things she'd done, betraying her friends and her selfishness, but there was nowhere else to turn. Elica Frey was desperate.

I know I have been a terrible person. I didn't think about Anna or how my actions would affect Bernie when I turned Anna in. All I knew was that

I had to get away from the Gestapo. I was wrong, but I was so afraid. They cut me and beat me. I was in such pain and so afraid. Jesus, please forgive me. I beg you to forgive me and spare my little boy. I am the sinner. I am the one who did wrong, not him. He is just an innocent child. He never did anything bad to anyone. I am begging you to please keep him safe and help me find him.

But there was no answer. Only the sound of birds chirping in the trees. An automobile horn somewhere in the distance. The quiet beating of her sad and lonely heart. *Anna is gone. She's probably dead, and it's my fault. Dagna is one of them, a complete nazi. She has become a demon. And now, I know that Bernie and her mother have been arrested because of my selfishness. Do I dare to hope that they could still be alive? Could Theo still be alive?*

Elica knew it was pointless to sit there in front of this house. She no longer had any reason to be there. So, she got up and began walking back home slowly.

Days passed, and depression lay its heavy hand on Elica's heart, leaving her tired and without enthusiasm for anything at all. She knew her mother was struggling and could use financial help. It would be a good idea for Elica to try to find work. But she was so tired that she couldn't force herself to get out of bed, get dressed, and go to look for a job. The looks on the people's faces, when they saw her with the angry red scar of the Star of David carved into her cheek, made her feel self-conscious. *I am ugly. The Nazis have taken everything away from me. My husband, the love of my life. All he ever did was to be born a Jewish man. My precious child, my sweet little boy. My friends. And my face. I am a shell of a person. Maybe I deserve what happened to me. I betrayed Anna. I didn't want to, but I was selfish. I had to find Daniel, and I thought it was the only way I might convince Dagna to help me. All the while, Daniel was already dead. I wish I had the courage to commit suicide. But I don't. I just lay here and keep hoping that, somehow, my Theo has survived.*

Elica avoided mirrors whenever possible. She covered the mirror in the bathroom with her towel as soon as she entered to avoid seeing her reflection. The girl who had once spent hours combing and plaiting her long wheat-colored hair no longer cared for herself. Even bathing became a monumental chore that she avoided, and often her mother had to nudge her to clean herself up. "You're starting to smell bad, Elica. I won't have it in this house. Now get up and bathe."

She'd forced herself to obey. But she no longer took pride in her appearance. The Jewish star the Gestapo carved into her once lovely face stripped her of any trace of her former beauty.

Elica knew her mother was losing patience with her. She would leave for work early while Elica was still in bed and return late at night to find her lying there, often weeping.

Sometimes Elica had nightmares of Dagna's smile when Elica had been under arrest. She would awaken trembling, sweaty, and twisted up in the sheets. *Dagna, how proud and almost joyful she was when she told me she was there when the Gestapo killed my husband. I can't believe Dagna and I were once blood sisters. We were once best friends. I guess I never really knew her.*

Elica's mind never stopped racing. She was caught up in the past and could not move forward.

Often, she wept out of guilt for what she'd done to Anna and her family. *If only I could turn back time, I would do things differently. Anna didn't deserve what I did to her. She had always been kind to me, a blood sister in the true sense.* She prayed Bernie had somehow survived. Anna too. But she doubted that either of them was still alive. But most of all, her heart ached for her son. *My Theo was just a baby. So small. So trusting.* She could see his little face, his first smile, when she closed her eyes. She would sometimes dream of his tiny hands gripping her fingers. Then she would awaken alone, and panic would set in. *I am helpless. I don't know where else to go to look for him.* Then the thought of his little body lying lifeless would enter her mind, and she would feel pain in her chest. Her left arm would throb, and a scream of terror would often escape her lips.

Weeks turned to months, and Elica still lay in bed, hardly eating, unable to rest or do anything else. Then one morning, Elica's mother walked into her room. She pulled open the drapes, and the sunlight flooded the room, burning Elica's eyes. Elica covered her eyes with her forearm.

Her mother said in a firm, loud voice, "It's time you got up and went to work. I am working hard, trying to keep a roof over our heads. At least when your father was alive, he sometimes helped me to make ends meet. Once in a while, he worked a little. But now, there is no one to help me. I am getting older, Elica. Soon I won't be able to work the way I do now. You are going to have to put the past behind you, get out of bed, and pull your own weight."

"How can I find a job, Mother? Look at me. I am ashamed of my face. I can't look anyone in the eye. Everyone who sees me is repulsed by me."

"Elica, you are still alive. There is nothing you can do about how you look. I need your help, so you must learn to live with your face as it is. There is nothing you can do to change it. Lying in bed all day isn't helping you, and it certainly isn't helping me. You must get up and find work. We need the money." Her mother was stern.

"Where? What kind of work can I do?"

"You can always find a job as a maid."

"No. I won't do that," Elica said firmly.

"Because you were always ashamed of me when you were growing up. You were ashamed that your mother was a maid. I always knew it."

"That's not the reason," Elica lied. It was the reason. She'd always wanted more than her parents could provide. That was part of the reason she had married Daniel. Daniel was not only handsome, but she was also crazy about him. But he was also a rich boy from a wealthy family. And the day they married, Elica began to plan to live as a wealthy woman in a big beautiful house like Anna's, far away from the working-class parents she'd grown up with. And now that all was said and done, she was faced with the same fate as her mother. "I can't do it. I can't go to work as a maid for some family and see them daily with my face the way it is."

"Well, don't be a maid then. But you must do something. I suggest you go to the wealthy areas and knock on the doors. Offer your services as a laundress and a seamstress. You can tell them you will pick up dirty garments, wash them, fold them, and return them. Beg if you must. But get some work. You must start bringing some money in. I can't carry this burden alone anymore."

"Don't make me do this, *Mutti*. Look at me. I can't go to people's houses and look them in the eyes. How can I ever bear it when they look at my face?" Elica cried.

Frau Frey pulled a small bottle from the pocket of her dress and handed it to Elica.

"What's this?" Elica asked, but she knew what it was. It was makeup. Foundation. She could use it to cover the scar. It might not be invisible, but at least it wouldn't be so red.

"It's makeup for the scar on your face."

"How did you get this? Makeup is hard to come by, and it's so expensive."

"Yes, that's true. It was expensive. But I hope it will help you to start living a normal life again. Cover the scar the best you can and get out of bed, clean yourself up, and go and find work."

Her mother turned to leave the room. As her mother left, Elica noticed that her mother had begun to walk with a slight limp, and a small hump had begun to form in her upper back. *She looks so old. Working hard all of her life has taken a toll on her.* Elica had always known that someday her mother would be old, but in her heart, she'd never really believed it. All through her youth, her mother had been strong and capable. And because of this, Elica believed her mother was invincible and would always be there for her to fall back on. Now she could no longer avoid her mother's mortality. Elica shivered when the reality hit her that someday, in the not-too-distant future, her mother would die, leaving Elica all alone to face this terrible world on her own.

CHAPTER THIRTY-THREE

Elica forced herself to sit down in front of a mirror. Looking at herself made her feel sick to her stomach. Not only was the scar deep and horrible, but she had neglected herself for so long that dark puffy circles were under her eyes, and her once beautiful hair was now knotty and lifeless.

The small bottle of foundation felt cold in her hand. The oil floated on the surface, and the color was at the bottom. She shook it hard. Then opened it and began to apply it over the scar.

It wasn't easy to hide the damage that was done to her face. The mark left by the Nazi's blade had etched deeply into her skin, like a brand. Remembering the bible classes she'd taken as a child, she thought, *It's like the mark of Cain.* She trembled. But she continued to layer the foundation until the redness was muted and the star of David was indistinguishable. It was still easy to see that her cheek had suffered a knife wound, but the shape was no longer apparent. People hated Jews, and the star of David symbolized all they despised. Even here in Austria, people were caught up in Nazi ideology. And even those who were not didn't dare to speak out lest they end up in camps beside the Jews they were trying to defend. It was clear that the best thing to do if one wanted to survive was to stay far away from anything that had any connection to Judaism.

People looked at her as she boarded a bus that would take her through the working-class area where she'd grown up and into a wealthy neighborhood with large houses and well-maintained lawns. The other riders glanced at Elica with pity in their eyes. She was ashamed and hated herself, but she was glad she had covered the scar with the foundation. She wondered if they would sympathize if they could see that her scar was a Star of David.

Elica couldn't bear to return to the neighborhood where she'd lived with Daniel or to the street where Anna had lived. But the road where she got off the bus was very much like both of those little neighborhoods. Most of these homes had once belonged to Jewish families. Now, however, they were owned by Aryans. They had been awarded to high-ranking members of Hitler's elite, the SS.

It took all the courage she could muster to walk up to one of the houses. Wishing she could turn around and run back home, she forced herself to go forward and stand in front of the door. Her fingers ran over her scar before she forced herself to knock. She felt like vomiting as she told herself, "I have to try to find work. We need the money. We'll be out on the street if we lose this place." Unsurprisingly, the woman who answered the door to this large, expensive home was a servant. Elica knew, because her mother had been friendly with many other maids, that many came from the country and had little education. And because of this, many of them were very superstitious. The woman who opened the door couldn't hide her shock and fear when she saw Elica's face. She crossed herself. And when Elica asked about work, she quickly said that nothing was available and closed the door. Although Elica would have liked to board another bus and go home, she went on to the next house. And then on to the next. Some were polite and apologized that they could not help her, while others just stared at her in horror and then slammed the door. But no one had any work for her. By four o'clock, Elica was tired and beaten. She had bus fare but didn't want to spend it, so she walked home. *I am branded, ruined for life. No one will hire me. No man will ever love me again. Only my Theo will love me. I have to believe he is alive. Because if he is not, I have no reason to go on.*

That afternoon Elica cut up vegetables and put them in a pot with water to make soup. *At least if I can't get a job, I can try to make myself useful.* Then she sat down on the old sofa and gazed out the window.

CHAPTER THIRTY-FOUR

To Elica's surprise, her mother was not angry that she couldn't find work. "At least you tried. And you made dinner too. Don't worry. I'll help you," she said. "I'll ask the woman I work for if she knows anyone who needs a laundress or a seamstress. If she can find you some work, I'll bring it home and deliver it when you finish. That way, you won't have to see anyone."

Tears were forming in Elica's eyes. She quickly wiped them with the hem of her skirt.

"Come, let's eat," her mother said. "You have been out walking all day. You must be hungry."

"Mother," Elica said as they sat at the kitchen table eating the steaming bowls of soup Elica had prepared. "I hate my life. I hate myself. I want to die."

"Don't say that. You must never say that. You don't want God to answer your prayer now, do you?"

"If Theo is no longer alive, then... why would I want to live?"

"Because you're young. You can still do some good with your life."

Elica felt a sting of anger. How could her mother not understand how hard this all was for her? She wanted to lash out at her and say, *"What good did you ever do with your life? You have never been anything but a maid."* But she controlled herself. Instead, she said, "I don't know what good I can do. I have made so many mistakes already."

"As long as you are alive, you can make things right."

"I've done terrible things, *Mutti.*" She thought of Anna and felt her eyes sting with tears.

"We all have. It's the times we live in. I'm sure you did things you should never have done. But now, you must try to make them right."

Elica nodded, and then there was a long silence. The hot soup was soothing and made her feel a little better. And she remembered how she'd felt when she realized that her mother was getting older and wouldn't always be there for her. Suddenly, she wanted to hold on to this moment forever. Just her and her mother sipping hot soup at the table in the kitchen of her childhood home. Her mother smiled at her.

"*Mutti,*" Elica said in a soft voice.

"Yes."

"I'm sorry for hurting you."

"I know. I know you are."

True to her word, Elica's mother brought home a basket of dirty laundry the following week. And that was the beginning for Elica. She had a job, not one she enjoyed, but at least it paid. And, from then on, Elica spent her days scrubbing and mending. Once a week, she ventured out to the market to purchase food. She would cover her scar with plenty of makeup and then wear a scarf tied at her chin. Pulling some of the fabric over to cover her cheek lightly, she hoped the scar was less noticeable. At first, she was sure people were staring at her, but as time passed, they seemed to grow accustomed to seeing her, and no one looked anymore.

CHAPTER THIRTY-FIVE

1943

One rainy spring afternoon, Elica was at the market. She stood in line to buy potatoes when she saw a boy she had known from school. She even remembered his name. It was Otto Alsdorf, and she recalled he'd been a handsome boy with golden blonde hair and light gray eyes. He'd been an athlete too. She closed her eyes and could still see him playing *Fussball* with the other boys, his blonde hair blowing in the wind. Then, ashamed, she recalled that they had been intimate once. It had happened before the Anschluss. They'd both attended the same church and one evening, the church had a cookout for their youth group. She remembered how she and Otto had flirted with each other during the entire outing. How he had made her giggle when he tickled her upper arm as she walked by him. And then, after the cookout was over, a group of boys and girls told the counselor that they were going home. But they hadn't gone home.

Instead, they slipped deeper into the woods, where they drank beer that one of the boys had left there the day before, knowing they would return after the cookout. Everyone was drinking, necking, and joking with each other. Otto and Elica sat together. He took a sip of beer for courage, leaned over, and clumsily kissed Elica for the first time. She was very receptive because he was strikingly handsome. They kissed a few more times and had a couple more beers. Then he took her hand and whispered in her ear, asking her if she would like to get away from the rest of the group and be alone. Her body was tingling all over. She wanted to be alone with him as much as he wanted to be alone with her, so she agreed. "Well, I'm leaving. I'm going to walk Elica home," Otto had told the others.

She smiled at everyone innocently. But once they were far from the group, Otto grabbed her roughly and kissed her passionately. Her desire was as strong as his, and she knew what would happen next. He wasn't the first boy she'd been intimate with. So, she would not stop him. She didn't want him to stop. One thing led to another, and before she realized it, they were lying on the ground, spent and tired. "It's late, and I'm sure your parents will be worried. We should get home," he'd said.

"Yes, you're right. They will worry." She sat up and pulled her full skirt back down over her thighs.

"Come on. I'll walk you."

She stood up, shook the dirt off her clothes, and picked the leaves out of her hair. They walked home in silence. He couldn't look directly at her. She wanted to ask him what was wrong, but felt uncomfortable and intimidated. So, she kept silent.

After that, he avoided her. And she was too ashamed to ask him why. It didn't matter anyway because two months later, she met Daniel. And although Daniel was dating Anna when Elica first saw him, she knew she wanted him. And Elica had no interest in any other boy from that very first day.

Elica glanced over at Otto. He was still handsome; his face was, anyway. He still had the same strong chin and chiseled cheekbones. But when he walked, she saw that he walked with a cane, and he hobbled like he had a wooden leg. She shuddered. It had been common knowledge among her neighbors that Otto and several of his friends had been conscripted into the army right after the Anschluss of Austria to Germany. *He must have lost a leg in the war.* She looked away quickly. Elica checked the fabric of her scarf. She pulled it looser to be sure it was draping over her cheek.

Otto spotted Elica and smiled. Then he hobbled over to her, his wooden leg and his cane thumping on the floor. "Elica Frey? Is that you?" he asked.

She swallowed hard, wishing she could disappear. *My face.* Her fingers automatically went to the scarf. She pulled it over her scar even more than before and held it firmly in place. "Yes, it's me," Elica said, not meeting his eyes.

"Otto Alsdorf here. Do you remember me?"

"Yes, of course," she said. Her hands were trembling as she held the scarf tightly. *Look at us, two broken souls. Our once beautiful bodies are now destroyed.*

"It's good to see you again," he said, smiling.

She nodded, trying to smile, but her lips were quivering. "How are you?" she asked him, but she didn't sound too excited.

"Except for having lost a leg, I'm fine, I suppose," he said, then laughed.

I don't know how he can laugh. He has a good attitude about losing his leg. "Did it happen in the army? In a battle?"

"A mine explosion," he said, shrugging. Then his eyes took on a faraway look, and for a few seconds, neither spoke. Then Otto cleared his throat and asked, "And you? How have you been? How are your parents?"

She shrugged. "I'm all right. My mother is fine. My father passed away."

"Oh, I'm sorry to hear it."

"Yes, well, he had an accident at work," she said, not wishing to discuss it anymore.

Otto seemed to sense her desire to change the subject, so he did. "Maybe we could go out some evening, have a beer or two. Or coffee if you like. Whatever you prefer. We could talk about old times," he said, his voice cracking.

"I'd love to, but I am swamped. I hardly ever get into town."

"Well then, how about now? You're already here in town. We could have a drink right after you finish shopping. What do you say?"

She felt dizzy. "I'm sorry, Otto, but I have to get home. I have work to do." It wasn't a lie. She had piles of dirty laundry from her customers lying on the living room floor waiting to be scrubbed. But even if she didn't, she wouldn't have wanted to spend the time with him. She hated being in town, and whenever she had to purchase food, she tried to get away from the prying eyes of her neighbors as quickly as possible. She longed to retreat to the safety of her home. To close the door and shut out the rest of the world. Looking at her hands, she realized they were red and chapped from all the scrubbing, and she tried to hide them.

"Not today, then. I understand. You're busy." He smiled, but his lips were trembling. "Well, how about tomorrow or the next day?" he asked.

"I don't know. I don't think so."

"Come on. It will be fun. And God knows we could use a little fun in our lives, huh?"

She nodded. "I have to agree with that." She looked at him for a moment, and for the first time, she thought about him rather than herself. *How difficult all of this must be for him. He was once a handsome man, but now he is standing on a wooden leg, walking with a cane. Everyone is staring at him, but he doesn't seem to care.*

"Well then? Will you go?" he asked again.

"All right. Yes, I'll go."

"Tomorrow? Two o'clock?"

"You don't have to be at work?"

"Not yet. I haven't been able to find a job with my leg. But I'm looking."

She smiled, "All right. Tomorrow. At two."

"Are you still living at the same address?"

"I am. I am living with my mother."

"Good. I'll be over at two to pick you up."

She smiled, but he couldn't see her smile because she held the scarf over the scarred side of her face. After she bought the potatoes, she began to walk home quickly, and as she did, she thought of Otto. *I've been so lonely. It would be nice to have someone in my life—a man to have a beer with or a meal occasionally. I haven't felt the touch of a man in a very long time, and I miss it. I miss the gentle caresses; I miss being held in the strong arms of a man. But how could I ever let him see my face? What would he think when he saw my scar? Could I tell him the truth? That I married a Jewish man, and the Gestapo carved a Star of David into my cheek? What would he think about that? Does it matter?*

Just look at him. He's damaged too. However, his body is destroyed because he followed the Nazis. He fought for them. So, everyone thinks that he should be honored. But people think I'm a criminal, and I'm despised. Maybe this is a mistake. I probably shouldn't have agreed to this date. But it seemed so hard for him to ask that I felt bad turning him down. Well, I promised him I would go, and so I will. Why not? I have nothing to lose, just my pride, and there isn't much of that left, anyway.

CHAPTER THIRTY-SIX

The following afternoon, Otto was fifteen minutes early when he knocked on the door of Elica's home. She was almost done getting ready, and she quickly grabbed her scarf and tied it under her chin. Then she held it over the side of her face as she opened the door.

"Come in," she said.

He handed her a small box of chocolates.

"My goodness, what a lovely treat. How did you ever get these?"

"Let's just say I have a lot of friends," he said, smiling.

"Would you like a piece?" she asked him.

"Oh no, thank you. They're for you."

She put the candy on the table in front of the sofa. He glanced over and saw the piles of laundry. She was ashamed of her work. But she saw the question in his eyes. "I couldn't find a job," she shrugged as she admitted. "My mother got me this work doing washing and mending for rich people. I'm not proud of it by any means."

"Work is work. And it's honest work," he said. "I have been looking for a job for months and can't find anything. So, I must tell you, I'd be happy with any work that brought me a few Reichsmarks."

She nodded, glancing down at her rough red hands. At least now, she wouldn't have to explain why her hands looked like they did. He would already know.

"Are you hungry?"

"Yes, a little."

"Good. I know a place that's not too expensive. We'll have a beer and a knackwurst. What do you say?"

"Yes, that sounds nice," she said, grabbing a light coat from the coat rack and slipping it over her shoulders.

"Ready?" he asked.

"I am."

They walked for a while until they came to a beer hall. It wasn't one of the nicer ones, but she understood. He didn't have much money, yet, even though he was not working, he'd brought her chocolates, which had to cost him a fortune, and now he was buying her lunch and a beer. Elica glanced up at him. Otto had shaved. *He tried his best to look good on this date with me.* And a sudden wave of tenderness came over her.

The only people inside the beer hall were drunks. It was too early for a real crowd to have gathered for an after-work drink. Elica was glad. She didn't have to worry about anyone staring at them. They found a table in the back and sat down.

"I suppose I should ask before I order. You do like beer and knackwurst, don't you? Or would you prefer something else?" he asked.

"No, it's perfect," she smiled. Her lips were trembling.

"I'll go to the bar and get us two beers and a couple of Brats."

She watched him go up to the bar. It was so obvious that it wasn't easy for him to walk. He limped on the wooden leg, and the cane clicked against the floor. She longed to take him in her arms and hold him. *What's the matter with me? I hardly know him. But I need someone so badly, and he is so kind.*

Otto brought the beers and sausages back to the table one at a time. Elica thought about getting up and helping him, but she didn't want to embarrass him, so she didn't move. Once he'd delivered everything to the table, Otto sat down. He was out of breath. "That was a lot of walking," he sighed. "I'm not used to it." He caught his breath, then smiled at her. "So, it's been a long time since I last saw you. What have you been doing? How have you been?"

"Eh," she said, feeling her depression crawl up to the surface again. "Not so good."

He nodded, "Yes, well, me either."

"I can imagine it must be hard for you," she said, looking down at the table.

"Am I that transparent? And I thought I did a good job of hiding my misery. You mean to say that you can see that I can hardly walk?" His voice had a hint of sarcasm. But then he smiled a big broad smile and let out a laugh. "Don't worry. I'm used to it. I have to be used to it, don't I?" He laughed again. She was surprised to see no bitterness in his laughter, which brought back memories of how contagious his laugh had been when they were young. He had been such a lighthearted and carefree boy. Then despite herself, Elica laughed too.

"Are you sorry you went to war?"

"Of course I am. Who could end up like this and not be sorry? But at the same time, I can't blame myself. I had no choice, and besides, at the time, I was convinced it was the right thing to do."

"So, you thought it was right."

"At the time, yes. I thought I wanted to be a part of Hitler's war to create an Aryan world. But once I got to the front and experienced battle, my mind changed, and I began to feel differently."

"Differently, how?"

"Ahhh, that's a loaded question," he said. "Let me see if I can explain. If I could go back and change things, I would. I would have left Austria before I was conscripted. I would have avoided war at all costs."

"You would have run away?" Elica asked, taking a sip of the dark, bitter beer.

He smiled. "Yes, I would have. So, now you know. I am a coward. But, yes, I would have run while I still had both legs and could run. Now I couldn't run if my life depended on it."

"Where would you have gone?"

"I don't know. Anywhere. Anywhere where there was no fighting, no blood, no death." He took a sip of beer. Then he raised his glass. "Let's make a toast to a place where there is no fighting, blood, or death. Heaven, maybe?"

She nodded. They clinked their glasses, and then they both drank.

There were a few moments of silence as they ate and finished their beers. Otto didn't go to the bar this time. Instead, he called a waitress over to the table and ordered another round of drinks. Then, in a serious tone, he turned to Elica and said, "Why do you wear it?"

"Wear what?"

"That scarf you constantly pull over the side of your face. What's under it? What happened?"

"Oh," she said, looking away from him. For a moment, she'd forgotten how self-conscious she was. "This?" She touched the scarf and mindlessly pulled it to ensure it covered her scar.

"Yes, that," he said.

Elica thought of a hundred different lies she might tell him. But in the end, she told him the truth. "I was married to a Jewish man. We had a child together, a son. One day, for no reason at all, my husband was arrested. I didn't know what to do. So, I went to the police station to see if I could find out where he was and if I could do something, anything, to get him released. Dagna was working there. Do you remember Dagna Hofer?"

"How could I forget her?" Otto winced.

"Well, I thought she would help me. I didn't realize she would torture me for marrying Daniel because he was Jewish. I was tortured and beaten, and then one of the Gestapo agents carved up my face."

"Where is your son?"

"I don't know. I had left him with a friend when I went to the police station, and by the time I returned, my friend and my child were both gone."

"Have you tried to find him?"

"I have, but I don't know where to look. Besides, I am ashamed for him to see me. When children on the street see me, they are horrified. My face is ruined. I look like a monster."

He didn't say a word. He just stared at her. She began to cry.

"Let me see your scar," he said.

"Here? Now?"

"Please..."

"I can't," she said. "I can't take off my scarf here. I just can't." Elica felt like running away. She stood up. "I'm going home. Thank you for the beer and the sandwich."

Quickly, Elica left the beer hall and began running down the street. She was holding the scarf over her cheek. *My face is horrible. It's like I'm the sideshow at a carnival.*

Otto called out to her, "I can't run, so I can't catch up with you, but I'm sorry. Please wait up for me. I want to talk to you."

I could keep running, or I could stop and talk to him. Elica's feet froze, and she waited for him. Getting there took him a long time, but he caught up to her.

"Thank you for waiting," he said, out of breath. Then he added, "Let's go to my apartment. We can talk more there."

"Where do you live?"

"Only a few streets from here."

"All right," she said. "But even though we're going to be alone, I don't know if I can show you my face. It's tough for me to do that."

"I understand. You can show me when you're ready," Otto said.

CHAPTER THIRTY-SEVEN

They walked together in silence until they came to a rundown building on the poorer side of town. Otto stopped and took the key from his pocket. "This is it. This is my palace," he said, winking at her as he opened the door. Elica followed him inside.

Otto's apartment was small, cluttered with papers, junk, and dirty. Elica could see it had been a long time since anyone had washed the floors or the windows. "Make yourself comfortable," he said, pointing to the tattered couch. There was a slight odor of sweat mixed with alcohol.

Elica sat down. Otto went to the shelf and poured them both a glass of schnapps. He brought the glass to her, limped back, and retrieved the second glass. Carefully, he put the glass on the scratched-up wooden coffee table and eased himself to the sofa beside her.

Everything takes a lot of effort for him.

"So, now that we're here, you can relax. It's just us, just you and me, yes?" he said.

"Yes," she nodded, but she was not relaxed. Not at all.

"I'm afraid I can't kiss you with that scarf covering your face, Elica," he said.

"I know," she answered, but she made no effort to remove the scarf. They sat there awkwardly, neither of them speaking.

Then Otto cleared his throat. "Do you remember that night we spent together after that cookout from our church?"

"Oh, that was so long ago. We were so young and innocent," Elica said, embarrassed because she did remember that she'd had casual sex with him that night.

"We went off alone together. I can still remember how we were hiding, so we wouldn't get caught by the counselors. We would have gotten into a lot of trouble. But we did it anyway, and then we made love. It was incredibly romantic, and I can remember it like yesterday. Every single moment of it. We were both whole then. Both of us were so perfect. I was tall and handsome, and you were magnificent. All the fellows in the church youth group said so."

"Did they?" She sighed.

"Oh yes, we used to talk about all the girls in the neighborhood. And everyone agreed that you were by far the loveliest. I was mad about you."

She turned to look into his eyes. "Well, it's rather strange that you say that because you acted so strangely after it ended. Then you never came by to see me again after that night when we were intimate. You said you would, but you didn't."

"Ahhh, so you do remember all of it."

She nodded, "Actually, yes, I do."

"I was young and stupid, I guess," he said.

"Why were you so uncomfortable?"

He laughed, "Would you believe me if I told you it was my first time? I felt like a fool. I didn't know what to do. And I was afraid you could tell it was my first time, and you thought it was rather lousy."

"I didn't. I couldn't tell, and I didn't think it was lousy. You should have talked to me," Elica said.

"As I said, I was young and foolish."

She shrugged. "I'm glad you told me. I often wondered if there was something wrong with me."

"No, Elica, nothing was wrong with you."

She smiled at him and gave everything he had just told her some serious thought. *That night at the cookout was a long time ago. We were both young and although he didn't call me after we were intimate, I can forgive him for the past. I am tired of being alone. I need someone to spend my time with. Someone to talk to, maybe even laugh with once in a while. And it would feel so good to be held, stroked, and touched. No man comes near me. I haven't even felt the warm touch of another man holding my hand or rubbing my hair since my Daniel has been gone.*

She reached for Otto's hand. But even as she did, she glanced down at her hand and felt sick to her stomach as she looked at the rough red skin. *This is what happens from scrubbing clothes with strong soaps.* He glanced at her ravaged skin, and she was suddenly embarrassed. She quickly pulled away, but he gently took her hand back in his. Then he kissed her palm. Elica shivered. She was ashamed, and she pulled her hand away again.

"I'd better go home now," she said, tucking her hand behind her back. She began to stand up, but Otto gently held her down.

"Please, Elica. Give us a chance. Don't leave." He reached behind her and took her hand again. This time, she didn't pull away. She allowed him to take it in his. Gently, he massaged her palm with his thumb as he held it in his own. Hot tears stung the back of her eyes. *I can't cry. It will ruin everything if I cry.*

He reached up and looked into her eyes. She was trembling as he slowly began to untie the scarf.

"No, please don't," she said, grabbing her scarf and holding it over the side of her cheek.

He stopped and looked into her eyes. "It's all right," he whispered. "I understand how hard this is for you. I know it's going to be equally hard for me when I take off my clothes, and I have to let you see my wooden leg."

She looked away and swallowed hard. *I have no idea what that will look like. I'm afraid I will be sick when I see it. And that's so unfair of me. He's willing to accept me. I should be willing to accept him.* Elica forced herself to smile as she let the scarf fall. Otto gently touched the raised flesh on her cheek.

"It's not so bad," he said.

"Really?"

"Really. You see it as much worse than it really is."

Her lips quivered, but she smiled as tears ran freely down her cheeks. Otto unbuttoned her blouse, and she allowed him to. Then he stood up, took her hand, and led her to the bedroom.

Elica lay down on the bed and watched as Otto removed his clothes. At first, she felt sick when she saw the stump that was his leg. But she took a deep breath and said, "It's not so bad, really." Then she managed a smile. "You see it as much worse than it really is."

Otto laughed. "Now you understand. We are meant for each other."

Elica nodded. Otto took her into his arms, and she surrendered to his gentle touch as they made love.

CHAPTER THIRTY-EIGHT

Early spring 1943 , The Gypsy Camp

After dinner, the Shero Rom, the head of the Gypsy camp, called a meeting. Once everyone gathered around the campfire, he stood up. His face was drawn, and he appeared anxious as he began to speak, "I know we have been comfortable here. But I think the time has come that we should begin traveling again. Some of you have brought it to my attention that you have seen Nazis in the forest watching our campfires from time to time. I assume they come to watch our women dance. And so far, they have left us alone. However, last week, we had a few visitors from another Romany family, and they told me to be careful of the Nazis. They said that the Nazis had been arresting groups of travelers and putting them into prison camps. Quite frankly, I don't trust these Germans at all. Since the visitors came, I have been unable to sleep. I've given this a lot of thought and decided that it is best if we go as soon as possible while we still can. We are very fortunate to have made it through the last winter at this camp. Because none of us like to travel during the winter, it's too difficult. But we have always traveled through the spring and summer, and the weather is perfect right now. I realize we have spent an entire year here, which is unusual for us, but it was pleasant, with plenty of game, fish, and fresh water. And thanks to the wonderful hunters and fishermen among us, we've had plenty of food, too. But now, I think this visit from the other clan is a warning and... well," he hesitated and said, "it's time to saddle up our horses and pack up our vardos. I would like to leave here sometime in the next two weeks. However, I won't make a final decision without hearing your thoughts. So, does anyone have anything they would like to say?"

A young man stood up. "With all due respect, I feel we might be safest here. The Nazis who patrol these woods know we are here and have left us alone. If they wanted to arrest us, they would have done so already. If we leave this place and travel, we may encounter new Nazis who might not be so kind or tolerant."

"I agree." Another man stood up.

"Sometimes, the Germans who come here to watch us dance want more. We refuse them. How long do you think they will allow us to do that?" A pretty woman in her mid-thirties asked. "The last time I refused to let a Nazi have his way with me, he became very angry. I was afraid. He didn't hit me or do anything to us but he could if he wanted to."

"We can't trust them. And, I'll say it again, in my opinion, I feel it is best that we go," the Shero Rom repeated. It was difficult for Anna to determine his age. His body was healthy and strong, but he'd begun to lose his thick black wavy hair, which was such a strong Romany trait, and his eyes were dark and troubled. "But I won't make this decision without all of you being in agreement. So, I say we take a vote on it."

The others agreed. And after the vote, it was decided that they would stay through the summer again and then through another winter.

The Shero Rom shook his head as he stood up to leave the area. But before he did, he said, "No music or dancing tonight." Then he extinguished the campfire, and the group began to disperse, everyone quietly making their way back to their vardo's.

On beautiful spring nights like this, when the weather was warm, and the sky was clear of rain, many men would sleep under the stars. But not tonight. Tonight, everyone was worried. The people all walked slowly. No one sang, talked loudly, or laughed, and Anna could see their hearts were heavy with the burden of their decision.

Then, in typical Romany fashion, unable to go to sleep in a sour mood, one of the musicians turned back to the center of the campground. He glanced over at the Shero Rom and shrugged, "I'm sorry," he said, but then he picked up his violin and began to play. "Music is the lifeblood of the Romany people, and we're Sinti, musicians at heart."

Everyone turned to look at the Shero Rom to see if he would be angry because he'd been defied. But he just laughed, threw his hands in the air, and said, "I was wrong to tell you not to play tonight. Music is life, no?"

"Yes," several people answered him in unison as they returned to the circle.

"My mistake. It's most important to be happy. So, please, ignore an old man's foolishness and enjoy."

The rest of the group abandoned their worries and their misery, and they, too, picked up their instruments. Sweet music filled the forest and drifted up to the sky. Anna, caught up in the magic of it, picked up her violin, and she, too, began to play. The women danced, entranced by the sound. And one of them began to sing a beautifully haunting song in her native language. For over an hour, the Gypsies played and danced and lost themselves in the music. And then, one by one, they began to head back to their vardos to retire for the night.

Anna made her way back toward the wagon she shared with Nuri. "Let's sleep outside tonight," Nuri said. "Under the stars. What do you think?"

"Yes, I'd like that. I'll go and get the blanket you gave me," Anna answered.

As they lay under the stars, Nuri said, "I think that's The Big Dipper."

"And that's the northern star."

"Do you like sleeping outside?"

"I do. I love it, in fact. My family was stuck in an attic in hiding. We lost track of time. Days faded into nights. There was no fresh air. This is far better."

"I can't imagine being stuck in an attic. Was it a small space?"

"Yes, very small, cramped. We were hungry all the time. Thirsty too. It was hard. But I would go back to it if it meant I could see my parents and my brother again."

"You have a brother?"

"I did. But he died."

"I'm so sorry."

"Yes, me too," Anna was about to cry. So, she said in a soft voice, "Perhaps we should get some sleep."

"Yes, I agree. Good night."

"Good night."

It was still dark outside when Anna stirred awake. She was startled at first to find Vano standing over her, watching her. "What are you doing here?" she asked.

"I'd like to talk to you."

"Yes, of course," she said. "But let's go for a walk so we don't wake Nuri."

He nodded. As they walked, he whispered, "What did you think about the meeting tonight?"

"I don't know what to think. I am afraid of the Germans. But at the same time, I am also afraid to leave here and travel because that would mean I would be going even further away from possibly finding my parents. And, I have to admit, in the back of my mind, I always hope they will somehow find me here. I know it's probably impossible, but I am always hopeful."

"I understand."

He smiled sadly at her, and they walked together silently for a while. She felt his gaze upon her, and when she looked up, she found he was looking down at her. Their eyes met. Neither of them spoke. For a moment, they stopped walking and stared into each other's eyes as if they were seeing each other for the first time. Then a smile broke on Vano's face. Anna smiled too. And then they began to walk again.

They walked under the light of a full moon until they were well into the forest and far enough away from camp to speak without disturbing anyone. Then Vano sat on a broken tree branch large enough to hold them both. He motioned for Anna to sit beside him. She did.

"I am not a man who has an easy time talking about his feelings," Vano said, his voice choked. "Even now, as I hear myself speaking, I feel like I sound ridiculous. Laughable even."

"You don't. I promise you that you don't," she said. "Please, go on."

"I am trying," he said, managing a smile. "I don't know how this happened. I tried to fight it. I tried very hard because I know how my brother feels about you. But when I saw you and Damien looking into each other's eyes. It almost killed me. I don't know how to say this, but... I mean... well... I mean..."

Anna looked down at the ground. She thought of Damien. She knew he cared for her, and she cared for him, too. But her heart belonged to Vano.

The stars poured light down on the earth as if they had been made of liquid silver, and the wind in the trees sent a shiver up Anna's spine as she sat with Vano. He was such a quiet man, but his eyes spoke to her, and as she looked into them, she could feel his emotions. He moved closer to her. She didn't say a word, but her heart began beating faster with anticipation. Again, they sat looking at each other for a long time. Then, without warning, Anna leaned in and kissed him. It was electric, and as their lips touched, she felt warmth wash over her. She was amazed at her boldness as she pulled away. Both of them were breathless. They smiled at each other. Then Vano took her into his strong arms, and she felt the power of him surge through her like lightning. But as they leaned in to kiss again, they heard a rustle in the bushes. Fear struck Anna, and she pulled away. This time, she was looking into his eyes with fear and worry. "Did you hear that?"

"Don't worry. I'll protect you," Vano reassured her. And then, there was another rustle in the bushes, and they realized they weren't alone.

Is it Damien? Sabina? Could it possibly be my parents? Is it Ulf? Or maybe it's someone else? It could be the Nazis. She trembled and grabbed his arm. He put his finger over his lips, motioning her to be quiet. Then he gently loosened himself from her grasp and walked to the bushes where the sound came from. He tore the bushes open, but there was no one there.

"We're alone," he turned to Anna.

"Are you sure?" she asked.

"I'm sure. I checked. There is no one there. It could have been a rabbit or a fox."

"Yes, you're right," she said.

He smiled at her and patted her hand.

Anna was soothed. She trusted Vano when he assured her that they were safe. The forest had become a place of peace and tranquility for Anna. Where she had once feared it, she now loved it. And especially because she was there with Vano. This had been their special place, and she felt a deep attachment to it. However, unbeknownst to both of them, a danger lurked just behind the thick trunk of an oak tree covered by the blanket of darkness. He stood as silent as a lion, a true predator, watching them and waiting for the right moment.

The following night after dinner, there was a campfire with music and dancing as usual. One of the women began to play a strange-looking instrument. It looked like something between a guitar and a bass. Anna walked over to her. She'd never seen an instrument like this before. She closed her eyes and listened. The music filled her completely. After the song was done, Anna said, "I've never seen an instrument like that before. May I ask what it is?"

"It's a lute. Some people call it a mandolin," the woman said.

"You play it beautifully," Anna said.

"Thank you."

Anna sat down on the ground beside Vano and closed her eyes while the fire danced. The women swayed to the music, which filled Anna's ears and transported her soul. The Gypsy band played for hours. And once they'd finished, and the campfire was extinguished, Vano asked Anna to walk again. She agreed. Nuri was sitting with them, so this time, there was no need to inform her. "I'll see you later," she said to Anna.

Then Anna and Vano got up and began to walk through the forest.

The sky was alight with bright, twinkling stars. A soft, gentle wind whispered a love song through the trees, and Anna felt like she was living in a dream. Her life had been filled with pain until she'd come to live among the gypsies. And although she still thought of her family all the time, she loved it here, living in nature. The Romany way of life had allowed her to see beauty in the world again. Someday, if this war ever ends, she will go into towns and search for her parents. But for now, she must accept things as they were. Standing under the protective branches of a weeping willow tree with her hair blowing softly in the wind, Anna felt she might just be as happy as she was when she was a child again.

Vano stood beside her. Anna trembled as she looked up into Vano's eyes. He was tall, built strong and thick like the tree, and smiling despite his trembling lips. "Words don't come easy to me, Anna," he said. Then, clearing his throat, he added, "But, well... I wanted to tell you that you've come to mean a lot to me."

Tears filled her eyes. It had been so long since she'd felt close to anyone. She had been lost since she was separated from her family.

But the way she felt about Vano made her think that she might begin a family of her own someday.

As she stood beside him, looking into his eyes, Anna remembered how frightened she had been while running through the forest alone, desperate, and unable to care for herself. A young Jewish girl desperate to escape the Nazis. Knowing all the while, the Gestapo would kill her if she were caught. It was Vano who had found her. If he hadn't, she would have died of thirst or starvation. Or even worse, she could have been captured. But he had been hunting, and when he saw her, he brought her back to the rest of his caravan. At the time, he seemed distant and paid little attention to her. But then, once she was back at the camp, she met Damien, Vano's brother. While Vano was quiet and kept to himself, Damien was the opposite. He was outspoken, vivacious, and fun-loving. And Anna was grateful to him because Damien set about making Anna feel at home in the Romany camp. He introduced her to Nuri, a beautiful and strong Gypsy girl who taught her to ride horses.

Anna and Nuri forged a friendship based on their mutual love of an auburn-colored horse by the name of Zino, which means red in Romany. Anna cherished the horse almost as much as she cherished the friendship between herself and Nuri. But Vano and Damien's mother, Lavina, did not relish having Anna live with the rest of the caravan. She told Anna that she could see that Damien was smitten with Anna, but she didn't want him to marry a girl who was not Romany. Anna didn't argue with Lavina. Because what Lavina didn't know was that although Anna adored Damien, she was not in love with him. And even if Lavina had never mentioned it, Anna knew she could never marry him. That was because Anna had always had a special place in her heart for Vano. But at that time, she believed there was no chance for her and Vano to be together. That was because Lavina told Anna that Vano was betrothed to Sabina. Lavina loved Sabina. She told Anna that Sabina was like a daughter to her.

"What about Sabina?" Anna asked in a small voice.

"What about her?" Vano asked, confused. He wondered why Anna was mentioning Sabina right now.

"Well, aren't you betrothed to her?"

"She may think so, but I have no intentions of marrying her. Not ever," he said.

"But your mother told me—"

"My mother would like me to marry Sabina, but I have no plans of ever fulfilling her wishes."

"Never?"

"No, never," he said, smiling.

Anna looked up into Vano's dark eyes and felt her pulse race. He put his arms around her shoulders, and she fell into them. He held her close. His skin smelled like cool fresh air, and his arms were warm and tender. He was taller than her by over a foot, but he bent until he was the same height and kissed her.

Oy Vey, I think I might be falling in love. Anna thought as she looked at this beautiful man who held her tightly.

CHAPTER THIRTY-NINE

Otto and Elica had a standing date on Wednesday nights. Occasionally, he would come to her house, bringing enough food and beer for their evening meal. But she went to his apartment more often, as it was far more difficult for him to get around on his wooden leg. She didn't mind. She found she was glad for the company. And as time passed, she grew used to his stump, as he called the short piece of flesh that had once been his leg. Seeing it no longer bothered her. His company gave her a reason to wear a dress and makeup to cover her scar. Elica found she looked forward to Wednesday nights and thought about Otto all week. Most often, their dates did not consist of anything outside their homes.

They never attended the theater, a concert, or even a film. But that was all right with Elica. When they were alone, she could pretend she was still the proud, beautiful girl she'd been before her face had been ravaged. Their evenings consisted of a meal and a few hours of lovemaking. This wasn't the glamourous life Elica had once dreamed of when she'd married the wealthy Daniel Goldenberg. Still, it was a break from her mundane existence of washing and folding laundry. Sometimes, when Otto came to dinner at Elica's home, she would cook for him. Nothing fancy, just soup or stew with thick, dark bread. But he seemed to enjoy a home-cooked meal so much that she tried to prepare one for him at least once a month. Sometimes, if Elica's mother was at home, and they didn't want to go into the bedroom, they would play cards after dinner. Although money was difficult for Otto to come by, occasionally, on a Friday or Saturday night, Otto would take Elica to a beer hall where he would treat her to a few dark beers and bratwurst.

Having sex with Otto was pleasant, if not earth-shattering. She could see the strain on his face when they made love because he had to hoist himself up on one leg. It made her uncomfortable, knowing he wasn't as swept away as she would have liked him to be. Most of their lovemaking consisted of kissing and gentle stroking. But Elica had been alone for so long that any human touch was welcome. Her mother disapproved of her relationship with Otto at first. After all, sometimes she'd heard them when they made love at her home. And she made sure to tell Elica that Otto was not Elica's husband. But one day, when her mother was ruthless with her comments about Otto, Elica explained her loneliness. After that, her mother stopped criticizing her. On the nights when Otto came by to see her daughter, Frau Frey slipped quietly into her bedroom and left Elica and Otto alone.

As time passed and the relationship between Otto and Elica grew, Elica found she longed for more from him. She was tired of spending her days alone and wanted more of his time. One night, Elica invited him to her home. She prepared a special dinner. It had taken all her rations to buy a chicken on the black market, but she'd gone to the butcher, and he had arranged it so she could purchase one. She did this because she wanted this night to be something she and Otto would never forget.

Elica carefully roasted the bird with a few potatoes and carrots. When Otto arrived, she'd set the table with her grandmother's dishes. Although she hadn't had enough money to buy candles, it looked lovely. She served him dinner, and he told her how impressed he was with this special meal. Elica's mother was not at home that night. She'd made arrangements to be out that night because she was aware of Elica's plans. After Otto devoured his chicken, Elica led him to her room, and they made love as they always did. Once they were finished, she lay with her head on his chest. Sliding onto one elbow, Elica reached up and touched Otto's cheek. She softly asked, "What do you think about us maybe getting married?" Then she cleared her throat, embarrassed by her boldness. She didn't look into his eyes as she said, "I am lonely. I believe you are too. As we get older, we need someone in our lives. It would be nice to have dinner together every night. And if you didn't feel well for some reason, I would be there to take care of you." She could hear herself. Elica knew she was begging, and it made her sick to think that this was all she had. But it was, and she held her breath in the darkness, waiting for his answer.

After a few long moments of silence, he said in a kind, soft voice, "Elica... I like you. I like you a great deal. You are very special to me. But I can't marry you."

She choked out the words, "But why Otto? Why?"

"How can I explain this?" He slid away from her and then used his arms to hoist himself up. Now he sat naked on the edge of the bed. Even in the darkness, she could see the shadow of the stump that had once been his leg.

"Please... explain. I don't understand. Have I done something wrong?"

"How do I explain this to you? I hope you will understand," he said, then she heard him sigh in the darkness, "Elica, you told me yourself that you were married to a Jew. And to make things worse, somewhere, you might even have a half-Jewish brat running around.

I can't marry you. A Jewish man was inside of you. He planted his seed inside of you." He was trying to sound gentle, but he sounded cold and harsh to her. She could tell that he was deeply sickened by the very idea of her having been married to Daniel. "You are tainted by the Jew. Don't you see? Don't you understand? What would people say if the truth ever got out?"

She was quiet for a moment. Her fingers immediately found their way to the scar on her face. She touched it and felt the raised skin. A single tear trickled down her cheek. "But you find you can easily lie here with me. You can have sex with me," she said bitterly. "But marriage? No, not that."

"Elica, marriage is an entirely different thing. Don't you see that?"

"Oh yes, I can see a lot of things. And although I am lonely. Very lonely. And... I am paying a very high price for my choices and what I've done," she hesitated. Then, in a firm voice, she added, "I refuse to pay this price. I refuse to be your backstreet girl. The girl who you come to for sex when you feel like it. How many women are standing at your door waiting for you? None, I would guess. You can hardly move, yet I accept you for who you are. I take you to my bed with your one good leg, and I never say a word about it."

She got up and put on her robe. Then she turned to him. "You have a hell of a lot of nerve to criticize my husband for being Jewish. You aren't even half the man he was. But of course, you never knew him. All you know of him is that he was a Jew. And that's enough to make you and your kind hate him."

"I don't hate him. You're right. I don't know him. But knowing he was a Jew is enough. I just can't have that stigma on me. Can't you understand Elica? Besides, what if your son surfaces? Then I would raise a half-Jewish child? I couldn't," he said.

She was trembling. And she was glad that it was dark, and he couldn't see that she was crying. She spoke to him in a low growl, "Get out of here, Otto, and don't ever come back. I never want to see you again."

They were both silent as he struggled to put his clothes on. Then she listened with tears spilling down her face as his wooden leg clopped on the floor as he walked down the hall to leave. Elica jumped when she heard the front door slam. He was gone, and she knew he was gone forever.

CHAPTER FORTY

A thunderous roar, followed by a large boom, shook the ground. Enzo had been lying on his bed, trying to please his mother by napping. But after hearing and feeling the explosion, he ran screaming from his room. Aria met him in the hallway and gathered him into her arms. Mateo was not at home. He was at the office. Aria ran to the telephone to try to contact him. But when she picked up the receiver and put it to her ear, she realized the phone line was dead.

There was another roar, followed by another boom.

"I think we're being bombed, Signora," the maid said, her voice shaking. "What should we do?"

"Bombed?" Aria asked. She felt as if she might faint. Mateo had been nervous and on edge lately but refused to tell her why. She knew he wouldn't tell her anything because he didn't want to worry her. Shielded from the truth, Aria had been oblivious to what was happening in the world and had no idea that things had gotten this bad. However, if she gave it some thought, she'd had a small glimpse into the dangers that had been approaching. She closed her eyes for a second and remembered how she had gone into town a little more than a week ago to shop for a new dress to wear to an upcoming gala she and Mateo planned to attend. Aria had been in the dressing room trying on an aqua-colored taffeta gown when she overheard two ladies talking in the dressing room next to hers. Aria had recognized them when she'd entered the store. They were the wives of officials in Mussolini's government. Their husbands were not as high up as Mateo, so Aria had never been introduced to them and didn't know them well enough to speak or say hello. But she couldn't help but hear them.

One said, "I am very worried, Maria. I'm sure you know that Allies landed in Sicily and that the Italian army has been unable to fend them off."

"Yes, I've heard. My husband says we're going to have trouble with Hitler. He's not happy with Mussolini," she whispered. But Aria heard her anyway.

"Yes, I know. My husband says the same thing. He says the Italian army is folding. Then there will be real trouble here. And yet, here we are shopping for dresses when the world might be coming down around our ears."

"That's the time to shop for dresses. What else can we do?"

Aria felt her throat go dry. She took off the dress and laid it on the dressing room chair. She'd been so frightened by what she'd heard that she quickly put her dress back on and left the dress shop without making a purchase. Foolishly, she rushed home to speak to Mateo. But he had been at work, and she didn't feel comfortable telephoning him to ask him about this. *I don't dare do that, just in case someone is listening.*

Aria was anxious all day because Mateo didn't arrive home until late that evening. Enzo had already been fed and was fast asleep. Mateo refused dinner, telling the maid he'd eaten at the office. Aria knew that he was worried, too. She searched the house for him and found him in his study. He was sitting behind his desk when she asked what she'd heard at the dress shop that day. "I'm worried," she said. "I'm really scared."

"No, no, my sweet darling," Mateo said in his usual comforting way. "It's all going to be fine—nothing for you to be worried about. I'm taking care of us. There are just a few problems right now. You'll see. It will be all right."

"But these ladies said that the Italian army was folding. What will become of us?"

"Shhh," he soothed her. Then he put out his arms, and she walked over to him and sat on his lap. He held her close to him and ran his hand gently through her hair. She lay her head on his shoulder. "I would never let anything happen to you or Enzo," he promised.

This promise was good enough for her. Mateo had never lied to her, and she trusted him implicitly. His serene attitude calmed her, and she sat in his lap for a long while. Then, as they always did, they went up to their bedroom and lost themselves in each other.

But now, as the bombs were raining down on Rome and she held her screaming child in her arms, the terrifying words of the women in the dress shop came rushing back at her. The house shook with each loud explosion. Enzo looked into her eyes, pleading with her to make this stop. His face was red with terror.

"Perhaps we should get in the closet or under the bed," the maid suggested.

"Yes, perhaps," Aria said, biting her lip.

But just as they were about to get into the closet, the front door flung open, and Mateo rushed inside. "Come, hurry. Follow me. We're going out to the country where you'll be safe."

"But where?" Aria asked.

"Do you remember the farm we went to recently? I have made arrangements for you and Enzo to stay there. Take the maid with you if she wants to come."

"I can't come with you. If you are going, I would like to get home to my family."

"Yes, of course. Go," Mateo said. The maid ran out the door without even stopping to gather her pocketbook.

"Perhaps you should pack a bag. You might be there for a few days," Mateo said. Then, still trying to sound calm, he added, "But please hurry. And... Aria?"

"Yes?"

"Pack all your valuables. You might need them."

She paused for a moment. She wanted to ask him why. But the look in his eyes told her not to ask anything. And although he was trying to sound calm, she knew him better. He was unnerved. The best thing to do was to pack as quickly as she could so they could make their way out of the city.

Mateo drove the car instead of his chauffeur, driving at break-neck speed as the bombs ripped the already ravaged city apart. With each loud explosion, the car shuddered, and Enzo let out a high-pitched scream. Black smoke rose in the air, and Mateo's face was covered in sweat. His hands were trembling. He turned to look at the child, who was still screaming, and yelled, "Shut him up!"

He'd never spoken harshly to Aria or Enzo before. She felt hot tears in the back of her eyes threaten to fall, but she knew he didn't mean to be rough with her. He was driving fast and needed all his attention to be on the road. After all, he was trying to protect them. So, she held Enzo in her arms and whispered into his ear, "Shhh, it will be all right. Shhhh, don't scream. Papa and I need you to be very quiet right now. Can you do that for me?"

Enzo nodded. He was whimpering. Then he put his thumb in his mouth, and she held him against her breast.

Finally, after what seemed like a lifetime of danger, they were out of the city. Although they could still hear the bombing in the distance, they were no longer in the middle of it. Enzo was exhausted from crying, and he fell asleep. Aria wanted to ask Mateo a million questions, but something in her husband's demeanor told her not to question him right now.

They arrived at the farm, and the farmer's wife immediately told the family to come inside. Enzo was still asleep in Aria's arms. Mateo reached for him, and Aria handed the child to her husband, who carried him. They followed the farmer's wife to their room, where Mateo gently laid Enzo on the bed. When they went to the farm a few weeks ago, unbeknownst to Aria, Mateo made these arrangements in case of trouble. He had paid the farmer very well for the room and also arranged for meals to be provided for his family. However, Mateo was not planning to stay with his family. He would leave them here, where he knew they would be safe. He felt obligated to return to the responsibilities he'd left behind. "I must return to work. Things are very shaky for Mussolini right now. I can't tell you much more, only that I know that Mussolini had some sort of argument with Hitler. And he has run away for the time being. I know where he is hiding, but I can't say. It's top secret. You understand, I am sure. It's better if you don't know anything. It's safer for you and the boy. However, I believe our leader will return soon and need all his men to help him regain power."

"You will be in danger," Aria said. Her hands gripped his coat. "I can't let you go."

"I must go," he said softly.

"No," she held tightly to his coat. He took her into his arms and held her close to him. She smelled his cologne, and tears filled her eyes.

"You must trust me," he said. "I'll be back as soon as I can. I promise you." Then he smiled and tried to make light of the situation. "Come on now, do you think I could stay away from my beautiful wife? You know how crazy about you I am. I'll be back very soon."

She nodded and loosened her grip. But something inside of her told her not to let him go. He kissed her softly. He then placed a kiss on Enzo's forehead. "It's going to be all right," he said to Aria as he winked and smiled. But she saw in his eyes that he was uncertain.

She began to cry. He turned and came back, taking her in his arms and holding her so tightly that she thought her back might break. But even so, she wished he would never let her go. But he did. Leaning down, Mateo placed a long, passionate kiss on Aria's lips. Then he turned, and without looking back, he walked out of the room. Aria listened as the front door of the farmhouse closed. She ran to the window just in time to see Mateo driving away.

CHAPTER FORTY-ONE

Ulf returned from work one evening, too tired to cook, so he'd stopped at a local tavern to pick up food he took home with him. He walked into his house and immediately opened a bottle of beer. He took a long swig, then sat down to eat. He ate slowly and was careful not to get any grease from the sausage on his Gestapo uniform. Sitting down in the living room, he gazed out the window of the home he'd been given by his department head when it was recently Aryanized. Ulf closed his eyes briefly, and his thoughts turned to Anna. He'd risked so much to rescue her, but in the end, she had not appreciated his efforts. Instead, she ran away from him as soon as he admitted he had been forced to participate in the execution of Jews. *She refused to see my point of view. She didn't care how hard things were for me. I had to kill those people. The least she could have done was try to understand. She never takes my side on anything. Typical for a Jew to fail to appreciate all I have done. Instead of saying, 'poor Ulf, it must have been hard for you to do your duty to the fatherland. But you had to do what was expected of you. I know you didn't mean it.'*

Instead, she got scared and looked at me like I was a monster when I admitted that I had killed people, most of them Jews. But what she didn't understand was that I had to do it. I had orders. I had to follow them. Besides, she should know that I would never hurt her. I've always loved her. I suppose it could be argued that I am obsessed with her.

I want her more than I have ever wanted any woman. Maybe it's because she's different. And I suppose I have been warned that Jews have magical powers, and she has cast her Jewish spell on me. This is why the Führer tells us to stay away from them. They taught us that a Jew could cast a spell on an Aryan man and ruin him. I have come to see that. And so, since she will not come to me willingly, I will take her and make her mine no matter what. As an Aryan, it is my right to control her. She is nothing but a Jew, a subhuman at best. So, there is no crime in keeping her for my pleasure.

Ulf was used to having his way. He had been born to a very wealthy father. His mother died when he was just a child. His father soon remarried a woman far younger than himself. She was a beauty who gave him two twin boys. Ulf's younger half-brothers adored and worshiped him. And in turn, he drank their admiration like a cool drink on a hot day. His father indulged his children, particularly Ulf. Perhaps it was because his father felt guilty that Ulf did not have his birth mother to care for him. But as he grew up, Ulf was given whatever he asked for. So, when he broke up with his fiancée and fell wildly in love with Anna, his father didn't say a word, even though Anna was only a nanny for his brothers, who had come to spend the summer with his family in Berlin. At that time, Ulf didn't know that Anna was Jewish. She was posing as a Christian.

While he was away at school, Ulf had been listening to speeches by Hitler, and he found he was enchanted with him and the ideals he was presenting to create a new Germany. Like his fellow followers of the Nazi party, Ulf had an extreme distrust of Jews. After all, he read all the works that Dr. Goebbels, Hitler's Minister of Propaganda, had published, and he was caught up in the glory of creating a fatherland where Aryans, like him, would rule the world. So, when Anna's friend Dagna came to his parents' home and told his family that Anna was a Jew, Ulf was appalled. He was angry that she'd lied, but he was also shocked to learn that she was Jewish. His stepmother had kept the news quiet because even though Anna had lied to them to get hired, his stepmother was still afraid that the party officials would blame her and her family for hiring a Jew. Anna was quietly let go from her job and sent home to Austria. Ulf tried to forget her, but the harder he tried, the more he wanted her. She sent him a letter apologizing to him for lying. But he didn't write back. He continued to fight his feelings.

Then the war broke out, and he was filled with bravado. He wanted to show the world he was willing to fight and even die for his Führer, so he enlisted in the army. He put on his uniform and looked in the mirror. Instead of a lazy intellectual college student, he saw a triumphant and powerful Aryan man staring back at him. However, war was uglier than he had expected. And as he watched his childhood friends fall on the battlefield, he secretly became disenchanted with Hitler. He began to see that the war effort was little more than a way for Hitler to increase his power. Somewhere in the trenches, with the blood pooling on the cool earth, he lost faith in Hitler's lies. He wanted out of the army. Ulf no longer believed that Hitler's efforts to conquer the world were to help Germany and the common German man. He'd seen too much death, hunger, and cold. He wrote to his father, who had connections with Göring, a high-ranking official in the Nazi Party. His father pulled some strings, cashed in some favors, and Ulf received a promotion that took him out of combat and put him into the Gestapo. While working with the Gestapo, he'd arrested plenty of Jews. He'd gone to their homes and taken them away with their children in their arms. He'd gotten tips from neighbors about Jews who were hiding, and he had pulled them from their hiding places without a thought about what would become of them. Quite frankly, he didn't care. All he knew was that he was away from the front lines, and Ulf was glad to be working for the Gestapo. It was nice to be safe. Besides that, as far as the Jews were concerned, he could do as he pleased. He had no one to answer to. If anyone, especially a Jew, refused to listen to him, he could shoot them without worrying about consequences. It was easy work for him. But as much as he tried to put Anna out of his mind, he still thought of her. *She is forbidden to me. And that makes me want her even more.* Because he was a man who had never had to accept rejection and had been given all he asked for, he was not used to wanting something he couldn't have. And so, his feelings for Anna grew into an obsession. After the Anschluss, when Austria welcomed the Third Reich and Hitler as their leader, Ulf asked for a transfer to the police station near Anna's home in Vienna. And because she had written him to apologize for lying, he knew her address in Austria. But when he went to look for her, she was gone. He doubted that he would ever find her. But at least he could try. He transferred from Berlin to work at the Gestapo in Austria near her home in hopes of finding her. Ulf didn't find Anna right away, but he did find Dagna, and he remembered that she had known Anna. He knew he had to be careful when he asked Dagna if she knew what happened to Anna. Questions like these could cause him a lot of trouble. Dagna replied that she had no idea, so he dared not ask anything more. Then, to his surprise and delight, a young Austrian woman came into the police station. She was searching for her Jewish husband. The Gestapo did not take kindly to an Aryan woman marrying a Jewish man. They beat and tortured the woman. Ulf thought they might kill her. But then, to protect herself, she decided to turn in a family of Jews. Ulf heard that she told one of his fellow officers that she knew a Jewish family named Levinstein was hiding in a home right in the neighborhood. He'd been elated. *Could it possibly be Anna?* He'd wondered. But he also knew he must act quickly. He must ensure that he and his partner would be the officers sent on the mission to arrest the Levinsteins. This was the only way he could protect Anna. And he knew he would probably be forced to kill his partner because he could not expect him to cooperate. Quickly, he took the papers with the address where Anna and her family were hiding from his superior officer's desk. Then he told his superior officer he and his partner would handle the arrest. He decided that once he'd made the arrest and had killed his partner, he would drive out of Austria and then release Anna and her family into the forest. But it would not end there. This, Ulf was certain, was to be the beginning of a relationship between himself and Anna. Ulf planned to return to where he'd left Anna and her family as often as possible and bring food and supplies. *She would be so grateful that she would give herself to me willingly.* He would fill himself with her until he had enough of her, and this obsession disappeared. Then, once he no longer needed her, he would turn her and her family in. As far as the killing of his partner was concerned, he would lie to his superior officer. He would tell an elaborate story about how when he and his partner arrived at the house, his partner had turned on him and freed the Jews who were living there. Ulf would explain that he believed his partner must have known them because he spoke to them before he set them free. Then Ulf would make himself a hero, telling his superior officer that he'd killed his partner but could not catch the Jews. Then he would ask for time off work to hunt down those Jews who had escaped. His superior officer would understand. He was certain of it. And he would use the time he had off from work to go and see Anna. It all seemed perfect until he went back to see her and bring her food, only to find she and her family were gone. *She'd caused me a lot of anxiety, running away from me like that.* And he decided that he would find her, and when he did, he would never let her go again. Then a miracle happened. He'd been working on a special assignment in the east when his coworker suggested they slip away and go to a Gypsy camp. He hadn't even wanted to go, but he was glad he did because it was there that he saw Anna. And then he knew he would be able to find her again. However, he must be careful. The Gypsies had guns. He would have to make a plan in which she was unknowingly cooperative. He would take her, but not by force. He would outsmart her and take her by his wits.

After Ulf finished eating, he went down into the cellar. It was a dark and dank place, with spiders hanging in webs from the ceiling. *Poor Anna. She will probably be afraid of these spiders. Perhaps I should take down these webs. My poor little Anna.* He thought, but then he remembered that she'd betrayed him. *But why? Why should I make things nice for her? She ran away from me. I don't owe her anything. If she hadn't been so eager to run away from me and had just trusted me, I would not have had to find a way to abduct her and then built this prison and put her in a cage.*

It had taken lots of thought and effort to acquire all Ulf would need to imprison Anna. And now, as he studied the prison he'd built in the cellar of his home, he was satisfied. *Once I capture Anna and put her in this cage, she will never escape me again.* He thought as he tested the lock on the large dog cage he borrowed from the police station where he worked. *I can keep her here in the cellar in this cage when I am not using her.*

It was strong. Everything looked perfect. Now, it was only a matter of putting his plan into effect. Ulf glanced at this watch. It was early, only seven thirty in the evening. *It's not too late to telephone my brothers.*

He walked up the stairs, picked up the telephone receiver, and dialed the operator. *I must be careful that they are not aware of my true intentions. They are only boys, just sixteen years old, so I can't tell them the truth. I must make them believe that I am their good, kind brother and that I have Anna's best interest at heart.*

"Hallo," Ulf said when the new maid at his parents' home answered the phone. "It's Ulf. I want to speak to one of my brothers, please."

"Of course. I'll let them both know you're on the phone."

It was a few moments before Ulf's half-brother Gynther picked up the phone. "Ulf!" he said excitedly.

"Hallo, Gynther. How are you?"

"I'm fine. How are you? Klaus and I miss you. We talk about you all the time. When are you coming to visit?"

"I can't come and visit. I'm too busy with work. So, I thought that perhaps you and Klaus would like to come and stay with me for a week or two. How does that sound to you?"

"Yes! We'd love to, but Mother would never allow it. She would say we have to go to school."

"Don't worry about your mother or school. I'll take care of everything."

"Mother will do what you ask, I'm sure, but what about the school?"

"As I said, don't worry about it. I have a big position now; people listen to me. So, I'll call and see what I can do about getting you out for a few weeks."

"Really? That would be so wonderful. I can't wait to see you. And Klaus and I are so proud of you. You do have a big job! Father says so all the time." Gynther was rambling, speaking fast and excited.

Ulf could hear Klaus, Gynther's twin, in the background. "Is that Ulf?" Gynther didn't answer Klaus. He was ignoring him.

"Let me talk to Klaus for a minute," Ulf said.

"Hold the phone. I'll put him on," Gynther said. He was still very excited.

"This is Klaus."

"How are you?"

"I'm fine."

"Well, good. It's good to talk to you both. I was just telling your brother that I will arrange to take you and Gynther out of school for a few weeks so you can visit me. Would you like that?"

"Oh yes, Ulf. I really would!"

"Good, then it's settled. I'll make all the arrangements and get back to you boys early next week."

CHAPTER FORTY-TWO

The Gypsy Camp

As time passed, Anna and Damien grew closer. He was kind and gentle, often funny too. But she saw him more like a brother than the potential lover she knew he hoped to be. They went horseback riding together. He even took her fishing. But, even though she knew he was in love with her, her feelings were not there. Whenever she saw Vano carrying wood for the fire, the muscles in his tan arms strong and capable, she found she couldn't take her eyes off him. Unlike his brother, Vano was a very serious man, hardly ever joking or laughing. The others asked him for advice. And sometimes, Vano, rather than the Shero Rom, was consulted to settle an argument. Although she had no confirmation of this, Anna had begun to believe that perhaps Vano would be the successor of the Shero Rom, who had no children of his own. If this were true, she was certain that Vano would be required to marry amongst his clan.

However, to Anna's surprise, Vano had become more attentive to her. Sometimes when she was caring for the horses with Nuri, Vano would come over to ask how they were doing. He would stay for a few minutes and try to make conversation. However, casual chats were difficult for him. He was awkward, self-conscious, and not easy with words and laughter like his brother Damien.

"He's definitely in love with you," Nuri said one day after Vano visited them and left.

"I don't think so," Anna said, dismissing her comment, although she secretly wished it were true.

"I do think so. In fact, I am pretty sure of it. And, to make matters even more interesting, I would venture to say that you're in love with him, too." She smiled and added, "Now, don't get me wrong, I know you like Damien, but Vano is the one you love."

"Oh, Nuri, maybe you're right. Maybe I do like Vano too much because his mother told me he is betrothed to Sabina."

"Never. He likes her, but she is more like a sister to those boys than a potential wife. I realize Lavina wants Vano to marry her, but he won't. You'll see. He feels the same way about Sabina as you feel about Damien."

"I wish I were as confident as you are about this."

"I'm looking at it as an outsider, and I can see more clearly because I am not a part of it." Then she added. "Do you want to ask the cards? We could read the tarot if you'd like."

"You read cards?"

"Of course, we all do. My grandmother taught me."

"Sure, I'd love to see what they say," Anna said.

"Let's finish with the horses, and then we'll read before lunch."

They finished brushing and feeding the horses. Then they made their way to Nuri's wagon. Anna sat down at the table. Nuri took a hand-painted wooden box out of a dresser drawer. Then she sat across from Anna and began to shuffle the cards. She handed the deck to Anna and said, "Shuffle these and think about what you want to know."

"I don't know what I want to know," Anna said. "I'm not sure."

Nuri laughed, "Most people have a million questions. You have none?"

"I don't know what to ask. And I'll be quite honest with you. I'm afraid of the answers."

"All right. I understand. Let's not read the cards, then. We'll just leave the future up to God."

Anna smiled and threw up her hands. "I'm sorry," she said. "I don't know how to do this. I've never read cards or tried to predict the future. It seemed like it would be fun, but then I kind of got scared."

"Don't be afraid. Let's just forget about it. What will come, will come. I just thought that if you knew the future, you could make plans. You know what I mean?" Nuri asked.

Anna let out a laugh. "When I was a child, my *bubbie*, my grandmother, used to say, *Mann tracht, un Gott lacht.* It's Yiddish, meaning that man makes plans and God laughs. It means that God has his plans for all of us, and whatever we plan makes no difference at all."

"Perhaps that's true. Your *bubbie*, as you call her, sounds like a wise woman," Nuri said. "Let's get some food. Are you hungry?"

"Yes, very," Anna said.

Anna thought about everything that Nuri had said. But she wasn't sure how she felt about Vano. He was very attractive, and she felt a pull to him, but she wasn't sure if she could spend the rest of her life like this. She wanted to go home. And it was hard to accept that the home she'd once known no longer existed. She had no home, and as for her family, she had no idea where they were. Anna longed to be loved, to have a husband and children. If she couldn't return to her parents, at least she would have something to hold on to. She was still a virgin. Before the war, she firmly believed she would be a virgin on her wedding night. She thought she would marry a Jewish man under a chuppah, a canopy, with her parents and brother at her side. Now, all of that was gone. It was little more than a bittersweet memory. But lately, she had begun to wonder what it would feel like to be held in a man's arms. *There is a good possibility that I may not live long enough to know what that feels like. With the Nazis hunting Jews, who knows what the future will bring?*

Perhaps I should just live for the moment. Let down all the moral constraints my parents instilled in me. Maybe I should taste love while I am still alive, while I can still do so. She felt guilty about having these thoughts. Anna's mother had told her that sex without marriage was the worst possible sin a girl could commit. She would never have considered doing something like this had it not been for the fact that her way of life was gone.

After lunch, Nuri returned to the wagon, but Anna needed some time alone. She went for a walk through the woods to study her feelings for Vano. *I care for Vano. I always have. Maybe Nuri is right. Perhaps this is what love is. I am not sure. When we kissed the other night, I felt like my body was on fire. And then the other day, when he looked into my eyes as he took the reins from my hand and our hands brushed, I felt a tingling inside of me that I had never felt before. I wanted him to kiss me.* Even as these thoughts crossed her mind, she felt ashamed. Her face grew hot and red, and she was glad she was alone. But she finally admitted to herself that she was not willing to die without ever having felt the physical love of a man. Vano was a perfect choice. *I think he cares for me, but I don't know if he loves me. Nuri thinks so, but I'm not sure. But what I do know is that he is kind and protective. And he stirs feelings of desire in me. So, I think he should be the one.*

That night, after the campfire was extinguished, Anna and Nuri were returning to Nuri's wagon when Anna saw Vano standing alone and watching her. She thought he probably wanted to go walking with her again. They had walked together several times since she'd kissed him that first night. Anna looked over at Vano. He smiled at her, and her heart melted. She turned to Nuri. "I think Vano wants to go for a walk. I'll be back early."

Nuri nodded. "I won't wait up for you because I doubt you'll be back early." Then she added, "Go on. He's waiting for you."

"Vano," Anna called out.

"Yes." A look of surprise came over his face when she called out to him. Anna walked over to where Vano stood by the fire. "Did you want to go walking tonight?" she asked boldly. Because he was so quiet, she found herself becoming more outspoken.

"Yes, I would like that," he said. "Let me help put out the fire first. Then we'll go, all right?"

She nodded. Then she blurted out awkwardly, "I have a letter for you. I wrote it for you." Anna wanted to tell him how she felt about making love to him. And it was easier for Anna to communicate through writing rather than speaking, especially about such an embarrassing subject. So, she had written to him, telling him she wanted him to be the first man she would make love with. She told him in her letter that she was a virgin and didn't want to die without ever feeling the love of a man.

"A letter?" He cocked his head as he asked, puzzled. "Why a letter? What's the matter? You can't talk to me?"

"Yes, I know I can. But I wrote to you because I had something personal, something I couldn't say out loud." She thought about it momentarily and then realized she might have shamed him. She didn't mean to, but he had a strange look on his face, and it suddenly dawned on her that he might not be able to read. She was holding the letter in her hand. He didn't take it from her. So, she whispered, "Vano, can you read?"

In a whisper, almost imitating her voice, he said, "Anna, can you hunt? Anna, can you fish? No, I can't read. And you can't hunt or fish."

"I'm sorry. Did I offend you? I didn't mean to."

"No," he sighed. "I'm not offended. I can't read. I never learned. It's not something that is important to us. We live off the land, so the things we learn have to do with survival. Reading is not one of them. But you can't hunt or fish because you never learned to do so. This was not important in the world where you grew up. Reading was. So, you learned to read. That makes us equal in our ways, no?"

"Yes, you're right," she admitted. Then she added, clearing her throat and being as brave as she could, "When we go walking tonight, I will tell you what is in my letter."

"I would be very curious to know. I would even be interested in learning how to read."

"Good," she said.

"Sit down for a few minutes while I finish here."

"All right," she said as she sat on a tree stump.

Once the fire was extinguished, Vano walked over to her. "It's done. Would you like to go now?" he asked. She could tell he was nervous.

"Yes, let's go."

He nodded.

Anna could feel the eyes of the rest of the group on them as they left the clearing together. She thought she saw Damien give her a hurt look as they passed by where he was sitting. Anna felt terrible about Damien. She wasn't sure what to say to him. She glanced back at him again, but he was gone. In his place was Lavina, watching with her eyes narrowed as Anna and Vano disappeared into the forest.

They walked for a while before Vano said, "Is something wrong, Anna? I mean, something must be wrong for you to have written a letter to me."

She didn't know how to say what she needed to tell him. It was difficult for her. So, she said, "Come, let's sit down."

He sat down on the ground, and she sat beside him. Until Anna came to the Gypsy camp, she'd been a quiet girl. She had never been as bold as she was now. Somehow, she found her voice and her courage. And, as she sat on the cool ground beside the most handsome man she'd ever known, she had decided that if this were to happen between them, she must initiate it because he would never do so out of respect for her. Vano was watching her silently, waiting for her to speak. Anna did not speak. Instead, she took his face in her trembling hands and pulled him down. Then she placed a warm kiss on his lips. He looked at her, puzzled. "Is this what the letter was about?" he asked.

"Yes, this and more," she said.

Now he realized what she wanted, and he took her into his arms and kissed her passionately. They kissed again and again, rolling on the ground in each other's arms. Then Anna clumsily put Vano's hand on her breast.

"Are you sure this is what you want?" he asked.

"Yes, Vano, I'm sure."

He looked into her eyes without moving his hand. "Anna?"

"Yes, Vano. Yes, this is what I want. We don't know what tomorrow will bring for us. This is a very dangerous world we live in. All we have for certain is today, this moment. I don't want to die without ever knowing what it's like to feel loved. Do you know what I am trying to say?"

He nodded. His eyes were sad, but full of affection. He kissed her again. Then he kissed her neck and her breasts. He worshiped every inch of her, and she was not ashamed. It was beautiful. More beautiful than she could ever have imagined. His eyes did not leave hers for a moment. And then he entered her. For a single second, it hurt. She wanted to cry out. But before she could scream, the pain gave way to pure pleasure.

Once they had finished making love, they lay together under the stars, Anna's head nuzzled in the crook of Vano's arm. "Look at the stars," he said. "You see that constellation over there? That's the big dipper."

"I know," she answered, running her fingers through the light dusting of hair on his chest.

"And that one over there, the bright one, that's Venus, the planet of love. It is guiding us tonight," he said, kissing her head.

She smiled and took his hand. He braided his fingers with hers. And they lay like that without speaking until they both fell asleep.

When they returned in the morning, Nuri was awake. "So, I was right," she said.

"Yes, you were," Anna smiled.

Anna and Vano walked every night after the campfire was extinguished for the next three weeks. Although no one mentioned it,

Anna was certain that everyone knew that they had become lovers. It was obvious in the way Vano sat beside her and held her hand during the music and dancing. When he went hunting or fishing in the morning, he brought food to her and Nuri first, then to his mother and Sabina. Damien seemed to know and to accept her choice. He was still friendly, but not as warm as he had been.

The age-old ancient language of physical love brought Vano and Anna close to each other. She felt closer to him than she'd ever felt to anyone—even her family. *I think Nuri is right. I am in love with him.*

One night after Anna and Vano made love, they lay together under a tree. Vano stood up and took out a small pocketknife. Then he began to carve into the trunk of a tree. "What are you doing?" Anna asked as she rolled onto one elbow.

"I'm carving a heart into this tree. Trees live for hundreds of years. And that means our feelings for each other will last hundreds of years."

"Let me help you. I'll put our names inside," she said, then stood up and scratched their names inside the heart. Anna and Vano. He smiled at her, and he began to deepen the letters, carefully carving them into the tree.

She smiled at him and sighed. Anna was glad she'd decided to become Vano's lover. Everything in her life seemed to glow these days. Finally, she felt the emptiness that was inside of her disappearing.

After Vano had finished carving their names, he lay down beside Anna and caressed her. She molded like clay into his arms.

"Well, anyway, I have something interesting to tell you." He cleared his throat. "I went to see one of the wise women. She read my tarot cards."

"Oh?" Anna said. "What did she say?"

"She couldn't tell me much. All she said was that you feel the same about me as I do about you."

"Do you believe that strongly in fortune telling?"

"I don't know," he said. "All I know is that I am pretty sure I am in love with you. And I'll be damned if it doesn't hurt me to know that my brother feels the same way."

There was a silence, a long silence, in which neither of them spoke. Anna reached for his hand and squeezed it. Then she smiled at him. "I know. I think the wise woman is right. I think I love you too."

They were both silent for a few minutes.

"You've made me happy," he said. "And sad. Sad because I have never done anything that would hurt my brother before. Never."

"I believe you. And I like Damien very much. But my feelings are not the same as the feelings I have for you."

He nodded. "I know. I can see it in your eyes when you look at me."

She nodded.

"I talked to Damien about it. He accepts us as a couple. But I know it hurts him."

"I'm sorry. I hate to hurt him too. He is a good, kind man. But he's not my man. You are."

He looked into her eyes. There was a moment of silence, then in a soft voice, he said, "I would like to marry you." Vano reached over to the place where his pants lay. He fished into his pants pocket and pulled out a large ruby ring. "This was my grandmother's ring. She gave it to me before she died. She told me to give it to the girl I was sure I wanted to spend the rest of my life with. Until I met you, I never wanted to give it to anyone. But now, I know you are the one, and I want to give it to you." He stumbled over his words. Then, in a small voice, he said, "Will you accept it? Will you marry me?"

She was excited and scared at the same time. Anna was trembling. She was at a loss for words. Her heart was beating so hard that she thought she might faint. "Yes," she said, "I'll marry you."

He took her into his arms and kissed her. She sighed, and then she realized why she had come to live amongst the Romany in the forest. It was because God had sent her here to find her *beshert*. It was Vano. He was the man who was destined to be her true love.

She thought about how her parents had always expected her to marry a Jewish boy. And when she was young, she believed that her husband would be a Jewish boy from her hometown. But that was a long time ago. A lifetime ago. Vano was here with her now. He was holding her in his arms, and it felt right. So right. "Yes," she repeated in a whisper, tears slipping down her cheeks.

"Yes, you will? You will marry me?" his voice was filled with joy and excitement.

"Yes, I will."

He kissed her. Then he gently pulled her down beside him and kissed her again.

"I know you spoke to Damien, but what about Sabina and your mother?"

"What about them?" he shrugged.

"Your mother hates me. She wants you to marry Sabina."

"I know. And I love my mother, but she's going to have to accept the fact that I can't marry Sabina just because she thinks she would be right for me. I wouldn't have married her even if I had never met you. Sabina is more like a sister to me. We've known each other all our lives. I couldn't see living with her as a husband, if you understand what I mean."

She nodded. "I do. But your mother won't."

"She will, eventually. At first, she'll be angry. She'll refuse to speak to me, but she'll warm up. You'll see. I know her. She can't stay angry with either of her sons for too long."

"So, you think everything will be all right? I mean, I will be living here among your people and want to be accepted. Until now, I think I have been tolerated but not necessarily accepted as one of them."

"It will be all right. They will all accept you because you will be my wife."

"Even though I am not Romany?"

"Yes, even though you were not born Romany. You will be Romany because you are the woman I have chosen." He smiled. "Tell me you love me," he said.

She giggled.

"Go on, say it. Please. Say it. I love to hear it."

"I do love you, Vano. We are going to be very happy. We'll have lots of children."

He gently put his fingers under her chin and raised her face so her eyes would meet his. "I love hearing that," he said. "I'll build us our own vardo. We'll have a lovely home. You're going to love it when we start to travel again. The world is such a magical place."

She was blushing, but she smiled.

"And as far as my brother Damien is concerned, we'll talk to him together. We'll go to him tomorrow after dinner before the campfire. We'll make him understand that we love each other. I want us to be a close family. So, I will talk to my mother too."

She smiled at him again as he helped her up.

"We should get back," he said. "I have to go hunting if we want meat for dinner."

"All right," she said.

He pulled her to him and kissed her passionately.

"I'm happy," he said softly.

"Me too."

Hand in hand, they walked slowly back towards the camp. Before they entered the camp and while the trees still hid them from view, Vano released Anna's hand. "You go and get some sleep. I'm going to go out and hunt. Sometimes I find that hunting is even better at night. Besides, I need some time alone to think about how I am going to approach all of this with Damien and my mother. I'll be back in a little while and see you in the morning. But don't say anything to anyone tonight, not even Nuri. We'll tell all of them together."

"Yes. I prefer to do it that way," she said, "and I promise, I won't even tell Nuri. Besides, my guess is that she is already asleep. That girl falls asleep as soon as she lays her head down. I've never seen anything like it."

He laughed. Then he gently placed a kiss on Anna's lips.

She put her arms around his neck. And then he looked around.

They were still hidden by the forest grass that they'd both come to love. He pulled her down and then sat beside her. She was in no hurry for the night to end. Vano lay her back down on the forest floor. "I can't get enough of you," he said. "Every time we make love, it makes me want you more."

She smiled. "I know. I've never felt anything like this, Vano. I've never been so close to anyone before. I mean, my family and I were close, but this is different."

"Yes, it is," he kissed her again.

"I never thought being with another person could be so wonderful. I want to spend the rest of my life feeling this way," she said softly.

And then the trees rustled behind them. Not a lot, but just enough to cause Vano to jump up quickly. Before he said another word, he ripped through the bushes and saw Sabina crouched down, listening. "What are you doing here?" he asked angrily. "How dare you spy on me?"

"How dare I spy on you?" She stood up and retorted, "I caught you fornicating with that Jew whore. Vano!" She put her hands on her hips. "You are pledged to me. We are betrothed." Sabina was trembling. She was short, but when angry, she appeared much taller. "I have been watching the two of you for weeks now. And Vano, I am sure you know what you are doing is wrong. I don't expect much of her. She is not one of us," she pointed at Anna. "But you should know better, Vano. If I told everyone back at the camp what you did, they would be disgusted by you. They would talk about the kind of man you have become, and it would bring shame to you and your family."

"I don't care what people say about me. Let them talk. I am not pledged to you. That agreement was made between you and my mother. I had no say in it, and I never agreed to it. So, you might as well know now that I have no plans of ever marrying you."

"You have turned into a real good for nothing. I'm sure she is responsible. Because before she came here, you were a better man," Sabina growled.

"I was the same. Less happy. But even then, I did not agree to an arranged marriage with you, Sabina. I like you. You've been like a sister to me. But I don't love you. And even if Anna were not here, I would not take you for my wife."

"I am going back to the camp. I've heard all I need to hear from you, Vano. Wait and see what kind of misery I can bring to you. I am going to tell everyone what I saw here tonight. Your mother will be furious with you. That much I can promise."

She stormed away.

Anna, who was sitting up on the ground, cast her eyes up at Vano. "What should we do?"

"Nothing," he said, dismissing Sabina. "Let her tell my mother about us. I don't care. I was going to tell her myself. But now, Sabina will do it for me."

Anna shook her head. "And Damien? He's going to find out, too."

"Maybe, maybe not. Either way, he's going to find out eventually."

"I don't want your mother to hate me. I don't want Damien to hate me, either."

"They'll be angry for a little while. Then they'll get over it. Don't worry so much. It will be all right."

He sat down beside her and took her hand in his.

"She's so angry," Anna said.

"Sabina is like that. She's hot-headed. But she'll get over it too. My guess is that my mother will try to marry her off to Damien. And I think that would be a good match."

"And what does Damien think?"

"I never asked him. But we'll find out, won't we?"

"You sound as if you are quite calm about all of this."

"I am. I've found the girl I love." He squeezed her hand. "And I am going to marry her. That's all there is to it."

They sat like that for a few minutes. Then Anna asked, "Are you still going to go hunting? Or should we head back to camp together?"

"I'm still going hunting. Nothing has changed. We still have to eat, don't we?" He smiled at her. "Don't worry about all of this. I'll work it all out. I'll go and talk to my mother as soon as I get back to camp."

Anna watched him as he turned and walked back towards the forest. She was unnerved by knowing that Sabina had watched them. But at the same time, she felt whole for the first time since she'd lost her family. Anna knew she would never forget her parents and her brother, and she would search for them as soon as it was possible. But she would marry Vano, and then for the rest of her life, she would have someone who loved her, children, and a home, even if it was unconventional. This lifestyle was certainly different. But she would learn to love to travel because she would be with her husband and her children. And she would be safe. The very idea of being safe gave her a warm, secure feeling inside.

Vano had already disappeared back into the forest. Anna couldn't bring herself to go back and face his mother and Damien alone, and she had no intention of going to bed. Sitting down under a tree at the edge of the forest, she took a moment to close her eyes and remember the events that had transpired earlier that evening. Anna savored the taste of Vano's lips on hers. She closed her eyes, and although she knew that there would be a lot of problems in the camp in the morning, she still felt no regrets about what she had done. Anna had come to love the forest and the quiet stillness of it. So, she felt she needed to take some time to be alone and to think things through. Anna looked up into the sky. *The moon is full tonight, and I can see very well by its light. Perhaps, I'll take a walk and gather some mushrooms. I can still remember which ones Damien said were safe to eat. I'll bring them back with me in a little while. And tomorrow, when we prepare our dinner, Nuri will be glad to have them. She loves wild mushrooms.*

CHAPTER FORTY-THREE

The man in his black SS uniform, hiding just a few feet away from the scene, watched and waited as the angry Gypsy girl made her way through the forest. It was a windy night, and her colorful skirts flew in the air as she ran. He'd followed her as she followed that young couple each night. The Gypsy man, who they called Vano, had almost detected him before, but he had gotten away just in time. The Gypsy girl was like a cat, a skillful huntress. She'd followed the couple unnoticed until she became too enraged to hide. And because she was so engrossed in watching the couple, he'd been able to follow her. But he was glad she had led him to this filthy scene between the Gypsy man and the Jew. He'd watched them, both of them subhuman, and he had burned with rage. But he still had been unable to look away. However, now, the Gypsy girl was returning to the Gypsy camp, where she would cause trouble. This would not be good for him. Because soon, all the gypsies would be in the forest, and it would be too late to carry out his plan. And he would have missed this opportunity. He followed close behind the Gypsy girl they called Sabina but still made sure to remain hidden behind the trees. She must have felt his presence or heard a branch crack beneath his feet because she stopped for a moment and whirled around. Then, in a shaky voice, she said, "Vano, is that you?"

She looked from side to side and repeated, "Vano."

The SS Officer came up behind her, and quickly, with one stroke, just as he learned to do in the army, he reached over and broke her neck.

Sabina never knew what hit her. She was dead instantly.

Ulf looked down at the broken body of the young girl and wiped his hands on his pants legs. *Filthy gypsies.* Then he went back to look for his actual target, Anna.

CHAPTER FORTY-FOUR

I t had only been a couple of weeks since Damien had taken Anna to gather mushrooms. She tried to remember everything he'd taught her, like where they grew and which ones were poison or safe to eat. Slowly, she headed towards the clearing. The moon was a bright ball of silver, and the stars twinkled like tiny diamonds. She knelt and studied the patches of mushrooms that grew wild between the grasses. But now, by the light of the moon, she was finding it difficult to distinguish between the ones that were safe and those that were not. *I thought this was going to be easy, but it's not. And I don't want to make a mistake and bring back dangerous mushrooms. Although, I'm sure Nuri would be able to tell if they were all right or not. Still, I'd rather not take the risk.* Anna was about to give up on gathering mushrooms and return to camp when she looked up and saw two teenaged boys approaching her. Her heart leaped with fear at first. But then one of the boys said, "Anna? Anna, is that you?"

They know my name. They must be boys from the Romany camp. Anna thought as she squinted, trying to see them better. But as they got closer, she realized they were not boys from the Gypsy camp. They were Ulf's younger twin brothers, Gynther and Klaus. It seemed like a lifetime ago when she had been their nanny one summer in Berlin.

Am I seeing things? Are these boys really here so far away from their home, or are they ghosts? How could this be? How is it possible that I would find Ulf's brothers, Gynther and Klaus, in a forest so many miles away from their home in Berlin? Even though she had adored them when she was their nanny, she was afraid. This was all so strange. And she knew these were dangerous times when a Jewish person must never let down her guard.

"Anna!" one of the boys called again.

Her first instinct was to turn and run away. After all, these were Ulf's brothers, and she had run away from Ulf. He had changed, and she was afraid of him. But she'd been frozen in place for too long, and now it was too late to get away. Gynther was running towards her.

"Anna, Anna! We have good news!" Gynther hugged her. Then his brother Klaus hugged her, too. "We missed you," Klaus said. "That summer you stayed with us was the best summer of our lives, wasn't it, Gynther?"

"Yes, it certainly was."

"What are you boys doing here?" Anna asked skeptically.

"We were looking for you. Ulf sent us to search for you. He has found your parents." Gynther had grown into an enthusiastic teen with a big smile. Klaus stood at his side, smiling, too.

Anna put her hand on her heart. Her mouth fell open. "My parents?" she said. "Ulf has found my parents? I was afraid that they'd been captured."

"No, they're fine. Ulf has them at his home," Gynther said, nodding as he repeated what Ulf had told him. "They are waiting for you. Ulf said that if we found you, we should bring you to him, and he would take you to your family."

She began to cry.

"Anna, don't cry," Klaus said, "please don't cry."

She fell to her knees and wept. "My parents. Are they all right?"

Her entire body was trembling. She was afraid of Ulf, but her desire to find her family was stronger than her fear.

"Ulf said to tell you that your parents are fine. Come with us. We'll take you to Ulf so that he can take you to your parents."

Anna thought about Vano. I should tell him where I am going. But he's hunting, and I don't know where to find him. "Can I go back to the Gypsy camp where I've been living and tell them I am going with you?" she asked Gynther.

"Ulf said to tell you not to say a word to anyone. He is putting himself and us in danger by doing this for you. He said that if we were caught, we would be arrested for aiding someone Jewish. So you must not let anyone know where we are going."

She considered what Gynther said for a moment. Then she nodded. "All right. I'll come with you."

As they walked through the forest, Anna studied Klaus and Gynther. They'd grown up so much since she'd last seen them. They had been nine years old when she'd spent that summer as their nanny. But that was such a long time ago. They were teenagers now, strong and handsome boys. "How have you boys been?" she asked.

"All right," Klaus answered. Then he blurted out, "Gynther and I don't like Hitler."

"You talk too much," Gynther said. "Didn't father tell you not to tell anyone what you thought of the Reich?"

"But this is Anna. Don't you remember how close we were to Anna? She was like a big sister to us."

"But she is Jewish. And father said never to trust Jews," Gynther blurted. Then he stopped walking and looked at Anna. "I shouldn't have said that. I'm sorry."

"It's all right," Anna said.

"But we're scared too. We don't want to get in trouble with the Gestapo. And our father says that Jews will do anything to save themselves. He said that A Jew would turn us in if they knew how we felt about the Nazis. They would do it to save themselves."

She looked at his young, innocent face, then she sighed. "Gynther, I would never turn you in."

"But our father said that the Nazis are killing the Jewish people. That's a terrifying thought. He says they're trying to create a world without Jews. And because of this, we must be careful all the time. We are not to trust anyone Jewish. They will do anything to protect themselves. But he also said not to trust anyone when it comes to how we feel about Hitler. He says other Aryans would be angry if we said anything against the Führer. So, please don't tell anyone what I said."

"Don't be afraid of me," she said. "I won't ever do anything to hurt you, boys."

"Ulf is brave," Klaus said. "He told us he rescued your parents despite the danger. I'm proud of him. I'm proud that he is my brother. I'm sick and tired of living in fear. I wish I had the courage to do something to stand up to them."

"Well," Anna said, "The best thing you can do right now is live and grow up. So, keep your thoughts to yourself. Your father is right. Don't trust anyone, Jewish or not."

As they came to the clearing, Anna could see Ulf standing by the door to his black automobile, smoking a cigarette. He wore his black Nazi uniform. The swastika on his armband made the hair on the back of her neck stand up, and she had a strong desire to run away. But then she thought of her parents. *I would give anything, risk anything, to see them again. I don't believe Gynther or Klaus would ever do anything to hurt me.*

"Anna," Ulf said as they approached. "I'm glad my brothers were able to find you. We've been out here every night looking for you. It's been a week now." Then he put out the cigarette and smiled at her. "I don't know why you ran away from me," his voice was innocent, yet she thought she could detect the slightest malice in the tone behind his words. "I did everything for you. I helped you and your family escape from the attic. I killed a man to keep you safe. And then... you ran from me?"

Anna caught a glimpse of the look that passed between Klaus and Gynther. They both looked confused and a little startled. She wasn't sure if it was because their older brother admitted to committing murder or because they found out all he'd done for her and that she'd run away from him, anyway.

"I was frightened, Ulf." *I still am. I don't know why I am frightened of you, but I am.*

"Of me? I don't know why you should be afraid of me. I have done nothing but try to help you. Perhaps it was because I said I had to do things I wasn't proud of. Anna, I was just following orders. I had to do as I was told. Please understand I had no choice. I would never have chosen to do those things."

"What things?" Gynther asked.

"Never mind. That's not for you to know," Ulf said to Gynther, and Anna heard the angry tone come into Ulf's voice again. She said nothing.

Then Ulf turned away for what seemed like a long time but was only moments. When he turned back, his face was calm and serene again. "Well, let's forget that stuff. It's in the past. I have good news for you. I've rescued your parents." He smiled.

She smiled back at him. "Anselm? My brother? Is he with them?"

Ulf shook his head. "I'm sorry. Your brother passed away before I was able to get to them. From what your parents said, Anselm was very sick. You knew that he was sick, didn't you? I mean, from what I understand, he has always been sickly. Sadly, this was all too much for him."

"Yes, he was always sickly," she said woefully. "But my parents? The boys said that they're all right?"

"Absolutely. They are perfectly fine. And once you are reunited with them, I will drive you back here to this area, and you will all be together again. And then, once again, if you allow me to, I will take care of you, Anna. I will bring food once a month, and I will help you and your family to survive."

"Where are they? Are they far from here?" she asked desperately.

I dare not tell him about Vano and me getting married. She turned as she slipped the ruby ring off her finger and hid it in her bra. *I know it's deceptive, but I won't tell him until he brings me back here with my parents. Then I'll explain. I'll make him understand somehow.*

"Yes, actually they are at my home. I've left Austria and moved back to Berlin," Ulf said warmly. "So, we have a long drive back to Germany." He took a deep breath. "Now, this is important. Anna, you must stay on the floor in the car's back seat and remain hidden under a blanket so no one will see you when we go through checkpoints. I'm wearing my SS uniform so that they won't stop us. But you will have to remain hidden. Gynther will sit in the front seat with me, and Klaus will sit back with you."

"I'd like to sit in the back with Anna as well," Gynther demanded.

"Very well, if you would like to sit in the back too, that's fine with me," Ulf said. He was growing impatient. He grabbed Gynther's arm and pushed him towards the vehicle a little more forcefully than he'd intended. "But, let's get going." Ulf smiled, trying to hide his annoyance with his brothers.

Everyone climbed into the automobile.

It was as it had been when Anna worked for Ulf's family as the boy's nanny. As they drove down the dark road, the twins uncovered Anna's face so they could see her, and although she was uncomfortable on the floor, she sat up on one elbow to speak to them. "You boys look so good. You've grown up so much," Anna said.

"We have. We're sixteen now," Gynther said. He'd always been the bolder one of the two. And even though they were identical, Anna had always been able to tell them apart because their unique personalities shined through on their faces.

"Sixteen," she said. "Why, you boys are men already."

"Yes, we are," Gynther said. "I have a girlfriend."

"Emma is not your girlfriend," Klaus corrected him. "You'd like her to be, but she's not. She says she doesn't even like you."

"Yes, she does. She is just saying that. We went to a film together."

"Yes, with a whole group of other people," Klaus sneered.

"Well, just look at you. You don't have a girlfriend at all," Gynther snapped at Klaus. "Who would ever want to be your girlfriend?"

"Stop arguing," Ulf said in a firm and commanding voice.

The boys stopped arguing and turned away from each other.

"How's school?" Anna said, trying to change the subject by making some normal conversation even though her own life had been anything but normal since she'd last seen them.

"School is fine. I'm the better student. I get better marks than Gynther," Klaus said proudly.

"That's because you're always at home studying. You have no friends, and you're lousy at sports."

"Boys. I said stop," Ulf growled.

If she hadn't been lying on the floor in the back of an automobile with a blanket covering all but her face, Anna would have thought this was a typical day and this exchange was an everyday conversation between two competitive teen boys. But nothing was normal for Anna anymore. She'd been through so much while running and hiding from the Nazis. Did the boys know what it had been like for the Jews? And if they did, what did they think about all of it? Anna wanted to ask them but didn't because she was afraid Ulf would get angry. So, rather than ask questions, she let the boys lead the conversation.

"What are you doing here? Have you been living on a farm or something? And why were you wandering around in the forest at night?" Klaus asked. His voice was so innocent that she wasn't sure how Ulf would want her to answer.

"I'm sure you boys must know things are bad for Jews in Germany, don't you? Well, things are bad for Jews in Austria, too. I had to hide so I could be safe."

"Yes, we know that the Jews are being treated badly in Germany," Gynther agreed. "From what we hear, Jews are in danger everywhere. They tell us in our youth group that the Jews must be controlled. We are told that they are dangerous, and we should be afraid of them and be careful when we encounter them. We are told we must report anyone who helps Jews, even our relatives. But don't worry, neither Klaus nor I would ever report Ulf for helping you. And that's because we know that you're different. You're not really like other Jews, are you?"

Anna had no idea how to answer that question. *This is a dangerous question, yet I feel I must answer it honestly.* "You know I have never lied to you, boys. So, I am not going to start now. You boys know and like me. And I know and like you. But in truth, I am no different from many other Jews. The Jews are not bad or dangerous. They are just people like you and me. However, you have been told a lot of lies by the Nazi party about Jewish people."

The boys looked at each other. She saw the confusion on their faces.

"That's enough," Ulf said.

"Let's talk about something else," Anna quickly changed the subject. She didn't want Ulf to become angry and decide that he'd made a mistake trying to take her to her parents. If that happened, it could lead to disaster for herself and her parents. So, in as cheerful a voice as she could muster, she said, "Guess what, boys, I learned to ride a horse. Have either of you boys ever ridden a horse?"

"I have," Gynther said. "He was too scared," Gynther tipped his head, indicating his brother Klaus.

"I wasn't scared," Klaus said defensively.

"Yes, you were. You were shaking and refused to get up on the horse's back."

"It's all right, Klaus. I was scared the first time, too. It's very high up," Anna said.

"Yes, it is, that's right," Klaus said, nodding. "How did you ever learn to ride a horse?"

Anna couldn't think of a lie. The truth came flooding out of her, and as soon as she said it, she was sorry. "I was living with a caravan of gypsies, Romany, they call themselves."

"Gypsies?" Klaus asked.

"What were they like?" Gynther asked. "I've heard they're even more dangerous than Jews. Were you afraid of them?"

"No, not at all," Anna smiled. "They were very kind to me. Their lifestyle is a little different, but they are wonderful people."

Ulf was quiet, but the three continued talking for a few hours until Klaus said, "Ulf, I have to go to the bathroom."

"Well, then we must stop, mustn't we?" Ulf said. He seemed a little annoyed. But he pulled over on the side of the road at the edge of the forest.

"Since we've stopped, let's take a few minutes and get out so we can stretch our legs," Gynther said. "Would that be all right with you, Ulf?"

"Yes, I suppose so. We might as well have lunch since we will have to stop, anyway," Ulf said, taking the basket of food he'd brought with him from under the front seat.

Klaus hopped out of the car and ran into the woods to relieve himself.

"Here, spread this blanket so we can have a picnic. Take Anna with you," Ulf said to Gynther. But as Gynther got out of the car, Ulf closed the door before Anna could get out. He turned to Gynther, and in a whisper, he warned, "Listen to me. Don't let her out of your sight. She gets very flighty, and she might run away again."

"Why would she?"

"Because she doesn't trust me," Ulf said.

"Why wouldn't she trust you, Ulf? You are going to marry her after all, aren't you? But I don't know how you can with her being Jewish. But you're so smart that I am sure you have thought of something. What are you going to do?"

Ulf was growing angry and frustrated. He had too much on his mind to answer these childish questions. "I don't know yet," he said. "All I know is that you are not to let her out of sight. She must not get away. Do you understand?"

"But you have her parents waiting for her at home. She wants to see them."

Ulf grabbed his brother's shoulders roughly and took him farther from the car. Anna was sitting up, watching. Ulf had an angry look on his face. "You're a man now. You're much stronger than your brother, so you might as well know the truth. I killed Anna's parents. I had to," he told Gynther in a whispered growl.

"But why?" Gynther looked at him, confused and frightened.

"Do you think we need more Jews running around? You know the laws. You know that we are Aryans, and it's our responsibility to get rid of them."

"I don't understand," Gynther said. He was trembling. "Are you going to kill Anna too?"

"No," Ulf was losing patience. "I love Anna. I always have."

"So why would you ever do that to her?"

"Because I had to." Then he added, "I found and killed them, and that's all you need to know. Make sure Anna doesn't find out."

"What are you going to do with Anna?"

"Eventually, I probably will have to turn her in."

"What does all of this mean, Ulf? None of this makes sense. This is not what you told Klaus and me when you said we would help you find Anna. You never said you would hurt her, or we would not have agreed to help you."

"What this means to you is simple... you keep your mouth shut about what you know and make sure you don't let her out of your sight. Not for a second. Remember, Gynther. I am your brother, and I know what is best. Anna is nothing but a Jew. She is really not your friend. She's a dangerous demon."

"That's insane. She was our nanny. She's always been our friend."

"Don't ask me any more questions. Just make sure you do as I say. Now go and get Anna out of the car. Tell her to sit on the blanket and wait for Klaus to return so we can all eat something."

CHAPTER FORTY-FIVE

Gynther couldn't take his eyes off Ulf as they were eating their lunch, and every so often, he would rub his shoulder from the pain Ulf caused when he grabbed him. Ulf was laughing and telling jokes as if things were perfectly normal. Gynther couldn't understand how his older brother could be so strange and unaffected by what he'd done to Anna's parents. Gynther could not get Ulf's words out of his mind. It horrified him as he watched his brother cheerfully tell a story about a party he'd attended for the Fuhrer's birthday. *This is madness.* Gynther thought. *Klaus and I are going to be conscripted into the army soon, and I don't think I can go and serve the fatherland. I'm afraid I might go mad if I am forced to go. Ulf has gone out of his mind. He lied to Klaus and me. He has murdered Anna's parents, and now he plans to turn Anna in. I must tell Klaus everything. I must talk to him about this as soon as I can get him alone.*

"I'm going to urinate," Gynther said when they'd finished eating. "You'd better come with me, Klaus. You know how you always have to go to the bathroom? Well, I'm sure Ulf won't want to stop again for a while."

"That's right. I won't. So, you go with him, Klaus. And hurry it up, both of you. I want to get back on the road. I have something I need to do."

Klaus followed his brother into the woods. Once they were far enough away from the blanket where they'd left Ulf and Anna, and he was sure Ulf couldn't hear them, Gynther grabbed Klaus's arm roughly. "What's the matter with you? That hurt," Klaus said, pulling his arm away and rubbing it where his brother had squeezed it.

"I'm sorry. I didn't mean to grab you so hard, but I have to tell you something. Something important."

"What? Tell me."

"Shhhh, whisper. Please," Gynther said. "No one can know. Especially not Ulf."

"What's the matter with you?" Klaus asked.

And then Gynther told him. He told him everything that Ulf had said.

Klaus was pale. All the blood had drained from his face. "Our brother killed Anna's parents," he repeated the words Gynther had said in disbelief. "I don't even know Ulf anymore. He's not like the brother he used to be. I'm afraid of him."

"I know. Me too. I think he would kill us if he had to," Gynther replied.

"I do too, but we can't let Anna down. We must find a way to help Anna. We can't let him hurt her. She saved my life in the lake that day," Klaus whispered.

"I remember, but how can we stop him?"

"I don't know. All I know is that we must."

CHAPTER FORTY-SIX

"Come on, boys. What the hell is taking so long? I thought you boys were just going to take a piss, not going on a nature walk," Ulf called out. "After all, I could just shoot the lot of you and be done with all of this. My life would surely be easier," he laughed. "Don't worry. I am just joking."

The twins looked at each other and saw the terror reflected in each other's eyes. "We have to be very careful. We must be sure he doesn't find out we are against what he's about to do, or he might just shoot her and us," Gynther said.

"It's so hard to believe that Ulf could do that. Do you really think he would?" Klaus asked.

"I don't know what he's capable of. All I know is that he told me he murdered Anna's parents. And I would never have thought he was capable of that."

"Boys, come on. Let's go!" Ulf called again. Then he turned to Anna. "You know how boys are. They can get lost in the woods so easily. So much to intrigue them there. They see an insect or a frog, and they are lost."

"Do you want me to go into the woods and look for them?" she asked.

"No, my dear. You stay right here with me," Ulf smiled a crooked smile.

Then the boys returned, quickly walking back to the blanket where Anna sat. Ulf asked, "What the hell took so long?"

"We found some frogs. We tried to catch them, but they were too fast," Klaus said.

"I see." Then he turned to Anna. "See, I told you about the frogs." Turning back to Klaus and Gynther in his most mature older brother voice, Ulf said, "Well, you boys are too old to be catching frogs, anyway. Now let's pack all of this up so we can get going. We wouldn't want to keep Anna's parents waiting, now, would we?" he winked at Gynther.

The twins stood so close to each other that they could feel the other tremble. "No, no, we wouldn't," Gynther answered in a small voice.

"Jump in the car. Let's go. Ladies first," Ulf smiled his most charming smile at Anna. A quick look of fear passed between Gynther and Klaus, but Ulf didn't notice. He got into the driver's seat of the auto.

After they were all in the car, Ulf started the engine. Then he began to drive. "I told all of you I have something I need to do before we can head back. So, I am going to make a quick stop in town. While we are there, you must keep a careful watch over Anna. You must make sure that no one sees her, or she could be arrested."

"What do you need in town?" Gynther asked.

"That's none of your business, little brother," Ulf said sweetly, but with an underlying threat that let Gynther and Klaus know they were not to ask any more questions.

They drove into town, where Ulf pulled up in front of a restaurant. "I'll be right back. Now, remember what I said about Anna getting arrested? We wouldn't want that, now, would we? So, make sure Anna stays hidden."

Ulf got out of the car and walked into the restaurant. Once he was gone, the boys looked at each other. Because they were twins and had always had a special connection, they both knew what the other was thinking. "We can't let her out here," Klaus whispered to Gynther. "It would be too dangerous."

"What?" Anna asked.

Gynther shook his head. "Nothing, nothing at all. Klaus just thought you might need to use the bathroom. But we don't think it would be safe here."

"I'm all right," Anna said, although she would have liked to use the bathroom.

CHAPTER FORTY-SEVEN

Ulf entered the restaurant. It was a small establishment owned and operated by a young husband and wife. He glanced around at the quaint little tables covered with stained white tablecloths and wondered if they would even have a phone. *If they don't have a phone, I'll have to wait until I get back. I don't have time to search for a phone in this small town.*

The owner was watching Ulf. He whispered something to his wife, and she quickly went into the kitchen. There was an older couple sitting at one of the tables. They stopped eating when they saw Ulf. *They are afraid of me.* Ulf thought, remembering that he looked very menacing in his black SS uniform.

"Can I help you?" the owner asked in a kind voice.

"Actually, yes, you can. Do you happen to have a phone I can use?"

"A telephone? Why, yes." The owner seemed calmed by Ulf's request, as if he were quite relieved that Ulf hadn't asked for something else. And for a moment, Ulf wondered what the man might be hiding. If he had been there on a different mission, he might have investigated this further. However, he had Anna and his brothers in the car. And he didn't dare search this place just in case he found something. Because if he did, he'd have to call in the local police to help him, and then there would be questions about the boys, and it would be a disaster if they found Anna. No, I'll just make the call I came here to make and then leave.

"Please, come with me. I'll take you to a phone. It's next door in the toy shop."

Ulf followed the restaurant owner several feet to the toy store. The old toy maker gave the owner a strange look when they walked in.

"Please, can you allow this officer to use your telephone?" the restaurant owner asked.

"I'd be happy to pay for the call," Ulf said cheerfully. He didn't want any trouble. At least not now.

"Of course. Yes, certainly," the old toy maker said. He led Ulf behind the counter, where a black telephone sat on the worktable.

"Excuse me. I am going to need some privacy," Ulf commanded.

The toy maker and the restauranter walked out the front door and waited outside. Ulf noticed the old man's hands were shaking as he walked away. *Definitely up to something.* He thought.

Once the two were gone, Ulf picked up the phone receiver and called the operator. He had the call connected to his superior officer, whose secretary answered, "Ulf. Where are you?"

"Never mind. I need to speak to your boss."

"Of course."

When his superior officer answered, Ulf did not mince words. "I haven't found the Jews yet, but I have good news. I've found a band of gypsies; they've set up camp in the forest. I'll give you directions as to where you will find them."

"Go on, tell me."

Ulf gave the best directions he could as to the location of the Gypsy camp. Then he added, "I think you might want to send troops to arrest them."

"We know about them. We've known for a while. No one has gotten around to arrest them yet."

"Why waste time? Get them now before they start traveling. Once they start their wandering, it will be impossible to find them again," Ulf said, then he added. "It will look very good on your record."

"You're right. It will. Why not? I'll take care of it today. Have you found any clues as to where the Jews you were searching for have gone?"

"Not yet," Ulf lied. Ulf had received this time off because he told his superior officer he planned to search for the Jews his partner had set free.

"Well, hurry up. We need you back here. Lots of work to do."

"Of course, I will hurry, *Obersturmführer*," Ulf dropped a Reichsmark on the worktable and left.

CHAPTER FORTY-EIGHT

Vano had just returned to the camp carrying several squirrels. He lay them down and ladled himself a large drink of water when Damien came running over to him, red-faced and sweating. "What's the matter with you?" Vano asked.

"Sabina is dead. I was hunting, and I found her body. She's been murdered."

"What? Take me to her!" Vano demanded.

Damien nodded. Then, with Vano beside him, he returned to the site where he'd seen the body.

"Oh," Vano exclaimed when he saw Sabina lying dead, her pretty young face covered with flies. He gently lifted her and saw by the way her body moved that her neck had been broken. Then he carried her back to camp.

Vano's mother saw them first, and when she saw Sabina, she let out a cry of pain. "What happened, Vano?"

Hearing the scream, the rest of the group came out of their Vardo's and gathered around Vano, Damien, and Sabina's body. The Shero Rom bent down to look at Sabina. "Who did this?" he asked.

Damien explained how he had found Sabina while hunting and how he'd brought Vano back with him.

"Nazis," the Shero Rom muttered. "I feel them surrounding us again. They come to watch our women. Who knows what they did to this poor girl before they killed her?" Everyone was silent with horror. "We must go. We must leave here right now. Gather your things, and let's begin to travel. Someone take Sabina. We will bury her when we stop."

"Where are we going?" a man holding a small child asked.

"I know of a hiding place where we will be in a clearing mostly covered by trees. It's not far from here. A mile, perhaps. Maybe a mile and a half. But, for now, it will give us some safety. Hurry! Please."

"But what if they are following us?"

"Then we will have to fight. We will have to kill them if they try to arrest us. Enough talk for now. Let's go."

Vano ran to Nuri's vardo in search of Anna. But he didn't find her. And Nuri told him she hadn't seen her since the night before. He searched the camp desperately, but no one had seen Anna. Then he searched the forest, but without success. Panicked, he ran back to his vardo, where his mother and Damien were packing up all of their things. "Did you find Anna?" Damien asked worriedly.

"No, not a trace of her. I'm very concerned. I came back here to tell you to go with mother, and I'll stay and wait for Anna."

"No," Lavina said. "You must come with us. You can't leave me alone like this."

"You won't be alone, mother. You'll be with Damien. I'll ask Nuri to help you once you and the group are settled."

"No, you must help me. You must come with us."

Vano let out a sigh. His mother was stubborn and insistent. But he loved Anna and had no plans of leaving her behind. Still, he knew he must travel with the group and help his mother settle in the hiding place where the Shero Rom planned to leave them. *It's only a mile or so from here. I will go with them, but I will return here on foot once they are settled. I should be back before nightfall.* "All right, mother. I'll travel with you. But then I must return for Anna."

"Anna is not for you, Vano. She is not the girl for you. Poor Sabina. She was the wife I hoped and prayed you would choose." His mother began to cry. She sat down in a chair. But Vano could not indulge her pain. He knew that there was no time to lose.

"Mother, this is not the time for this. We need to get packed and get on the road."

CHAPTER FORTY-NINE

The Gypsies were ready to travel in less than two hours. The Shero Rom called them to the center of the clearing. "My friends, you have done well. You have packed quickly, and now we are all ready to go. Line up your vardo's behind mine, and let's begin. May God be with us. And good road to all of you."

"Good road," the group cried in unison. Then they began to line up.

Vano was heartsick with worry for Anna as his brother strapped the horses to the wagon. He watched the forest, hoping to see her come running out to him. But she didn't. He jumped from the wagon one final time and asked Nuri again if she'd heard anything from Anna. But she hadn't. Vano climbed back up into the driver's seat of the wagon and held the whip in his hand as he had done since his father had died when he was only twelve. And then the Shero Rom let out a cry, his whip snapping the ground close enough to horses to start them walking forward. The caravan was on its way.

A strong breeze danced through Vano's dark hair as the Romany made their way out of the old familiar camp site. *Anna.* All Vano could think about was Anna. A mile took a little over an hour to cover because of the length of the caravan. Vano drove the wagon, but he was lost in thoughts of Anna. The sun burned bright and yellow in the sky. The birds chirped, and the forest was alive. However, Vano hardly noticed it. In fact, if he hadn't been so fixated on Anna, he would have seen the large troop of Nazi soldiers as they came up from behind on horseback. The Gypsy men saw them and began shooting. Vano, hearing the gunshots, was immediately brought back to the present. He looked around him and saw that they were in trouble. He nudged his brother, who nodded at him. Then he and Damien pulled their guns and began shooting. Vano was a good shot, but there was only one of him, and most of the other Gypsy men were mediocre at best. They tried, but for the most part, they were too nervous to hit their targets, and because of this, they were knocked out of their wagons and held at gunpoint. Then they raised their hands in surrender. Vano did not surrender. He kept shooting. And he hit two soldiers, but then he ran out of bullets, and before he could reload his gun, he was pulled down from his wagon and forced at gunpoint to get in line with the rest of the gypsies. *I can't be arrested. I must get back and find Anna.* He thought. But then, as his mother was being forced out of the back of her wagon, she tripped and fell to the ground. A young, arrogant blond soldier kicked her, declaring she was too slow at getting up. Vano rushed at the Nazi, but he hit him with the butt of his rifle, and Vano fell. Damien helped his mother get back up on her feet. He glanced at Vano, and he and Lavina followed the others into the lineup. The Nazis rode their horses through the caravan, pouring gasoline on the wagons. Anyone who was left inside came rushing out when they smelled gas.

Then the Germans set the wagons on fire. Large orange flames filled the sky as they ate through the wooden vardos, and gray smoke billowed, sending a message to God in heaven. The Romany way of life was turning to ashes before them. "Look around you? You are disgusting Gypsy pigs. You have forced us to waste gasoline to burn these filthy homes of yours. I'm sure they were filled with diseases.

Disease you were spreading to our Aryan population. Say goodbye to this mess." One of the Nazis shouted. Then, at gunpoint, the gypsies were forced to walk to the road. Some of them looked back longingly as the vardos were swallowed by fire. Once they arrived at the road, an open-air truck waited for them. The women wept as they moved their colorful skirts out of the way so they could climb on board. Some of the men wept too, but Vano was angry. He knew he was trapped, like a caged animal. *Anna,* his heart cried out in a silent scream. *Anna, where are you? How can I protect you if I don't know where you are?* Vano ached to charge at these arrogant Germans. He was sure he could take them if they fought with fists and not with guns. He told himself he would fight them all single-handedly if he had to. But he knew that he dared not stand up to them because they had guns, and they would shoot. His mother would be doomed if he was killed because his brother was not strong enough to protect her. Vano also knew that he would not be able to shelter his mother forever because he hoped that if he were patient, he would find a way to escape and find his way back to Anna.

CHAPTER FIFTY

After Ulf finished making his phone call to headquarters, he walked outside, where the two business owners stood very close to each other, whispering. "Thank you for letting me use your phone," then he went back into the restaurant where he purchased three pastries. When he got into the car, he took one of the small cakes and handed the other two to Gynther, "Now, remember your manners, boys, ladies first. Offer one to Anna."

"But we each want our own," Klaus said.

"Yes, so here is a dilemma for you. Which of you is willing to give your pastry up so she can have one? Which of you will it be?" Ulf said as a wicked smile came over his face. He was obviously enjoying himself.

Ulf's gone crazy. Gynther thought. But he didn't challenge his brother. He knew he had to play along until he could find a way to set Anna free. "It's all right. Here Anna, take mine," Gynther said.

"No, no, no," Anna said, "let's split one. Half is plenty for me."

Gynther split one of the apple tarts. He gave half to Anna, then ate the other half himself. Klaus took the other tart, and the three of them ate.

"Thank you," Anna whispered.

Gynther smiled.

"You too," she squeezed Klaus' hand.

"How do you like those tarts?" Ulf asked.

"Good," Gynther replied. Then he stole a look at his twin brother. They'd always had an unspoken language between them. And now, as they looked into each other's eyes, Gynther could see that Klaus was as frightened as he was.

Ulf had no idea that Gynther was distraught due to what he'd told him. And Ulf was not yet aware that Gynther had shared his fears with Klaus. Ulf thought he knew his younger brothers.

At first, I was reluctant to tell either of the boys the truth about what I was doing with Anna. In fact, I planned to keep it from them indefinitely. And I still feel that it's best that Klaus be kept in the dark. He's far too weak and sensitive. Sometimes he is so weak that he makes me ashamed of him. However, Gynther is different. He is more like me. Gynther is tough. He is more of an Aryan soldier than his brother. So, he understands that if Germany is to regain its place as a world power, we can't have Jews running free. They are too detrimental to society. And I am sure that once I have the time to explain things to him, Gynther will understand why I couldn't just let Anna escape.

A half-hour after they had left the little town, they were back driving along the edge of the forest. They drove for a few hours, and then Klaus said, "I don't feel well. I need you to stop the auto."

"What?" Ulf's voice was filled with annoyance. "What's the matter with you?" *This is why I can't talk to him about anything. He's weak, always getting sick, always crying. I'm sure he got sick from something he ate.*

"I think I'm going to vomit."

"Damn. You've always been such a little girl. I suppose it's either motion sickness or the food you ate," Ulf groaned. "All right. Hold on. Don't puke in my automobile. I'll never get the smell out." He quickly pulled off the road and parked the car. Klaus jumped out quickly and ran into the woods.

"It's getting dark. I'm going with him," Gynther said. "He's sick, and I don't want him to be alone."

"Go ahead," Ulf said, "But hurry up. I want to keep moving."

"May I go too, please? I have to go to the bathroom?" Anna asked softly.

"Yes, I suppose you might as well. But it's getting dark. And it's dangerous. I'll go with you."

"I'm all right alone," she said.

"No, I insist," He smiled.

All of them got out of the car. Anna walked behind a bunch of bushes and crouched. Ulf stayed close by. But Gynther ran into the woods, calling out for his brother.

"I'm over here," Klaus said. When Gynther ran up to Klaus, he saw that his brother had vomited and was very pale. "We can't let him do what he wants to Anna. We just can't."

"I know. It makes me sick too. But what can we do?" Gynther asked. "We're powerless. He's strong and has an important job. We can't tell him how we feel. He wouldn't listen, anyway."

"I don't know what to do. But what I do know is that Ulf used us. He used us to find Anna and make her trust him."

"I know. I know."

"He killed her parents, Gynther. Our brother is a murderer. He killed Anna's parents." Klaus grabbed his brother's arm and clutched it tightly. "He's going to kill Anna too. I'm sure of it."

"You really think so?"

"Well, you said he told you that he would turn her into the Gestapo when he was done with her. What does that mean when he's done with her? I don't like the sound of any of this. All I know is that if he doesn't kill her, the Gestapo will. She's Jewish."

Gynther looked into his twin brother's eyes and saw his reflection. "We can't do anything about it. We have to just go along. We can't even tell our parents when we get home. They can't do anything. And I don't even know if they would if they could. We just have to accept it and be kind to Anna."

Klaus let go of his brother's sleeve. "I can't. I won't," he said, and although he'd always been the shy and quiet one, he ran out of the forest and over to where Ulf stood. Klaus' face was colorless, and he was shaking. But he planted his feet and then looked up at his older brother. Ulf cocked his head. "You're sick, huh?" he said matter-of-factly.

Klaus didn't answer. Instead, he clenched his fists and mustered up his courage. Then, somehow, he found his voice. "You killed Anna's parents?"

Anna walked out from behind the bushes. She was trembling because she had heard Klaus and was shocked at the words he'd said.

"Well, did you? Is it true?"

"What difference does it make?"

"A lot of difference," Anna said. "It makes a lot of difference to me. What did you do, Ulf?" Tears were burning the back of her eyes.

"Shut up, Jew," Ulf said to Anna. It was nearly dark, and the shadows played on Ulf's face, making him look almost inhuman. His eyes were red and bloodshot from not sleeping. "This is between my brother and me."

"You lied to us. You lied to Gynther and me. You told us that if we helped you find Anna, you would reunite her with her family. And you never meant to do that."

"You have always been weak and pathetic. But now, your brother is on my nerves, too. The two of you are nothing but a pain in my ass," Ulf said.

"I won't let you do it. I won't let you hurt Anna. I won't," Klaus was clenching his fists.

Ulf looked at Klaus, then started laughing, and his cruel laughter echoed through the forest. "Just look at you. You're just a boy. And a weak one at that. A coward. You have no power; you can't stop me," he said. Then he added, "I'll tell you what. To sweeten all of this, how about if I let both of you boys have a go at her right now? Right here."

"A go at her? What does that mean, exactly?" Gynther asked as he stood at Klaus' side.

"You're teenagers. You know what it means."

"No, Ulf. Absolutely not," Klaus said. "We will not force ourselves on Anna. Isn't that right, Gynther?"

"He's right, Ulf. We won't do that."

"Just let her go, Ulf," Klaus said.

"For a little weasel, you have quite a big mouth. It's time you shut it, or I'll shut it for you."

"I won't let you do it. I won't," Klaus insisted. "Let Anna go. Run Anna. Run."

Anna was still stunned. She was glued to the forest floor. Ulf pulled his gun and turned to her. "You run, and I'll shoot you dead. I swear it." Then he turned to Klaus and hit Klaus in the face with the butt of his gun and, at the same time, kicked him in the shin. Klaus flew across the grass and landed on his buttocks. His lips and nose were bleeding. Anna started to run, but she didn't get far. Ulf was after her, and he was too fast. He caught her with one arm around her neck and threw her to the ground. Then he began to rip her dress open.

"Don't, Ulf. Don't do this," Gynther said, "You hurt Klaus badly. He's bleeding. Please stop all of this. Don't do this to Anna. Klaus is right. Just let her go."

"You boys are worthless because you're spoiled. You're weak. That's what you are. Weak. An embarrassment to the Aryan race."

Anna was crying, but Ulf held her down. He was strong, and she was no match for him. He turned to look at her and undid his pants. "You've been denying me this for too long."

Klaus got up quietly. Ulf didn't notice because he was too engrossed in Anna. Then Klaus ran at Ulf full force but didn't know how to fight, and Ulf looked up. He grabbed Klaus and threw him to the ground. Klaus hit his head on a large rock, and blood began to pool under him. Gynther ran to Klaus, "Klaus, get up. Get up!" Gynther was hysterical. "He can't get up. He's not answering." He started crying loud, wrenching sobs. Then he turned to Ulf, who was tearing Anna's panties off. "You killed him. You killed our brother!" he said in disbelief. Then he began to cry.

"Stop crying. Stop it, or you'll be next."

But Gynther had always been the athletic brother, stronger than Klaus, who had always been the person he was closest to in the world. Gynther was filled with rage. As Ulf climbed on top of Anna and started to guide his manhood inside her, Gynther came up from behind and hit him with a rock on the back of the head. Ulf fell on top of Anna. He lay upon her, stunned for a moment, unable to move. But she was still terrified and shaking. His head was bleeding profusely, and the blood poured onto her face and the bodice of her dress, but he was still alive. He stood up slowly and went after Gynther, who was suddenly stunned, frozen in his tracks.

Anna pulled her skirt down and covered herself. Ulf punched Gynther in the face, and Gynther fell. Then Ulf began kicking him in the ribs with his jackboots. He hadn't realized that his gun had fallen on the ground. Anna picked it up. She had never fired a gun before. She had never killed anything. But she knew she must act quickly and without remorse because she knew for certain that only one of these men would be leaving this forest alive. If she didn't shoot Ulf, she was sure that he would kill Gynther. So, while they were busy fighting, Anna aimed. Her hands shook, and her heart felt like it might explode, but she pulled the trigger, and Ulf fell. The bullet had entered his chest.

The loud bang echoed through the forest, followed by an eerie silence that sent a chill down Anna's spine. The gun fell from her hands onto the blood-soaked forest floor.

"I think he's dead," Gynther said as he walked slowly over to Ulf. He put his fingers on Ulf's neck, but there was no heartbeat. "He's dead."

Anna nodded, "I know. This was horrible. I would never want to do this to you or Klaus. I am the cause of all of this. I am the reason you lost your brother. I'm sorry, Gynther."

"No, you're not the reason. Ulf was. It was Ulf who killed Klaus. You didn't do it. He lied, and he killed your parents. Working with the Gestapo changed him. He wasn't the same anymore. I guess our real brother died long ago when he went off to fight for Hitler."

"I don't know what to say."

"I don't either. But what I do know is that you had better get out of here. Run, Anna, and good luck to you."

"Chances are we'll never see each other again," Anna said. "But I'll never forget you boys."

"Klaus loved you, and so do I. Now, you must go, Anna. Go and be safe."

"But what about you? How will you get home?"

"I can drive. I've stolen the family car at night and driven before. I'll go back into town and tell them that my brothers had a fight between them and that they killed each other. No one will ever know that you were here. Run, get out of here, and hurry."

She nodded. But then she ran over to Gynther and put her arms around him. She felt his wet cheek against hers, and she knew he was crying. But she dared not stay another minute. So, she ran.

CHAPTER FIFTY-ONE

Anna ran as fast as she could, the branches of the trees and bushes scratching her face and arms. But she didn't feel any pain. She was numb. She kept running until a white-hot pain in her chest grew so strong that she had to collapse under a tree and struggle to slow her heartbeat and breathe.

Every path in the forest looked the same. And there was no way to determine what country she was in. Ulf had been driving all day. But Anna had been under a blanket in the back seat of his car, and she had no idea which direction he'd gone in. *I believed him. I wanted to believe him. But he killed my parents. He murdered them, and who knows what he would have done to me had we ever reached our destination.* A shiver ran down her spine. It felt so much like a human fingernail had run the length of her body that she turned to assure herself that no one was there. *And Klaus. He murdered poor Klaus. His own brother. And Gynther. He will never be the same. He will have to live with all the memories of what happened. And he will have to live without his twin. I sensed something wasn't right with Ulf. I knew it. But I wanted to trust him because I wanted my family back.* Tears began to form, hot behind her eyes. She was thirsty and hungry and so tired. *Now I know that*

I will never see my parents or my brother again in this life. Only after death will we be reunited. But how will I ever find my way back to Vano?

Anna knew it was dangerous to sleep outside, exposed to the animals and the elements. But there was nowhere to go. "Vano," she whispered to the stars. "Vano, if you're out there, please come and find me. I made a terrible mistake. I was thoughtless, and I was a fool. I wanted so badly to find my parents that I chose to believe that Ulf would return all three of us to the forest where you are. But I should have known better. I wanted to trust him. I longed to believe that I would somehow see my parents again. And now, I will probably die because of my foolishness."

Exhaustion overcame her fears. She couldn't keep her eyes open. Anna felt herself fall into a deep, dreamless sleep, unable to move.

It was well after sunrise when Anna awoke. Her mouth tasted like sandpaper, and her head ached. *I need water.* She stretched and stood up to look around her. Then she began to walk, not knowing if the direction she was walking in was leading her closer or farther away from Vano. All she knew was that she must find water.

At one point, she could see the road from where she hid, protected by the trees and bushes. She saw a small, well-kept farm on the other side of the road. Anna sat down on the ground, still hidden by trees, and watched the farm until a young man walked out of the house and made his way into the barn. *I wonder if he has horses in there that he is going to feed. If he does, he will also give them water. Maybe I can try to break in tonight. And perhaps there will be at least a little left in the bucket.* She shuddered with fear. *What if he catches me and turns me in? He looks like he is just a farmer trying to keep up his farm, but I don't know anything about him. What I do know is that I can't trust anyone. I would love to run out and beg him for some water, but I dare not. He could easily turn me in. There might be a reward for turning Jews in. I must wait until dark and when all the lights are off in the house before I go into the barn and look for water.*

Night, Anna knew, was her friend. It was safer to sleep during the day and do what needed to be done after sundown. So, she hid inside a bunch of bushes. It was far from comfortable, but she lay there watching the birds fly through the trees, watching a spider spin a web, and waiting until the darkness blanketed her. Then, afraid and alone, she scrambled out of the bushes and made her way toward the farmhouse. The door was unlocked. She entered slowly. Her vision was not clear, but she was able to see enough by the moon's light. And she saw a tall brown horse in a stall. A few feet away, she eyed a bucket half full of water, a pile of carrots, and a half-eaten cabbage. Slowly, to not alarm the horse, she went to him and allowed him to smell her breath. Then she gently rubbed and patted him on the nose. "Good boy," she whispered in the darkness in a soft, sweet voice. The horse nudged her gently with his large head. And then, carefully, she drank from his bucket of water and ate two of his carrots. As she was about to eat a third, the farmer, who she thought was in the house fast asleep, entered the barn. He held a kerosene lamp. "Who are you, and what are you doing here?" he asked harshly.

Anna dropped the carrot. Her hands were shaking. Her heart was caught in her throat, pounding so hard that she couldn't answer.

"I asked you a question. Who are you? And why have you broken into my barn?"

He held the kerosene lamp up so he could see her face.

Anna began to weep. There was silence save for the sound of her soft whimpering. The man seemed a bit unnerved as he walked towards her. He held the lamp closer and looked down at her. Then he let out a laugh. "You're a woman?"

"Yes," Anna whispered.

"Damn it. Why the hell did you choose my barn? Couldn't you have gone to hide somewhere else? This is the last thing I need," he groaned. Then he said, "Well, all right. Just get out of here, and I won't hurt you."

Anna stood up; her knees were weak. She wanted to run, but she was frozen by fear.

"I said go. You're free to go. Just go now before I change my mind and turn you in."

Anna began to run, but she tripped over something hard hidden by a pile of hay. She fell flat on her face. The farmer looked at her. At first, he glared, then he began to laugh.

"Who are you? Why did you come here, and what's your name?"

"Anna," she said. "My name is Anna. I escaped from a crazy Nazi who wanted to kill me." She had to tell him the truth because she couldn't think of a lie that would sound any better.

"And you bring this kind of trouble here to me? I am nothing but a poor farmer. I have a sick sister who is bedridden to take care of. I don't need trouble with the Germans. This Nazi will come looking for you. You must go, Anna."

"He won't come looking for me," she said. "I can promise you that."

"And why not?" The farmer studied her. He was a tall, thin man with long muscular arms and legs. Not particularly handsome but pleasant enough to look at. His chin was strong but lined with stubble, and as Anna looked closer at him in the lamp's light, she saw that his eyes were not cruel. He was nervous. He was cautious, but he wasn't cruel.

"He's dead."

"You killed a Nazi?" the man asked, and she heard the horror in his voice. She wondered if perhaps he was a friend to the Germans.

"I didn't kill him. He died in an accident."

"What kind of accident?" he asked suspiciously. "We were driving in an automobile. He fell asleep and hit a tree."

"And you survived?"

She nodded. "Yes, and I ran before anyone came."

"I see," he said. Then, after a few seconds of silence, he added, "No one saw you?"

"No one saw me."

"All right. Come on. I'll help you. Follow me."

Anna didn't know what to do. She thought about running away

as they walked out of the barn. But she was hungry and, for some reason, not afraid of this man. So, she took a chance and followed him into the house. Once inside, he turned on a light and looked at her. Then he nodded his head. "You're a Jew, aren't you? That's why you had all this trouble with the Nazis. Isn't it?"

"No, no, I'm not," Anna protested. She imagined him calling the Gestapo and having her picked up.

"You are. It's all right."

"I swear to you, I'm not."

"I can tell," he smiled. "No need to be afraid of me. I'll help you if I can. Although I do have to admit, I wish you had gone elsewhere. I don't need the trouble," he said, shrugging. "But you didn't. You came to me. So, I have to believe that God sent you here. And if he did, the least I can do is get you something to eat. You are obviously very hungry. I saw you eating my horse's carrots."

She nodded. "I am hungry."

"All right. Sit down," he said, pulling out a chair for her at his kitchen table.

She sat.

He took a hunk of cheese from the pantry and cut her a piece. Then he cut her a slice of hard, stale bread. He set both of them down in front of her and poured her a glass of water from a pitcher on the table. Anna gobbled the meal as if it were the most delicious thing she'd ever eaten. He watched her eat in silence. When she finished, he said, "My name is Iwan Bosko."

"Thank you for everything," she said. "I don't know where I am. Can you tell me, please?" Her voice was small and full of gratitude. "I'm trying to get back to my family." It was true. She knew her parents and brother were dead, but now she was trying to get back to the caravan of Romany people and her fiancé. This was the only family she had left. If she could only find her way back, she would marry Vano and have children. Then she would have a place in this terrible world once again.

"You're in Slovakia," he said.

She felt tears form in her eyes, then she shrugged. "Thank you for telling me. But I guess it doesn't really matter. I am lost, and I don't know where we were camped. So, I have no idea how to get back. All the forests look the same."

"I don't know if this will help, but we could go into the forest and walk around until you see something familiar. I can't promise you will find them, but I will help you try."

"The group I am searching for are gypsies. I hope that's all right."

He smiled. "I happen to know where a group of gypsies keeps camp in the forest. Perhaps they will be the same ones you are searching for."

"Oh!" she gushed. "How can I ever thank you for helping me?"

"No need for gratitude just yet. As I said, I am not sure we will find anything at all." He smiled. "Now, I have a truck that I use to make produce deliveries from my farm to the German headquarters. They require farmers to deliver most of our crops to them. So, I can use this truck to drive along the road as close to the forest as possible. Then we'll have to park the truck and go on foot the rest of the way."

There was a long silence. "Why are you helping me?"

He looked away and said, "Let's just say I have my reasons."

"No need to explain," Anna said. "I'm glad for the help." She was still a little afraid that perhaps he was planning to turn her in. She'd heard that the Nazis rewarded people for giving Jews up to the Nazis. But she was afraid to ask him any more questions. She didn't want to make him angry.

"It's all right. I'll tell you. I hate the Nazis, too. I work hard trying to make this farm produce a decent crop. They come, and they take almost all of it. They leave me barely enough to live on."

"I understand," she said, and she did.

"Stay the night, and we will leave at dawn."

In the morning, Anna woke up to find that Iwan had already boiled potatoes, cabbage, and turnips for their breakfast. He served her a large bowl, along with a hunk of dark bread and a small slab of margarine. She was famished, and the food was hot and nourishing. They ate in silence. But once all the food was gone, he turned to her and said, "I want you to know that you are not a prisoner here. You can go any time you'd like."

This set her mind at ease. She nodded. "I understand and appreciate everything you're doing for me."

He smiled. "So, let's go and see if we can find this Gypsy camp."

CHAPTER FIFTY-TWO

Iwan and Anna got into the truck, and he drove. It was several hours before they arrived at the area that Iwan thought might be the place where he'd seen a Gypsy camp. It was difficult to be sure if this was the area. Everything in the forest looked so familiar and yet, at the same time, so unfamiliar. They walked for a while but saw nothing. "I can't be sure exactly where I saw the camp," Iwan admitted. "I know it was somewhere around here." They walked for hours and finally were ready to give up when Anna stumbled upon the tree where Vano had carved their names. She was giddy with excitement. "Look, look at this." She showed him the carving in the tree trunk. "Now, I am sure that I know where I am." She smiled. "The Romany camp should be very close to here. I know just how to get there. Follow me."

Anna hiked through the familiar landscape. She remembered everything and knew exactly where she was now. Her heart was light. Soon, she would see Vano, Nuri, and the red horse once again. She began to run, and it felt like her feet had wings. The sun broke through the canopy of treetops and filtered down on her. *Just a few minutes, and I will be back in the safety of Vano's strong arms. I'll lay my head on his chest and tell him the horrors I've just gone through. He will listen in his quiet way. I can hear him promise to make things all right.* She was so excited to be close to the Gypsy camp that she wasn't paying attention to her feet. She tripped over a large overgrown tree root that jutted from the ground and almost fell. But she caught herself and ran faster towards her goal. Iwan was following close behind her. But her heart sank when she came to the clearing and found it empty. Fear struck her like a bolt of lightning. Running as fast as she could, she ran into the middle of the clearing where Nuri's vardo had stood. She looked around her in disbelief. The wagon was gone. But tracks were still there where the wheels had been embedded into the ground. She looked across the field and saw the wheel tracks, including those from the wagons that Vano and Damien owned. But not one wagon remained. Anna fell to her knees.

"They left without me," she said softly. Her voice choked up with disbelief. "I don't know where they have gone. But I must assume that they were threatened by the Nazis and forced to start traveling again. But I can't believe Vano would leave here without me."

Iwan stood at her side. He didn't say a word. He just watched her as she put her face into her hands. Then she began to cry. "Vano said he loved me. But he left without me," she was crying softly. Then she cleared her throat and turned to Iwan. "Thank you for everything you've done. I'm sure you would like to return home. So, I'll stay here for the night camp out and see if he shows up. He might not have gone. He might still be in the forest waiting for me to return."

"His wagon is gone, Anna."

"I'm going to stay and pray he returns. I have nowhere else to go."

"You can come back to the farm with me," Iwan said gently.

"No, thank you. I can't leave until I am sure that he will not return for me."

"Then I will stay with you. You can't stay here all alone. It's too dangerous."

"I've slept alone in the forest so many times that I forget how dangerous it can be," she said.

"Well, it can. It can be very dangerous. You've been lucky up until now. But let's not test that luck anymore. All right?"

"All right," she agreed. "So, you'll stay with me?" She was still surprised.

"Yes. I wouldn't feel right about leaving you here. So, I will stay with you. However, I will not force you to let me stay. If you prefer, just say the word, and I will go back home."

"But I thought you said you had a sister who was ill and bedridden."

"I lied," he admitted.

"Why?"

"Again, I have my reasons," he sighed. "Because it is a lie I tell the Nazis so that they will give me a larger ration of my crops. They have yet to want to see my sister. That's because I told them that she had a contagious disease. Did you know the Nazis are terrified of becoming ill?"

"I had no idea," she cocked her head and looked at him. "But please stay with me. I would be so grateful not to have to face another night in the forest alone," she said. Although she hoped and prayed Vano would return, she knew, deep in her heart, that he would not.

As the sun set, Iwan and Anna lay down on the ground. They slept close enough to each other for him to watch over her, but far enough apart to satisfy her need for modesty. And, of course, she didn't want Vano to think that she and Iwan were lovers if, by some miracle, he returned. It was a warm night, which was good because they had no blankets or food. Anna awoke just as the sun was beginning to rise to find Iwan already awake. He was sitting with his back against a tree and waiting for her.

"Do you want me to stay with you any longer?" he asked.

She shook her head. "No, thank you for everything. I appreciate all of it. But you can go back home now."

"What are you going to do? Where are you going to go?"

"I don't know," she said as tears formed in her eyes. "I have nothing left. I have no family and no place to go. I guess I'll stay right here."

"That's absurd," he said, "you'll starve to death."

She shrugged.

"I suppose the best thing to do would be for you to come back home with me," he said. "At least you'll have a safe place to sleep and food to eat."

"I..." she stammered, "I don't know how to say this, but I am not the kind of girl who would sleep in your bed."

"Of course not. I wouldn't expect as much from you. Do I look like the kind of man who would help a woman to get something from her?"

"No. You are a kind and good man. But are you sure you want another mouth to feed?"

"I'm sure."

"What will you tell your neighbors? What will you tell the Germans if they come?"

"You will pose as my sister."

"You mean the sister who you made up. The bedridden one?"

"Yes," he said. "But I didn't make her up. She was sick and died. I just never told anyone. Come on. Let's go. I'll explain everything on the drive back."

CHAPTER FIFTY-THREE

As the old truck wound around the dirt road, Iwan began to speak. "I hope I can trust you," he said, and it seemed he was talking more to himself than to her.

"You can trust me," she said.

But he wasn't listening. He drew a long breath. Then he said, "I had a wonderful little sister. She was my best friend, even though she was several years younger than me. But she was very delicate. Typhoid went through our town, wiping out so many people. Our parents got it first. They were old and weak, and they died quickly. But then Kalina got sick. There was no money for a doctor. The Germans took everything we had and everything we could grow. They barely left us with enough to eat. I don't know if a doctor could have helped her. She was very sick. But she was young, only fourteen, and because of her age, I thought she would be strong enough to make it. She didn't. I buried her next to my parents and my fiancée in our garden."

"You were engaged to be married?"

"Yes, that terrible fever took them all. All but me. It left me to live all alone with nothing but my memories," Iwan said bitterly.

"I'm sorry."

He shrugged. "No need for you to be sorry. It's not your fault." Then he went on, "Kalina was the last to go. I stopped speaking to the neighbors. I didn't want to see people. I stayed on my farm, and when people I knew from church came to see me, I made them feel unwelcome. I was pretty heartbroken. In fact, I was so upset that I buried my sister without a gravestone. So, I never told anyone that Kalina was dead. The rations the Germans allowed us to keep from our harvest were pitiful. So, I made up a story. I told them my sister had this very contagious disease, a rash that burned the flesh. I said that she was bedridden upstairs. I told them they could go up and see her if they wanted to, but if they did, they would be subjected to possibly catching the disease. And there was no cure."

"Oh, my goodness. Weren't you afraid they would go up and see that no one was there?"

"The Nazis?" he laughed. "Not in a lifetime. You should have seen their faces. They are scared to death of diseases. And so, I have been getting rations for Kalina and myself. It gives me a little extra food."

"But now that you have me living with you, you might find you don't have enough."

"I'll have enough. I'm resourceful. I have some pretty good ideas of what to do to make sure both have enough food. And because the Nazis think you're my sister and have this terrible contagious disease, there is a very good chance you will never see another Nazi again."

She smiled. Then she said, "You're really quite smart."

"Yes, I suppose I am. At one time, I was hoping to go to study at the University. But then the fever came, and my uncle died and left the farm to my father. My father was hardly making a living, so he decided to move us all out of the city and onto my uncle's farm. I was born and raised in the city but had to learn to work on the farm. Then my parents got sick and died. The Nazis came, and between all of it, I never had the opportunity to continue my studies."

"And your sister got the fever before you left the city."

"No, she didn't get the fever until later. But she was one of the reasons my father was eager to get us out of the city. She had gotten herself into trouble."

"You don't have to discuss this if you don't want to."

"It doesn't matter now. She was pregnant when we left the city. I knew the boy who was responsible. He was a friend of mine. He refused to marry her. He said it wasn't his baby. My parents were furious with her. Because she wasn't married, my parents wouldn't permit her to have a doctor or a midwife present when she gave birth. She lost the baby anyway. It was stillborn. It weakened her, and she was sickly after that. Nothing life-threatening. Just headaches. Her hands shook. She was tired all the time. Most of all, she was very depressed. I wanted to kill the boy who had made her pregnant. But I had no way to get back to the city. I didn't have any money of my own. So, I stayed at the farm and tried to cheer her up." He hesitated. "It didn't work. Nothing worked. She hardly ate and almost never spoke to my parents at all. Then, after they died, she would sometimes talk to me, but not often. Then one winter day, I went up to her room to tell her that dinner was ready, and I found her in her bed, very sick. She was running a high fever and sweating profusely." He cleared his throat. "Three days later, she was dead."

Anna gasped, "Oh, I am so sorry."

"Yes, well, nothing to be sorry about. You had nothing to do with it," he said. "Anyway, as I said, I never reported her death. And since the neighbors hardly saw her anyway, no one questioned me. Everyone just accepted that I had a sickly sister living upstairs in her bedroom."

CHAPTER FIFTY-FOUR

They returned to the old farmhouse late that night. It was comfortable, and the furniture was lived-in but clean. After they ate the rest of the soup left over from breakfast, Iwan showed Anna to his sister's old room. It had a nice soft bed and a dresser with a mirror. "You should be comfortable here," he said. "And please feel free to wear the clothes in the closet. They should fit you. Kalina doesn't need them anymore, and there's no reason they should go to waste."

"Will seeing me in your sister's dresses make you uncomfortable?"

"I've learned we can't be too sensitive about anything during war. We must live for the moment, and although we never forget the past, we must put it behind us if we hope to survive. Do you know what I mean?"

She nodded. She knew what Iwan meant because she felt overwhelming sadness when she thought of her family or Nuri, Damien, and Vano. But Iwan was right. She must live for the present. So, Anna tried to keep her thoughts on what was required of her now. She had chores to do, and she did them without complaining. Anna kept the house clean and weeded the vegetable garden at night so no one would see her. During the day, she scrubbed the laundry and cooked their food. Being busy kept her from dwelling on the past.

Before the sun rose, Iwan went outside to work the land. He came in for an afternoon meal, then went back out to continue his work. But, after dinner, Anna read to him some of the forbidden books he kept hidden. Sometimes they played cards, and sometimes, they took walks around Iwan's property after dark. As the weather began to change and spring passed into summer, they sometimes took a risk by going to the river after sunset for a quick swim. But they only went after dark so that no one would see Anna. They came in wrapped in towels and laughing from the effects of the cool, clear water on their skin and hair.

Fall brought colder weather. When Iwan went into town to purchase supplies, he acquired a large ball of yarn. He'd gotten it as a trade for a few potatoes. It was thick and gray, if not pretty, it was at least practical. "It's enough to make a sweater for you," he told Anna. "Do you know how to knit?"

"Actually, yes, I do." She remembered when she'd been very young, and Elica had taught her. "My friend taught me when we were about nine years old." She smiled at the memory of Elica.

"Do you know what happened to her?"

Anna shook her head. "I have no idea. I hope she is all right. But I worry that she might not be. Her husband was Jewish, and he was arrested. She went to the Gestapo to try to help him."

"That's a dangerous position to be in. She must have been very brave to go to the Gestapo. I would never do that for any reason," he said.

"I know," Anna thought. Then she felt guilty as she stared into the fire. *I am Jewish, and because of that, I am putting Iwan in danger by being here, but I can't leave. I don't know where I would go or what I would do.*

As if Iwan had read her mind, he said, "It's all right, Anna. I'm willing to take the risk. I'm glad for the company. I've been alone too long."

"Do you think anyone will ever find out I'm here?"

He shrugged. "I'd like to say no. But anything is possible."

They didn't discuss it any further.

Anna began to knit at night as they sat by the fire. It was harvesting time, and Iwan worked hard to bring in the crops. The first thing they did when the sun went down, and it was dark enough for them to go outside unseen, was to bury some of the potatoes they harvested to hide the extra food from the Nazis. Iwan told Anna that if he gave the Nazis the percentage of his crops they expected to be given, he and Anna might have starved.

Each day, Iwan loaded up barrels of potatoes, cabbages, and carrots. "I hate that I am forced to give them my crops," he told Anna when he came inside. She was careful to avoid the windows. They'd put up shades on some of them. So that she was able to go out of her bedroom each day to prepare dinner and have it ready by the time Iwan came in each night.

And each night, Iwan said the same thing, "Damn those Nazi bastards. They should only choke on those crops they steal from us. It drives me crazy that my hard work supports the German war effort. I don't want to see them win. I'd like to see them all drown."

"I know," Anna agreed as she ladled some stew onto two plates.

"What can we do? If I don't show them a decent harvest, they will stay here longer than we'd like. They'll investigate this place to find out why."

"So, we give them what we have to, and we keep what we can steal," Anna said. "It's all we can do."

He nodded his head. They ate in silence.

"When do you think they'll come for the crops?" she asked.

"Soon," he said, "I was thinking maybe you should be hiding upstairs. I'll do the cooking for a while. And I'll do the laundry too. I don't want them to come here and find you walking around. It's best if they think you're upstairs and still sick."

"Yes, but I feel bad that I won't be of any help around the house."

"It's all right. Then, after they've collected our harvest and gone, you can come back out. All right?"

She nodded.

CHAPTER FIFTY-FIVE

For two weeks, Iwan watched and waited, but the shiny black automobile that brought the Germans each year did not arrive. He was almost beginning to believe that perhaps something had happened, and they would not come this year. But then, on a cold November morning, the dreaded black car rounded the corner. Iwan looked up from his work as he was clearing a patch of land and sighed. He thought of Anna. His heart was beating wildly. He ran into the house. "Anna, are you upstairs?"

"Yes," she called down.

"Stay there. Stay in bed. They're here."

Iwan forced himself to put on a courageous face as he walked outside to meet the Gestapo's automobile. The car stopped in front of his little farmhouse, and two men wearing long black leather coats got out.

"Good morning," Iwan said as cheerfully as possible.

"Good morning, Herr Bosko," One of the Germans smiled. He looked warm and comfortable in his dark uniform and coat. "May I assume that you're all ready for us?"

"Yes," Iwan said. "I've packed up my harvest. It's right over there." He pointed to the barrels of vegetables. Then he held his breath, hoping the German would not notice that his bounty was short because he'd been burying potatoes to ensure he and Anna would have enough to eat during the winter.

The Nazi walked over to the barrels, looked inside, and nodded. "A fairly decent harvest for a farm this size," he said. "I'll send the truck by this afternoon to pick it all up."

"Yes, all right."

"And by the way. Your neighbors? You know them, I am quite sure, the Czarneckis? Well, you won't believe this, but they have been arrested." The Nazi's voice was cheery, as if he were bringing good news. But the undertone was dangerous. And Iwan secretly shivered.

"Oh?" Iwan felt faint. "I don't really know them very well."

"Yes, well, it seems they are an underhanded bunch. After everything Germany had done for them, these ingrates were stealing from the Reich. They took more than their share of their harvest. Greedy, I suppose. However, I must admit, I was sorry for them. I truly was." He didn't sound sorry at all. He spoke mockingly, as if he were cautioning Iwan not to steal from his fatherland. "You see, it was all very unfortunate. We had to haul all of them away. And they had little children. We took the children too. Because, of course, we couldn't leave them at the farm unattended. I don't enjoy doing this, but thieves are thieves. I'm sure you understand. Germany can't tolerate that sort of thing, or everyone might do it. Then we would have trouble feeding our soldiers. And, of course, our army must be our first priority." He shook his head. "As it is, we are very generous with our farmers." He smiled, but his smile had underlying malice. Iwan tried to smile, but his lips were quivering. He was worried that perhaps the Nazis knew about Anna and that he and Anna had stolen from the harvest. He couldn't be sure that he and Anna had not been seen. And, if they were seen by a neighbor, they might have been turned in. After all, reporting a crime like this would surely result in a reward. A reward like extra food, something that the poor people would be inclined to do anything for. Even though they all knew that a crime like this could be punishable by death. Perhaps this Nazi already knew. Perhaps he'd come to arrest Iwan and Anna and was just toying with Iwan before taking them away.

The Nazi walked over to the area where Anna and Iwan had planted the potatoes and stood on the very ground where the potatoes were hidden. Sweat ran down Iwan's armpits. If the Nazi had been informed by someone as to where to look, and he happened to overturn that earth, or even if he looked more closely at the carefully covered ground, he would see that the land had been recently dug up. However, the Nazi didn't seem to notice. He just strutted around for a few more minutes. Then he sighed and said, "Well, it's a good thing you didn't know the Czarneckis better. You would be mourning right now. You see, I have a feeling they might all be dead soon. Even those sweet little ones. Ah, well, it's sad, very sad." He smiled.

Iwan kept his eyes glued on the Gestapo agent. Meanwhile, he was trying not to let his face show his fear.

"Well, I'd love to stay and talk with you, but I must go now. There are more farms in this area I must visit today."

The German got into his car. His shiny, polished, black boots caught a ray of sunlight as he climbed in and closed the door. He waved to Iwan. And there was the menacing smile again. Then he pulled away.

Iwan fell to the ground. His body was like rubber. He lay there breathing heavily, unable to move. And for a few moments, he couldn't stand up. Finally, he sat up and bent over at the waist, trying hard to catch his breath. When he was able to get up, he stood. Then he ran to the house to tell Anna what had transpired.

CHAPTER FIFTY-SIX

Anna was trembling in her bed when he walked into her bedroom. "Are they gone?" she asked nervously.

"Yes, they're gone. But they're sending a truck this afternoon to pick up the crops. So, you should stay here in bed today. It's best that they don't see you at all."

"Yes, I will," she said.

"I'll prepare something for dinner. I'll put up a soup right now," he said.

"No need. I baked bread yesterday, and we have a little cheese and an egg left. That should be all right," Anna said.

"Yes, that will be fine. I won't cook anything."

She got up and went to him. "Are you alright?" she asked.

"Yes," he smiled. Then, trying to make things lighter, he said, "I realize you want to eat the bread and cheese because you don't like my cooking."

She laughed a little, but neither of them was able to relax.

"Anna," he said seriously, "please don't forget, you must not leave this room unless it's absolutely necessary. And even then, don't do it. I left you some water in case you're thirsty and a bucket in case you need to relieve yourself. Do you understand me?"

She nodded.

"I'll come and get you later when I am sure it's safe."

CHAPTER FIFTY-SEVEN

That night, Iwan came late to Anna's room. He brought another pitcher of water, two glasses, a couple of plates, the bread she'd baked the day before, and the small block of cheese. He brought a small bowl containing a single hard-boiled egg cut in half. It was very dark outside, and although she was hungry, she didn't complain.

"They're gone. They took a long time to load the trucks. I brought our dinner up here. I thought we would eat together."

"Did they notice that we had taken some of the potatoes?"

"No, thank God. I was worried all day," he said as he gave her a plate and took one himself.

She nodded.

"Are you hungry?"

"Yes, very."

"Let's eat."

After eating, they went into Iwan's room because he had a fireplace, and it was a cold night.

A warm, welcoming fire blazed in the fireplace when Anna walked into the room. They sat by the fire together.

"Did they pick up the barrels?"

"Yes, they did. Right before I came to your room."

"So, we're all done with them now?"

"Yes, and I am so relieved. At least that's over for another year," Iwan said.

Anna nodded in agreement.

"And soon, the winter will be here."

"Do we have enough firewood?" she asked.

"Yes, I have plenty. But now we have to preserve some of the fruit from the garden and even some of the vegetables. Do you know how to preserve fruit and vegetables?"

"I don't think so," she admitted.

"I'll teach you. We should preserve as much as we can for the coming months."

They ate quietly for a while. Then Iwan said, "You know, I've often wondered why everyone I cared for died from the fever, yet I never caught it. All of us were living here, all in the same house. They dropped like tiny sparrows. But not me. I lived. And for a long time, I lived with guilt for having survived."

Then Anna took his hand. "I know what you mean because everyone I loved was taken from me, too. My parents, my brother, and my fiancé. My neighbors and my dear friends. In fact, there are still so many people who I haven't accounted for. I don't know if they are still alive. I might never know. And..." She hesitated, then sighed, "... and I can't understand what happened with Vano. He said he loved me. We were engaged. I don't know why he left without me. I might never understand it. He said he loved me, but he left with the rest of the Gypsies when they moved on. Or maybe something happened. Maybe something terrible happened."

"It could have. In the times in which we live, anything could happen, Anna."

"That's so true. I hope he's all right. I hope the entire group is still safe." But she wondered if he had gotten scared of how close they'd grown and left without her or if something unthinkable had actually happened.

"Were you actually engaged?"

"Oh yes, I have his grandmother's ring. I believed that we were going to get married. Maybe he wasn't really serious." She looked away because her face grew red with shame as she remembered the nights she'd spent naked in Vano's arms under the stars. *If he left without me of his own choosing, then he broke my heart. He didn't have to say he loved me. I never asked him to. And if he hadn't, I wouldn't feel bad at all. But he did. He swore his love for me, and then he left. It doesn't make any sense. Well, at least I'm not pregnant.* She thought. *This could all be much worse.*

"Maybe the group of gypsies had to go because they got word that the Nazis had found them."

"Maybe, but I still think he should have found a way to leave me a message or something," Anna said.

"But how?"

"I don't know. I don't know," Anna said, shaking her head. There was a long silence. Then Anna said, "At least you know what happened to your fiancée. Not knowing makes it worse. But I have to be honest, I would rather he left me than hear that he'd been hurt in some way. I still love him. I will always love him."

"Oh yes, I sure do. She died a terrible and violent death," he said.

"I'm sorry. I shouldn't have brought it up. I didn't mean to stir up old pain and memories."

Then he tried to smile as he touched her shoulder. "It's all right. It's no one's fault. Besides, if you want the truth, I wasn't in love with Christine. She was a girl who needed a husband, and I was a fellow who needed a wife. Sometimes, it's like that when you live on a farm. I was hoping we would get married and have sons who would help with the work."

"You weren't childhood sweethearts?"

"Not really. I knew her from the time we moved to the farm. But I wouldn't have called us sweethearts."

"Was she very beautiful?" Anna asked.

"No. I wouldn't have called her beautiful. She was tall and big-boned. A strong farm girl. Her father had three sons and a daughter. The boys stood to inherit their father's farm when they got married. It was a decent piece of land, but by the time they split it up, nothing would be left for his daughter. Christine needed to marry a man with land of his own. Our betrothal was little more than a business contract. A marriage of convenience."

"But you were friends?"

"Yes, we were friends. But far from romantic lovers," he admitted.

There was a long pause, then Iwan asked, "What was he like?"

"Who?"

"Vano, the man you were going to marry."

"Oh," Anna said. She put down her knitting needles and gazed out the window at the darkness. "He was romantic, like a hero out of a book. He was tall and handsome with dark, wavy hair. And, of course, living with a band of gypsies was so different from the way I grew up. I guess you could say the whole thing was rather romantic."

"How did you grow up, Anna?"

She smiled at him. "Like a nice Jewish girl from a fairly affluent family."

"In town?"

"Yes. We lived in Vienna."

"And did you have only Jewish friends and neighbors?"

"Oh no, my best friends, my blood sisters, were two gentile girls. I miss them."

"Blood sisters?"

"Yes, we made a pact when we were eight to always stand by each other. Then we cut ourselves and mixed our blood." Anna looked at her hand where the girls had cut themselves many years ago.

He smiled. "That was brave for a group of eight-year-olds."

"We weren't that brave. We didn't cut that deep," Anna said, smiling.

He nodded. "This may sound crazy, but in a way, I'm glad for the war and the upheaval it caused in my life."

"You're right. It does sound crazy," she laughed. "But I have to ask, why would you say that?"

"Well, because I know that if Hitler had not gone mad trying to take over the world, I would never have met you."

She smiled at him. Then let out a little laugh. "I suppose that's true." Anna liked Iwan well enough. And she was grateful for all he had done for her. But if she had the power to change the way things had happened, she would never have heard the name Adolf Hitler. Anna would prefer to be home with her brother and parents, all still alive. *I would probably be married with children. I would spend my afternoons taking care of my children and visiting with Elica and Bernie. And even though I would never have met Vano or lived among the gypsies, I would have my family and blood sisters.*

CHAPTER FIFTY-EIGHT

Aria and Enzo were still staying at the farmhouse. Before he left, Mateo had arranged everything for his family to keep them safe. And although he could not stay there with them, he visited them as often as he could, which turned out to be every other month. He had a telephone installed at the farmhouse so that he could call and speak with his wife once a week. And he did call almost every Sunday, at six o'clock. Once in a while, he missed his phone call, but he would make it up by calling later in the week.

Aria begged Mateo to leave Rome and stay with them at the farm, where she believed that he, too, would be safe, but he refused. He said he was not a coward and owed Mussolini a great deal. And so, he would not abandon Mussolini in his hour of need.

Whenever he came to the farm, before he returned to Rome, he gave Aria whatever money he had, which had diminished due to his party losing favor.

One rainy, gray afternoon, Aria and Enzo were upstairs in their bedroom. It was a lazy day, so Aria was reading Enzo a story from one of the children's books Mateo had brought. After Enzo drifted off to sleep, Aria put the book on the night table. She was going to take a nap when she heard the farmer and his wife speaking loudly, in fearful tones, downstairs in the kitchen.

Aria placed a soft kiss on the top of Enzo's head and got out of bed. She quietly opened the door to the bedroom and listened.

"The men in town are all talking about it. They say that Mussolini was hung upside down in the Piazzale Loreto in Milan," the farmer said, his voice shaky, "along with several of his top men."

"Who would do that?"

"I don't know. Germans maybe? Partisans. No one knew exactly. They only know that his body was hanging in the square where those fifteen partisans were shot last August. And it's not just him."

"I heard that there were problems between Hitler and Mussolini. But I thought they had worked things out. I know Mussolini ran away and hid for a while. But then, Hitler put Mussolini back in charge again, didn't he?"

"I thought so. But it could very well have been Italian partisans. That's my guess. There are a lot of people who don't like Mussolini. You know this as well as I do. But no one dared speak out."

"Yes, of course, I know. We never liked him much, either. But we kept quiet. It was safer. Then, of course, the Leonis came to stay here at the farm, bringing us extra food and money. Listen, we need to know what is going on. So, I'll go back into town and see if I can find out more this afternoon," the farmer said. "If Mussolini is dead, there's a good possibility that Aria's husband is dead, too. If he is, there won't be any more money. And we can't afford to keep Aria and the child unless we get paid."

"I know. You're right. Go into town and find out what you can. See if you can find out if Signore Leoni is all right. He didn't telephone on Sunday last week."

"Has he ever missed a Sunday call?"

"Yes, once or twice. Aria didn't seem too worried at the time."

"Poor thing," the farmer said. "She didn't know."

"No, neither did we. Do you know when this happened?"

"I'm not sure. But I'll find out when I go into town. Don't say anything to Aria until we have more information," the farmer said.

Aria put her hand over her mouth. She was already worried because she hadn't heard from Mateo in over a week, which wasn't like him. She got back into bed, pulled Enzo to her, and held him tightly. Then she closed her eyes and said a prayer.

CHAPTER FIFTY-NINE

Aria was in a state between sleep and wakefulness. But if it hadn't been for Enzo shaking her, she would have stayed like that without moving. "I'm hungry, mama," he said as he looked into her eyes.

"Yes, of course, you are," she whispered. Then she looked outside. It was already dark. *How long have we slept?* She asked herself. But she knew why she had not gone downstairs for dinner. It wasn't because she was asleep. It was because she was afraid of what the farmer was going to say. He should have returned by now. Somewhere deep inside of her, she already knew the truth. Although she hoped and prayed that she was wrong. But if she were to look deeply into her own heart, she could recall the exact moment when she felt something terrible had happened to Mateo. It had been on the evening of the 28th of April. After dinner that night, the ground was still wet from an afternoon rain. Enzo had insisted that he needed to get out and play before dark. She loved to indulge him, so she agreed. And so Aria had been outside playing ball with Enzo. His clothes were dirty. She glanced at him as he picked up the ball, which was wet with mud. "The ground is too wet to keep playing, my love, and it's getting late," she said. "Let's go inside, and we'll come back out first thing tomorrow. I promise."

"But mama, please?" Enzo said.

She didn't have the energy to argue. Suddenly, out of nowhere, she felt a terrible ache in her chest. The stabbing pain was so bad that she had to walk over to the chair outside and sit down. Grasping her bosom, she closed her eyes. Aria was panting. She could not catch her breath. But then, in her mind's eye, she saw Mateo's face. His eyes were filled with pain. A little gasp rose in her throat and escaped her lips. "Mateo," she whispered. Then shaking her head, she refused to believe it, but she knew he was dead. Enzo must have seen the look on his mother's face because he dropped the muddy ball and came running to her. He shook her hard. "What's wrong, Mama?" he asked.

"Nothing, darling. Nothing," she said because, in fact, nothing was wrong. She told herself it was just her imagination, born of fear and nothing more. But now, as she and Enzo walked down the stairs to the kitchen in the little farmhouse, she knew it was all true. Mateo's death was not something she had imagined. Mateo had come to her that evening, and it was probably to say goodbye.

Enzo ran into the kitchen and sat down. Everyone else followed. Once they were all sitting at the table, Enzo was given a slice of brown bread with margarine and a glass of fresh unpasteurized milk. Aria sat beside him. She couldn't touch the food. The farmer's wife was buttering a slice of bread. Aria watched her, waiting, terrified of what she already knew the farmer would tell her. This farmer had not been educated and was not a genteel man. He had faced a lifetime of hardships, drought, evil governments, illness, and of death, and so when he had something to say, he was direct. "I'm sorry," he said as kindly as he could. "I found out that your husband was killed."

After a long pause, Aria looked up with her eyes filled with tears. "Are you sure? Are you sure it was him?"

"I'm sure."

Aria let out a painful wail. She didn't ask how he knew for sure that it was Mateo. She didn't ask how it happened. Or even who did it. None of this mattered. The only thing that mattered was that Mateo was gone. She had felt an emptiness since that evening when she felt her husband leave the earth. And now, she knew for certain that it had not been her imagination.

The farmer cleared his throat. "I was thinking about it. And since your husband was part of Mussolini's regime, it's probably best if you and the boy find another place to stay. It's too dangerous for the wife and me to have you here. I'm sure you must understand."

Then the farmer's wife added in a gentle voice, "We are just poor farmers, and we can't afford to get into trouble. I'm sorry. I truly am. We like you and the child. But it's just too dangerous for us. I hope you understand, but you must go as soon as possible."

Aria nodded. She was in shock, but she understood. These were plain people. Non-political. They were just trying to survive. Aria's misery filled every ounce of her being. She had lost her beloved, and now she and the child were on the street. Her heart raced with fear. *If those responsible for this find Enzo and me, they might kill us, too.* She wanted to beg the farmer to shelter her, but she gathered her courage. "We'll leave tonight. After Enzo finishes eating," she said. "Can you drive us into the city?"

"No, I'm sorry," the farmer insisted. "You must get there on your own. I can't be seen with you."

Aria nodded. *I expected as much.*

She went upstairs to pack. As she emptied the drawers, she realized that it was best if they traveled light. So, she loaded their most practical clothing into their suitcase. As she did this, her eyes fell upon the toy gun Mateo gave Enzo. Rage filled her. *Why must men make wars?* She threw the toy gun against the wall, and it broke. Then she looked down at the rest of Enzo's toys and saw the puppet. Aria was transported back to that day on Enzo's birthday when Mateo had entertained them both like he was a ventriloquist. She felt her knees buckle, and she fell to the floor and began to cry.

It is getting late, and I must be strong for Enzo. There was no time for tears. She had to hurry and leave. She'd promised the farmer and his wife. But first, she must disguise herself and the boy as much as possible, so they can make their way safely out of town.

Aria covered her golden hair with black shoe polish to disguise her appearance. She did the same for her son, who giggled. He found it funny to see himself with black hair in the mirror. Aria smiled at him sadly. Then she picked up her suitcase and held Enzo's hand, leading him out into the blackness of the night.

Enzo was not in good spirits when they walked out of the farm-house. He was clearly frightened.

"Where are we going, Mama?" Enzo asked. "It's dark outside."

"To see some old friends," she said in a shaky voice.

"Are you crying?"

"No. No, Enzo, my love, I'm not crying. I'm all right."

"Where's papa? Are we going to meet him somewhere?"

"No, I'm sorry, but he won't be coming with us."

"Will he come and meet us there next week?"

"I don't know. Can you please stop asking me questions? It's a long walk to the train station. Let's save our energy. All right?"

"But it's dark outside, and I'm scared of the dark. I want papa."

"I know. I want him too," Aria said as tears spilled down her cheeks. She was glad it was dark outside, so Enzo could not see her crying.

They caught the train that took them back toward the church and the orphanage where Aria and Mateo had adopted Enzo. It was nestled quietly in the alps between Italy and Switzerland. When a guard came through the train car in the middle of the night and asked them where they were headed, Aria told him they were on their way to the convent to visit Aria's sister, who was a nun. Fortunately, no one recognized Aria as Mateo's wife. After they got off the train, they boarded a bus. Enzo was tired of traveling, and he became fussy. Soon the motion of the bus rocked him to sleep. Several hours later, Aria awakened him gently. He was groggy and cried a little, but she picked him up and carried him down the stairs and off the bus. Then she put him down and got their suitcase. He rubbed his eyes with his little fists, and it touched her heart. She began to cry. *How am I ever going to go on without my husband? We were such a happy family. And now, it's just me and little Enzo.* Tears fell down her cheeks. Aria wiped them away quickly. Then she bent down and kissed her little boy.

With Enzo's small hand in hers, Aria walked three miles from the train station to the orphanage. Halfway there, Enzo complained that he couldn't walk anymore, so Aria lifted him. With one hand, she carried him, and in the other, she held their suitcase. By the time she arrived at the orphanage the following afternoon, she was covered in sweat and exhausted. She hadn't eaten since the morning before she heard the news. And she was very hungry. But most of all, she was desperate as she knocked on the door.

An old graying heavy-set nun opened the door. "Can I help you?" The nun asked.

"I'm here to see the mother superior."

"Come in and wait here," the nun said. "And who may I tell her is calling?"

"Please, just tell her it's a desperate woman badly in need of help."

The old nun eyed Aria suspiciously, but she didn't say a word. She turned and left the room.

Aria watched Enzo's face to see if he had any memories of the orphanage. But if he did, he gave no indication of it. He sat stiffly pressed against Aria.

When the Mother Superior entered the room, there was a look of shock on her kind, old face. "Why have you and the boy returned? Is something wrong? Are you bringing him back to us?"

"No. I don't want to do that if I can help it. I love him. He's all I have left," Aria said, "but I need help. Can you help me, please?"

Just then, a group of young nuns walked by the main room where the mother superior sat with Aria and the child. Among them was

Viola. She turned and saw Enzo and his mother, and her face went white with fear. She walked away from the group of nuns and walked over to where the three of them sat. "Mother," she said, "please, may I ask why this woman and the boy have returned?"

Aria looked up at Viola.

"This is Viola. She brought the child to us," the Mother Superior explained. "He was the son of a friend of hers. The child's birth mother never returned to search for him, so we assumed she might be dead. However, I am certain that Viola is concerned to see that you have both returned. Aren't you, Viola?"

"Yes, Mother, I am."

"Well, let's all go into my office, and we'll see how we can help you, Signora Leoni. That's your name, isn't it?"

"Yes, you have a good memory, Mother," Aria said.

"I do."

The three women and the little boy walked into the office of the Mother Superior. "What do you call him?" Viola asked Aria.

"Enzo," Aria said.

Once the Mother Superior's office door was closed, Aria's shoulders fell, and she broke into tears. Enzo climbed into his mother's lap and began to cry too. Neither of the nuns spoke. They waited until Aria composed herself. A few moments passed, then Aria cleared her throat and told them everything that had transpired.

"My husband was a decent person," she said. "I know many people were unhappy under Mussolini's rule. But Mateo was not a cruel dictator. He was only a man working at a job."

"Perhaps not the best job," the Mother Superior said. "But that is not important anymore. Right now, we must concern ourselves with your safety and the child's safety."

Seeing his mother cry obviously frightened Enzo. He was pale and trembling while sucking his thumb.

"Perhaps you might like to go and play with some of the other children so we can talk to your mother," the Mother Superior addressed Enzo softly.

He shook his head violently and huddled his body closer to Aria's. "No," he said vehemently.

"All right. All right. You may stay here with us."

"What should we do, Mother?" Aria asked.

The Mother Superior hesitated, then she addressed Aria, "Keeping the two of you here with us could be dangerous for the rest of the children living here. So, we can't do that."

"But please, don't put us out on the street. If you can't take me in, I understand," Aria said, "But I am begging you not to send Enzo away. Although it would break my heart to be parted from him. I would do it if it meant that he would be safe. I would do anything to ensure his safety."

"Very well," the Mother Superior sighed. "Then that's what we shall do. Enzo will return to live here with us. And I am sad to say, Signora Leoni, but you must go."

Viola, who had been quiet until now, said in a small voice, "May I speak, Mother?"

"Yes, of course."

"Do you have any money?" Viola asked Aria.

The Mother Superior cocked her head. "Where is this going, sister? We don't accept payment for our help," she told Viola.

"No, please don't misunderstand. I don't want you to give the money to me or to the church. I am asking because if you have enough money to rent a room and get yourself started, I will lead you and Theo, I mean Enzo, through the Alps into Switzerland. It's a dangerous journey. But I believe we can make it. I've taken others before this. And if I can get the two of you across the border, you won't need to be separated. You can stay together. Once you are in Switzerland, you will both be safe. Then I will return to the convent. Mother, is it all right with you? You know I have done this before. I can do it again," Viola said firmly.

The Mother Superior nodded. "It's all right with me. But it's up to Signora Leoni. This must be her decision, as it is not without risk." Then she turned to Aria. "So, what do you want to do, Signora Leoni?

Would you prefer to leave the boy with us, or do you choose to take the risk and try to cross into Switzerland?"

Aria hesitated for a moment. She looked at her son with the black shoe polish clumping in his golden hair and bright blue eyes, and her heart ached. "I want to try to make it to Switzerland."

"Very well," Viola said, "I'll take you. Bring as little with you as possible. Do you have a pair of heavy boots?"

"I don't think so."

"It's all right. I have a pair. I'll give them to you. Be ready to leave early tomorrow morning before sunrise. I want to get started as early as possible."

"We'll be ready," Aria answered.

CHAPTER SIXTY

I wan was loading cabbages into a large barrel on a hot afternoon in the autumn of 1945 when Russian soldiers walked down the lane and came marching right up to him. He looked at them nervously because he had no idea what they wanted. He feared that they might be planning to billet at his farm. This would bring an angry troop of Nazi soldiers, and Iwan was afraid that there would be fighting on his land. However, there was an entire troop of them and only one of him. So, he had no choice but to allow them to do whatever they planned.

"Comrade," the soldier called out to Iwan. "We've come to let you know that the Nazis have been defeated. The war is over."

"What happened? When did it end?" Iwan asked.

"Spring of this year. The Allies won," the Russian smiled. "Damned Germans are finally where they belong. At the bottom."

The rest of the Russians laughed. Iwan tried to laugh, too, but he wasn't sure how he felt about these soldiers. He was afraid that the

Slovak people were still in danger and that they just might have traded one terrible group of invaders for another.

"So, do you have some food for a group of hungry soldiers?"

"Yes, of course," Iwan said.

Anna was in her room. She never came out during the day but could see the Russian soldiers from her window. At first, Anna had felt terrified seeing the Russians in their uniforms standing outside with Iwan. Then she saw Iwan walk up to the front door of the farmhouse with the soldiers at his heels. He was acting carefree, but Anna knew him well enough to know he was frightened.

She listened closely as the soldiers spoke to Iwan. She heard one of them say that Hitler was dead and that Germany surrendered in May of that same year. Anna was flushed. She felt hot all over. This is what they had prayed for. It was so miraculous that she felt overwhelmed by the news. She stood up, ready to go downstairs and greet the soldiers, but before she did, she fainted. When she awoke, the soldiers were gone, but Iwan was at her bedside. He was wiping her forehead with a cool cloth. "How do you feel?" he asked.

"I'm all right. I heard the soldiers downstairs. I guess I must have fainted."

"Yes, you did."

"Is it true? Is the war really over? Are the Germans really defeated?"

"Yes," he smiled. "We made it," he said. "It's over."

She was trembling. "Are we sure it's true? Are we sure it's over?"

He nodded, "I believe them."

Anna sat up in bed. She was dizzy. "Oh, I'm a little bit dizzy."

"Here, let me prop up some pillows for you," Iwan said. "Don't try to get up too quickly." He propped up the pillows behind her head, and she sat up, looking at him.

"Does this mean it's safe for me to leave this room during the day now?" she asked.

"Yes, I suppose it does."

"I guess it also means I should be leaving here..." Anna said.

His face fell. "What? Why? Where are you going?" he asked.

She shrugged. "I don't know. I never expected to survive," she admitted. "I don't know where to go. I only know that I want to find Vano, Elica, and Bernie. My parents and my brother are gone. God bless their souls. But I need to see if I can find Vano and my blood sisters."

He looked forlorn. "I was... I was..."

She cocked her head. "What is it?"

"Nothing, never mind," Iwan said. "I'll take you into Salzburg if you'd like. That would probably be a good place to start looking."

She nodded. "Yes. I didn't expect you to leave the farm and go with me, but I would like that very much. I don't want to go alone."

"I'll go with you."

CHAPTER SIXTY-ONE

I t took them a couple of weeks to get everything on the farm ready so that they could leave. But once the crops were harvested and stored, Iwan and Anna went to Salzburg, Austria. It wasn't what Anna expected. The city was full of displaced persons wandering aimlessly around without homes or families, desperately in search of their loved ones. There were camps for those who had been robbed of their homes and now had no place to return to. She and Iwan went to several of these displaced persons camps, where they inquired about Vano, Elica, and Bernie. But no one could help them. No one knew anything about the Gypsies, or Elica, or Bernie. Anna scanned the lists of people who had left their names because they were searching for anyone they might know. But she didn't recognize any of the names on the lists. Anna put her name and contact information on the lists, hoping someone from her past might come and search for her. Iwan didn't put his name anywhere. When Anna asked him why, he answered, "I have no one left. There is no one who would be looking for me."

Weeks passed. Iwan and Anna should have been canning fruit and vegetables. But they let the work on the farm go, as they spent hours searching the displaced persons camps and speaking with red cross workers. Finally, they came to a camp where Anna spoke to a woman who had been a prisoner at Auschwitz. She was Jewish but knew of a group of gypsies at Auschwitz. And she told Anna about them. "The Nazis had kept the gypsies together. They kept families in the same little area. They didn't separate them like they did the Jews."

The woman was young, but she looked old. She was skinny and frail. The bones jutted out of the skin on her face, making her look like a skeleton. Iwan couldn't bear to look directly at her. When she spoke to him and Anna, he had to look away. But he should have been used to it by now. They had seen so many people who looked like this walking the streets of Warsaw. The displaced persons camps were full of them. Half dead, half alive, walking corpses. But even though they'd seen so many of them, looking at them still made Iwan shiver. But Anna was not going to be put off by anything. She was determined to find any trace she could of her loved ones. So she asked the woman to please tell her what she remembered. They spoke for a while. At first, the woman talked about her family. She told Anna how she had lost her mother at the camp when they had first arrived. The woman told Anna about the horrible doctor in the white coat who had stood in judgment of the group when they'd first arrived. "His name was Dr. Mengele, but we called him the angel of death. He sent my mother to the gas that very first day."

Anna listened because she knew that the woman needed to talk. But then, in a very gentle voice, Anna asked the question she had been waiting to ask, "What do you remember of the Gypsy camp?"

The woman closed her eyes. "I don't know. I remember it. That's all. So, what do you want to know?"

"Do you know where the band of gypsies came from? Were they camped when they were arrested? Or were they traveling? Had they been camped in Slovakia when they were arrested?"

"How would I know?" the woman said sarcastically. "I don't know where they came from. Gypsies are travelers. They could have been anywhere. Besides, the camp wasn't made up of just one group of gypsies. It was more than one group; it was lots of different groups. I'm sure those Nazi bastards collected them from all over the place. The same way they collected everyone else they hated."

"Can you remember any of their names?"

"You mean the gypsies or the Nazis?"

Anna bit her lower lip; she must not lose patience with this woman. She could see that the woman had been through hell. The least she could do was remain calm and be as gentle as possible. "Not the Nazis. Do you remember any of the names of the Gypsies?"

"Let me see. I knew a woman by the name of Mala. And I was also sort of friendly with a woman named Lavina. Both of them were older than me. Forties or fifties, maybe. It's hard to tell."

Anna's heart raced. *Is that a common name? Is it possible that Lavina was the same woman who was Vano's mother? Could it be that her Gypsy family had been in that camp in Auschwitz? Maybe Vano never left that area where we were staying without me. Perhaps the Gypsy camp was discovered, and everyone was arrested. Is it possible that Vano is alive, and he's looking for me, too? Maybe this woman can help me find him.* She put her hand on her heart. Then, softly, she explained, "My fiancé was Romany, one of the Gypsy people. Lavina was my fiancé's mother's name." The words stuck in her throat, which was so dry it felt like sandpaper. "Do you remember if the woman you knew by the name of Lavina had any children? Did she have two sons?"

"Yes," the woman said. "Two boys, twins. Nice boys. Strong boys."

Anna felt dizzy, but she was determined not to faint. She was so close now that she was terrified of what this woman might tell her, yet she had to know. "Do you know what happened to them?" Anna asked.

"Yes," the woman said, shaking her head and closing her eyes. She wiped a tear from her cheek with a bony finger that had a sharp, torn-off fingernail. "I'm sorry. I'm so sorry. The Nazis liquidated the Gypsy camp."

"What does that mean?" Anna asked impatiently. She was losing her calm because she was filled with desperation.

"It was a terrible day. You see, The Nazis made the gypsies play their violins. I heard the haunting sound. It was like the violins were crying. They played beautifully, so beautifully. So sad."

"What happened to the Gypsies, to Vano?" Anna interrupted her. She was nervous and practically yelling now. She grabbed the woman's arm and shook her. "What happened? I need to know. Tell me, please."

"The Nazis, Mengele, you remember I mentioned him? Dr. Mengele? He was there at the selection when we arrived. You remember I just told you about him? He was a horrible man. A sadist."

"Please..." Anna said. The room was spinning, turning dark, and she was ready to faint again. "Please, I must know. Tell me what happened to Vano."

"Like I said, Mengele made the gypsies play their music. But it wasn't their regular music that they played. Mengele forced them all to march to the music at gunpoint all the way into the gas chamber. And when everyone else had gone, he sent the musicians too."

"What is a gas chamber?" Anna said, shaking the woman again. "I don't understand all of this."

"It's a big room that the Nazis built where they gas a lot of people all at once. They killed large groups of people, large groups, all at one time. Then they sent their bodies to the crematorium, where they burned them. That was how it was for the Gypsies. The Nazis murdered the entire Gypsy camp all at once. They called it liquidation, but it was murder. I saw Lavina and her sons, those tall, handsome boys. I think one of them was called Damien, and you're right; the other was Vano. That must have been your fiancé. Anyway, I saw them with my own eyes. They all walked together into the gas chamber. There was a young girl with them, too. She might have been Lavina's niece because she never mentioned having a daughter. She was a pretty thing. I think Lavina told me her name was Nuri? I suppose that's some kind of Gypsy name. Maybe she was twenty years old? Could have been younger. I don't know for sure. Lavina was leaning on her, and she was holding on tightly to Lavina's arm, almost holding her up, as they walked in. So brave. It was a very sad day. Such a waste."

"You're mad," Anna yelled at the woman, shaking her head in disbelief. "This is madness. It's not true. It can't be true. I refuse to believe it. I refuse." Iwan took Anna into his arms and held her tightly. She began hitting his chest with her fists, but he held her anyway. She was sobbing when one of the red cross volunteers walked over to them.

"Everyone at Auschwitz knew about the gas. We saw the bodies waiting to be burned in the crematorium. We all knew it was just a matter of time before it would be our turn to go to the gas. We were waiting to die. And if the Nazis hadn't lost the war, and the Soviets hadn't liberated us, we'd all be dead."

"No!" Anna screamed. She covered her face with her hands and shook her head.

"We lived with that knowledge every day of our lives. And, yes, it was torture. Because we knew."

"Are you alright?" The young volunteer asked Anna.

"Tell me, please tell me, it's not true. Tell me that this woman is insane."

"What is it?" the volunteer asked. "What do you want to know?"

"It can't be true."

"Please tell me what the woman said."

"She said that the Nazis put people into a gas chamber and murdered them. Then they burned their bodies. And she also said that they killed an entire group of gypsies, men, women, and children. How could something so terrible be real? Please tell me that this woman is crazy. Tell me she has gone out of her mind. Please, tell me she's crazy, please." Anna was begging, crying, pleading. She was on the verge of hysterics.

The volunteer took Anna's arm and gently escorted her to a seat.

"Please, sit down," the volunteer said. She was a young woman, but she looked thoroughly exhausted. Her hair was coming loose from the twist at the nape of her neck, and her dress looked like she's slept in it. But her eyes were kind. Iwan followed behind the volunteer and Anna. He seemed to be very distraught because his face had lost all color. The volunteer offered Iwan a chair. He sat. Then the volunteer sat beside Anna and took her hand. "I'm sorry to be the one to tell you this, but it's true. I know it's hard to believe, but the Nazis murdered many people that way. Not just Jewish people, but Romany and plenty of others, too. Then some died of disease and starvation. The Nazis were very cruel, and this has been a terrible war."

Anna began to weep like she had been fatally wounded. Iwan knelt at her side and took her in his arms. He held her for several long moments. No one at the DP camp looked at them. They had seen plenty of weeping and faced more than their share of tragedy. "I lost everyone I knew," Anna said to the volunteer. "Everyone."

The young woman nodded.

Iwan got up and stood behind Anna. Then he put his hands on Anna's shoulders. "Let's go home," he said.

She got up and leaned against him, and they left the DP camp together.

That night, they drove the old truck out of Warsaw and returned to the little farm. It was a cool night, and Anna couldn't get warm. She was shivering as they walked inside the house. Iwan helped her to sit down in the living room. Then he placed a blanket over her legs and went into the kitchen, where he put a pot of water on the stove for tea. Neither of them had eaten that day. "Are you hungry?" he asked in a gentle voice.

"No," she said, "I can't eat. But you go ahead and have something. You must be starving."

He grabbed a hunk of bread that had begun to mold and peeled the green off of the crust. Then he quickly ate it. When the tea was ready, he brought a cup to Anna, who gratefully sipped on the hot liquid. After a while, she asked, "How could this have really happened? I can't imagine such a terrible thing."

He nodded.

"How could these men have killed whole groups of people at a time? There were little children in that Gypsy camp. And they gassed so many Jewish people too. I think of my neighbors and relatives and wonder how many died this way." She shook her head. "How horrible it must have been to see other people murdered and to know you were next in line. I'm glad my parents and my brother weren't murdered that way. They died, yes, but at least they weren't in that place that she mentioned. Auschwitz."

He nodded.

There was a long silence. Then Anna said, "I know you've asked me to stay, but I don't feel right about it. You have been kind enough to keep me here and protect me through the war. I don't want to take advantage of you and your kindness. I should probably go and find myself a job somewhere."

"I don't want you to go, Anna. I love you. You aren't taking advantage of me. Not at all. You've done more for me than I can ever express. You've brought life back to me and to this little farm. Stay here with me. Please. You don't have to love me. I know that your heart is somewhere else. But give me a chance. I'll be a good husband."

"Are you asking me to marry you?"

"Yes, I am," he said.

She nodded. "I care very deeply for you, Iwan. But you're right. My heart still belongs to Vano."

"I know. I understand that. But, Anna, he's gone. And... I'm here. I'm alive. I can be your partner, your friend, your life companion."

She nodded. "And you're a wonderful man. A good friend."

"Marry me. Please don't go, Anna. You have nowhere to go and nothing to return to. Stay here with me."

She was planning to go back to Austria to see if she could find Bernie or Elica. But there was no guarantee that either of them had survived. *I could get back to Austria and discover that they were both taken by the war. Maybe he's right. Perhaps I should stay here and marry him. I do like him very much. And we get along well together. Maybe we can be happy.* After a long pause, Anna looked into Iwan's eyes. They were kind eyes, and she thought of all they'd endured together. "I will marry you."

His face lit up. She smiled at him because the joy he was radiating was contagious.

CHAPTER SIXTY-TWO

1948

Anna's arms rested on her growing belly. At the same time, she knit a baby blanket as she and Iwan sat in the living room listening to the radio when the news about Israel becoming a state was announced. She was so touched by the news that tears formed in her eyes, and she put her hands on her heart. "Finally, the Jews have a Jewish homeland," she whispered. "A place where Jewish people can go and live in peace. A land where they won't be persecuted for their religion... finally."

Iwan smiled at her.

"I wish we could go there."

"To visit?"

"Maybe, maybe to live someday," she said.

"But the farm," he said. "We'd have to leave the farm."

"I know. I know you don't want to leave the farm."

He looked at her, hesitated, then said, "Would it make you happy?"

"Yes. Very. And I am sure they need wonderful farmers like you there," she winked at him jokingly.

"Before we decide to sell our farm and move, let's find out more about what life might be like in Israel. It's far away. And I'm sure it's very different."

"You would really move to Israel for me?"

"Anna, I love you. I would do anything for you. But let's look into this further before we sell the farm."

She nodded, smiled, and touched his hand.

CHAPTER SIXTY-THREE

That summer, Anna gave birth to a tiny girl. She was born premature but had a strong will to live. And although she was very small, she fought hard for life. After a week of uncertainty with Anna and Iwan keeping vigil at the hospital, the child's condition began to improve. Anna wanted to call the new baby Leah, for Anna's mother, whose name had been Lillian. Anna explained to Iwan that it is the custom in the Jewish religion to name a child after the dead. And Iwan agreed to the name. He was happy to indulge her.

Three years passed. There had been no more talk of Israel, and the farm was prospering. They were both up before sunrise each morning, and they worked hard. Leah was growing up fast. She was already walking and talking. Although Leah was a strong-willed and demanding child, she brought so much joy to the young couple that they could hardly contain themselves. She made them laugh, and the wonder and amazement she expressed at everything around her made Anna feel that there was still magic in the world. And because of the gentle ways of her adoring husband, Anna began to fall in love with Iwan. It wasn't that she forgot her parents, her brother, or Vano. Despite all the Nazis had stolen from her, Anna began to love life again.

CHAPTER SIXTY-FOUR

On a cold morning in early March, with the help of the local midwife, Anna gave birth to their second child. He was a hearty little boy they had agreed to name Michael for Anna's father.

The midwife went out into the hallway, where Iwan was waiting. "You have a son," she said.

"And my wife?" he asked anxiously. "Is she alright?"

"She's fine. You can go in now."

Iwan entered the bedroom, where Anna lay smiling, covered with a fresh white sheet. "He's a beautiful boy," she said proudly. Then she added, "Where's Leah?"

"The midwife brought her daughter to watch Leah for me. She's still here."

He walked over to the bassinet and looked at the baby. "He's really special," he said.

"I think so. Both our children are special."

"That's because they have a very special mother," Iwan said, kissing her.

"And... an extraordinary father."

He smiled.

"Now that you have given me two wonderful children, what can I do for you?" Iwan asked as he lifted his newborn son.

"You know what I want," she said softly.

"Yes, I know, and it may surprise you, but I have been looking into it."

"What did you find out?"

"I found out that there are communal farms in Israel. We can get passage on a ship with the help of some Jewish organizations. Then we can live on one of these farms."

"What is a communal farm?"

"They call it a *kibbutz*. Everyone has a job. Everyone works together. Everyone lives together and eats together. I don't know if we'll like it, but I am willing to go because it's what you want."

"You're so good to me," she said.

"You're good to me, too." He kissed her. "Look at our beautiful family that you grew in that belly of yours."

She reached for his hand. "I know you are taking a big risk selling the farm and moving. And I shouldn't ask, but I have to. I have one more request," she said softly.

"Of course, my sweet princess. As if this moving across the world for you is not enough. Do tell me, what else can I do for you?" He was trying to sound sarcastic, but he didn't mean it, and she knew he didn't.

"Stop mocking me," she said, shaking her head. But she knew he wasn't serious; he adored her and would do anything for her. "Before we leave Europe, I would like to go back to Austria and see if I can find Elica and Bernie."

"All right," he said. "Do you know where to begin to look?"

"I've already tried all the DP camps when we looked for Vano. They had no record of either of my friends. I tried writing to Elica, but she never answered. I don't know if she ever received my letter. So, when we get to Austria, I'll start at Elica's home."

"You do understand that they might not have survived the war. I just don't want you to be hurt."

"I'll be hurt if they didn't survive, of course. I will. I'll be heartbroken. But I know there's a good possibility that they didn't make it. Still, I need to know what happened to them, Iwan. I need to see them again, at least one last time if it's at all possible."

"All right. We'll take the children and go to Austria."

CHAPTER SIXTY-FIVE

Iwan made all the arrangements for himself, Anna, and their children to take a train to Austria. They packed lightly because they didn't plan to stay long. Anna said that after she went to Elica's childhood home, she would go to her old neighborhood to see if anyone had survived. "Those are the only two places I know of to look for my old friends."

It was the night before they were planning to leave. The children were both asleep. Iwan sat on the sofa, and Anna sat on a chair.

"I am worried that this visit to Austria is going to be painful for you, and I wish you weren't insistent about going," Iwan said.

"I know you're right. Going back to Austria is going to open a wound if I find out that they didn't make it. But at least I will know what happened to them."

"That's why I've agreed to go. I want you to be happy and at peace when we move to Israel. Israel is so very far away, Anna. And there is a good chance we won't ever have enough money to return to Europe. But you're sure this is what you want?"

She'd been knitting a sweater for Leah. She stood up and put the yarn and knitting needles on a chair. Then she walked over to him and sat beside him. Taking his hand in hers, she brought it to her lips and kissed it. "Yes, I am sure," she said. "I don't want to stay here. I don't feel right about raising my children in a place that could do the things that were done to my people. I want them to have the freedom to walk the streets without fear. I want them to be able to celebrate the Jewish holidays if they choose to, without hiding. Israel is the only place on earth that I know of where they will be protected."

He sighed. "So, we will go and live in Israel." Then he kissed her hand. "But tomorrow we will go to Austria. Now, sweetheart, please don't be disappointed if we don't find anything. You realize that we might not find any trace of them. Nothing at all."

"Yes, I know that. It's been a very long time and a terrible war. But I have to go." She looked into his eyes. "I know. I've never said this before. But it's time that I do. I love you, Iwan. You are a good man, and you're the best thing that's ever happened to me. You are kind and wonderful, and I am so lucky to have found you."

There were tears in his eyes. "I never thought I would hear you say those words," he said, "but I always hoped."

They kissed softly. Then, quietly, so as not to awaken the children, he took her hand and led her to the bedroom. He closed the door behind him and took her into his arms.

CHAPTER SIXTY-SIX

Anna and her family checked into a small hotel when they arrived in Austria. Then Anna asked Iwan to watch the children for a while so she could take a walk. "Are you sure you want to go alone?"

"You don't even know where I'm going," she said.

"You're going to see your childhood home, right?"

"Yes, you're right. How is it you know me so well?" she laughed. Then she added, "I want to see it. I am certain it was Aryanized during the war. You know what that means, don't you?"

"I think so. The homes of Jews were stolen by the Nazis and given to German families, right?"

"Yes," she said. "But I want to see the house where I grew up, anyway."

"Are you sure you don't want me to come with you?"

"The children are tired. Look at Leah. Her eyes are half closed. And Michael is already nodding off. I'll be back in less than an hour."

"All right, but please be careful."

"I will," she said.

Anna walked through her old neighborhood. The houses looked

the same. But the blonde-haired, blue-eyed children playing on the grass reminded her that the Jewish families who once lived there were gone. There was no trace of the Jewish business where she had once shopped. The dress store where her mother had bought her dresses was no longer called Finkelstein's. Instead, a large sign outside that dress shop said, "Heidi's elegant frocks." The synagogue at the end of the street had been burned to the ground. Only the skeletal remains of the structure still stood. In the middle of the ashes, she saw a small wooden piece of what she was sure had been an *Atzei Chayim*, the wooden polls that held the Torah, the sacred Jewish scrolls. It was broken and charred. Her heart ached as she looked at the destruction. There was no point in going to her old house and knocking on the door. She knew she would not be well received. So, Anna walked slowly back to the hotel. On her way, she stopped at a bakery that had once been a Jewish bakery but no longer was. She bought some cookies for her children. And as she made her way back to the hotel, she broke off a small piece of one of the cookies. She ate it as she remembered how they went to a house of *shiva*, a house of mourning. After a funeral, her mother instructed her and her brother to always eat something sweet to take away the sadness.

When Anna entered her room at the hotel, Iwan stood up and put his arms around her. "I'm glad you're back. I was worried." The children were both fast asleep. The excitement and the train ride had worn them out.

"I'm fine," she said, "but thank you for worrying."

He shook his head. Then he saw the bag. "What did you buy?"

"Cookies."

He took one.

While Iwan finished the cookie, Anna lay down on the bed. "Take a nap. I'll wake you for dinner," he said.

Anna fell asleep almost immediately. She woke up a half hour later, and her face was wet with tears. She knew she'd been dreaming but couldn't remember her dream.

CHAPTER SIXTY-SEVEN

The following morning, the children woke Anna up early. She stretched, lifted Michael, and took Leah's hand, leading her down the hall to the bathroom, where she bathed both children. Then washed. By the time she returned, Iwan was dressed and ready to leave. The family headed downstairs to a small bakery, where they ate breakfast.

Iwan carried Michael, and Anna held Leah's hand as they waited for the bus to take them to the neighborhood where Elica grew up. When the bus arrived, they boarded and then rode in silence. Anna was shivering even though the weather was nice. Finally, she recognized the old, familiar bus stop. *How many times, when I was a young girl, did I take a bus to this area to see Elica?* "This is the stop," Anna said to Iwan.

Anna got off first. Then she helped her daughter down the stairs and reached up and took Michael as Iwan climbed down.

"Mama, where are we going?" Leah asked.

Anna was surprised it had taken her daughter this long to ask. "We are going on a little adventure. I'm hoping to find a childhood friend of mine."

"Papa said that if you don't find your friend, you might be sad, and Michael and I should be on our best behavior."

Anna let out a short laugh, then she shook her head. "You little minx," she said affectionately. "So that explains why you haven't asked me where we are going. Your father told you where we were going?"

"Yes, this is Austria, right? Isn't it?"

"Yes, that's right, we're in Vienna, Austria. This is where I grew up," Anna told her daughter.

"I have a lot of things I would like to know about how it was when you lived here, Mama."

"Ahhh, I see, Leah," Anna said. Leah was brilliant. Everyone said she was advanced for her age, and she always asked questions. Usually, Anna took time to explain things to her daughter, but today, Anna didn't feel like answering questions. She was lost in her own thoughts.

"I want to see where you went to school and where you lived when you were my age."

"I understand, Leah. But not today, all right? Maybe another day," Anna said, trying to be as patient as possible, but her nerves were on edge.

Leah gave her mother a hurt look. And if things had been different, Anna would have embraced Leah and apologized. She would have found some way to make her daughter smile. However, today, she was too nervous to focus on anything but the emotions from the past that were engulfing her.

Finally, Anna and her family arrived at the old wood frame house where the Frey's had lived when Elica was a girl. Frau Frey, Elica's mother, had been the maid at Anna's parents' home, and that was how Anna and Elica had met and became best friends. Anna had always thought of Frau Frey as a second mother. And her family had been generous to the Freys. But when the Nazis took over Austria, Anna's family was in trouble. Anna's father asked Frau Frey to help them. He begged her to hide Anna and her brother in their home.

However, Frau Frey said she was too afraid. She explained that she couldn't put her own daughter, Elica, at risk. And so she had gently refused to help Anna's family. Anna's father said he understood. After all, it was a crime to hide Jews. And he knew he was asking a great deal. Finally, it was Bernie and her mother who came to the rescue. They hid Anna and her family until they were arrested. The arrest occurred while Bernie was in Italy, so Anna never knew what had happened to her. And since Anna and her family were taken from the attic, they never saw Bernie's mother and knew what had happened to her. Anna always hoped that somehow Bernie and her mother had escaped.

Anna knocked at the door. When it was opened, she was suddenly transported back to her childhood. Frau Frey stood in the doorway. She looked so much older than Anna remembered. Her hair was white now, and she was very thin and frail. In a creaky, uncertain voice, she said, "Anna, is that you?" *Elica's mother can't be that old. But she certainly has aged poorly. Poverty and the war have taken a toll on her.* Frau Frey didn't smile. She just stood there staring at Anna in disbelief, as if she had seen a ghost.

"Yes, it's me, Frau Frey," Anna cleared her throat. She didn't feel like introducing this woman to her husband or children. Because even though her father had said he understood why Frau Frey had refused to help them, Anna had never understood. She'd grown up feeling that this woman was a part of her family. But she'd been sadly mistaken because when Frau Frey had to make a choice, she'd chosen to turn her back on the Levinsteins. "Is Elica here?" Anna asked, not looking into Frau Frey's eyes.

Anna saw Frau Frey's hands shaking as she nodded, "Yes, she's here. She's living here with me. She's out in the yard hanging up the wash."

Anna didn't say another word. She just turned and walked to the back of the house. Iwan and the children followed Anna. When she first saw Elica standing with her back toward them, Anna could see that she was very thin. "Mama, who's that?" Michael asked.

Elica whipped around quickly at the sound of a strange voice in her yard. She turned so quickly that she didn't have a chance to cover her face.

Anna gasped in shock when she saw the angry red scar that was raised from the skin on Elica's cheek. Then Anna quickly tried to hide her horror. But the children were not so courteous. Michael shrieked. "It's a monster, mama," he said.

Leah quickly hid behind her mother when she saw Elica's face.

Anna cleared her throat. "This is my friend, Elica," she told the children. Then she walked over to Elica and hugged her.

Elica began to cry, and then so did Anna.

"My face," Elica said, touching the scar.

Anna didn't say a word.

"Dagna was responsible for this."

"Dagna? What happened?" Anna asked.

Elica told Anna how she had gone to the police station to ask Dagna, who was working there, to help her find her husband, Daniel. "But you know how much Dagna hated Jews, and because Daniel was Jewish, she hated me for marrying him. She watched while this terrible Gestapo agent carved this Star of David on my face, and she didn't try to stop him. She just laughed. I always knew she was jealous of me, but I thought she was still my friend. She wasn't. You should have seen her face. I still have nightmares about it. It was as if she was deriving some sort of sick pleasure from seeing him carve me up. I never really knew her, Anna. But she is a horrible person."

Anna put her hand on her throat. She couldn't speak.

But Elica was weeping and growing hysterical as she told the story. "It was horrible, Anna. I was locked in the prison in the basement at the police station for a long time. They tortured and beat me. I was terrified and in horrible pain. I am so sorry. I am so sorry." She fell to her knees and covered her face with rough, red hands. "I didn't mean to do it. I was young then, and scared, and so selfish." She hesitated and wiped her eyes with the back of her hand. "I was in such terrible pain, Anna. From the beatings, from the cut on my face. Oh Anna, oh God. What have I done? Forgive me. Please forgive me."

Anna cocked her head. "For what? Forgive you for what?"

"It was me. I did something terrible, Anna. I told Dagna where you and your family were hiding. I told them so they would let me go. She let out a cry. I put you and your family in danger. I knew Bernie was on her way to Italy to take Theo to an orphanage. So, I assumed she and Theo would be safe. But I don't think she was safe, Anna. I've tried, but I haven't been able to find her. She isn't here in town. I guess she never returned. So, I destroyed all of you. It's all my fault. A day doesn't go by that I don't feel guilty. I regret what I've done. I am so sorry."

Anna's mouth dropped open. She gripped onto the fence to keep from falling. Iwan immediately went to her side. He put his arm under hers to give her strength.

Elica was still talking. She was going on about how she'd worried about Bernie and her son Theo, but Anna didn't hear her. She couldn't believe what Elica had said. *Elica turned us in.*

Leah, not understanding what was going on but seeing how upset her mother was, tried to change the subject of the conversation. "We are going to live in a *kibbutz* in Israel."

Anna looked down at her daughter as if seeing her for the first time.

"Yes, we are. We are going to live on a *kibbutz* in the Golan Heights," Leah proudly repeated what her mother had told her for months. "A land where Jews will be safe."

"She looks just like you," Elica said as she looked at Leah. Elica's voice was small and apologetic. Defeated by life itself. Then Elica added, "She's beautiful."

"Don't you even look at my children! You are a monster. How could you do that to me, to my family? My parents and my brother are dead. Bernie and her mother might be dead too. I blame you. If you had kept your mouth shut, we might have survived the war. It's your fault. You deserve to feel guilty. And it's no wonder your face is carved with the mark of Cain. You're a traitor. You were never my real friend," Anna growled. Her face was red, and her fists were clenched.

"Anna, please, I am sorry. I am so sorry. You can't know how sorry I am."

"I only know what the consequences were of your actions. I don't care how sorry you are. It doesn't matter."

Elica gasped, "I never meant…"

"What did you think would happen? You stupid little fool. You were always thoughtless, inconsiderate, selfish, and careless. I always forgave you because I believed that was just how you were. But not this time, Elica. Not this time. I can't forgive you for this. You're going to have to carry it with you to your grave because you will never have my forgiveness." Anna grabbed her daughter's hand. "Let's go," she said to Iwan.

"Anna, don't leave here like this. Please…" Elica begged.

Anna turned and walked out of the yard, with Iwan carrying Michael as they walked behind her.

"Mama, you're hurting me," Leah said.

Anna realized how hard she was gripping her daughter's tiny hand and released it. "I'm sorry," she said, bending down and hugging her daughter. "I didn't mean to hurt you."

"You're crying, mama," Leah said. "You're scaring me."

Anna nodded. "I know. I'm sorry, my little darling. I didn't mean to hurt or scare you." She pulled Leah into her arms and held her for a moment. Then she gently took her daughter's hand, and the family went to catch the bus back to the hotel where they were staying.

Anna was silent the entire ride back. She held Leah close and looked out the window as the bus passed all the places she remembered from her childhood.

When they returned to the hotel, the children said they were hungry. "Would you like to go and get something to eat?" Iwan asked Anna.

She shook her head, "Please. Just take them and get them something. I need a little time alone."

"All right," he said. Then he put his hand on her shoulders and looked into her eyes. "I'm here for you if you want to talk."

"I know."

After they left, Anna thought about all that had transpired. It was hard to believe that Elica had turned on her. But what was not hard to believe was that Elica had expected forgiveness. *That's just the way she is. It's the way she's always been.* Anna thought of Bernie. She remembered how she'd met her blood sisters at the park and how they'd shared all of their feelings. They talked about everything important to them at the time. And they kept their important moments in that little tin box they buried under a tree. They'd kept the bright red lipstick that Dagna had stolen, and their mothers forbade them to wear in that box. Elica kept keepsakes like buttons and pencils that she'd found that had belonged to boys she liked. And when Anna was forbidden to see her friends because she was Jewish and they were not, they left messages for her in that box. She would sneak away and read the messages, and they kept her connected to her blood sisters. Anna wanted to open that box. She needed to see it one more time before she left Austria forever. She took a pencil and paper from her handbag and wrote a quick note, which she left for her husband.

Then she walked to the bus stop, where she caught a bus that let her off right by the park. It wasn't a far walk from the bus stop, not even two full blocks. The old oak tree still stood, just as Anna remembered it. The leaves shone green and yellow in the sun. Anna sat down on the ground under the tree. She wished she'd brought something with her to dig up the box. But she hadn't, so she grabbed a branch and began to dig. The box was right there. Not buried very deeply. Almost like it was waiting for her. She lifted the box and opened it, and the memories came pouring out just like evil did when Pandora opened her box. There were letters filled with declarations of love for local boys from Elica and Dagna. There were love letters to Elica. And there was that red lipstick. It was all melted now, but it brought back the day when Elica, Dagna, and Anna had put it on and worn it into town. They'd felt so grown up. She closed her eyes, and she was suddenly a child again. She remembered that trip they'd taken when they went to work in Berlin for the summer. *Bernie was so smart. She figured out how to make papers for me. What a good friend she was.* "Bernie, what happened to you?" Anna said aloud, but the only answer came from a blackbird in the tree. *I will never forget you and all you tried to do for me and my family.* She looked down at the pile of love letters written to Elica. They were tied with a white ribbon that had long since faded to yellow. But when she took them out of the box, she saw another letter. This one was not a love letter. It was in Bernie's handwriting and said, "To Elica." Anna took the letter and opened it. She read it in silence. Bernie's letter said that if either Anna or Elica found this letter, she was probably dead and that as soon as she finished writing, she was going to leave Austria and travel to Italy to drop Theo off at an orphanage. At the bottom of the paper, she wrote the address of the orphanage so that they could find Theo again. *Theo might be alive.* Anna thought. *Should I give this letter to Elica, or should I rob her of her son like she robbed me of my family?* Anna took the letter and stuffed it into her handbag. Then she put the box back into the ground and covered it. After taking one last look around the park, Anna walked back to the bus stop. The bus arrived a few minutes later, and she was on her way back to the hotel.

Iwan was sitting in a chair, waiting. Anna could see that he was nervous when she entered the hotel room. Both children were asleep. "I was worried," he whispered, careful not to wake the children. "It's getting dark."

"I know. I'm sorry."

"I brought you a sandwich. You should eat something," he said gently.

"I can't."

She took the letter from her handbag and gave it to him. "Read this."

"What is it?"

She explained how she and her blood sisters had always left messages for each other in a tin box in the park. "I found this."

"What are you going to do with it?"

She shrugged.

"Elica doesn't deserve you bringing this to her. Let her wonder what happened to her child for the rest of her life. Let her suffer like you do," he said.

Anna didn't answer. She placed the letter on the table, took off her dress, and got ready for bed. She lay down beside Iwan, but she didn't speak. He gathered her into his arms and held her close to him. Finally, she heard his steady breathing and knew he was asleep. It was the middle of the night. She gently freed herself from his grasp and climbed out of bed. Then she sat down on the chair by the window. It was there that she remained until sunrise the following day.

Leah woke first. She got out of bed and sat down beside Anna. Even though Leah was just a child, Anna could tell that Leah sensed that something was still disturbing her mother because she was quiet. Michael stirred. He was looking for his sister, and because he felt the absence of Leah in the bed beside him, he jumped up and climbed into Anna's lap. Anna patted his head, but she didn't speak.

When Iwan woke up and stood up, he ran his hands through his disheveled hair. Then he glanced over at Anna. "Have you been up all night?"

"Yes," she said.

"I'll go to the restaurant downstairs and see if I can get us some coffee," Iwan said, shaking his head.

"Iwan."

"Yes."

"I am going to go and give this note to Elica. I don't want to carry this burden of hatred with me when we leave Europe. I want to close all the open ends in my life here in Europe and start over in Israel. Let her find her son. It does me no good to hurt her just because she hurt me."

"Are you sure you want to see her again?"

"Yes, I feel that I must. However, I know that this will be the last time."

"I'll go with you."

"No, please stay here with the children. I'll be back soon." Anna stood up and slipped on her dress. Then she kissed her son and daughter.

Michael started to cry, "Don't go, Mama. That monster lady made you cry yesterday." Anna looked at her children. *I have my children. She has nothing. And although she did something terrible to me, that is between her and God. I will not be responsible for keeping a mother from her child. I will leave this place blame-free. Whatever she has done is her sin, not mine.*

CHAPTER SIXTY-EIGHT

Anna arrived at Elica's house an hour later. Elica was kneeling on the floor and scrubbing sheets in a washtub when Frau Frey answered the door.

"Anna, I knew you would come. I knew you would forgive me." Elica got up. She ran over to Anna and hugged her tightly. Anna stood like a soldier. She didn't return the hug.

"Do you remember the tin box in the park where we kept our trinkets when we were children?"

"Of course," Elica said. She was crying softly.

"I went there yesterday. I went to the park, and I dug up the box. I found this. I think it's for you."

Elica took the letter and read it. Then she looked up at Anna and put her fingers to the scar on her face. "I don't want to see him," she said. "At first, I thought I did. But now, I just want to hide here in the safety of my home."

Anna was appalled. "You don't want to see your son just because you have a scar on your face? I have a scar on my heart, but I came here to bring you that letter because I wouldn't want the responsibility of having separated a mother from her child."

"I can't let him see me. I couldn't bear to see the horror in his eyes."

Anna stared at Elica. In the past, she would have taken the time to encourage Elica. She would tell her how much Theo needed her. Elica always had to be coddled. And, in the past, Anna hadn't minded. But not anymore, not today. "It's your choice. I am giving you this letter. Now it's no longer my responsibility. I know I have done what is right. You have to do what you think is right."

"Do you forgive me, Anna?"

"Yes, I forgive you, but I can't forget what you did. You have my forgiveness, but not for the reasons you might think. I don't want your friendship. I forgive you because I must let go of hate and anger so I can go on with my life. I'm leaving Europe now. I wrote the address of the *kibbutz* where I am going to be living at the bottom of the paper. I don't want to hear from you unless you find out anything about Bernie. And if you find her, please give her my address. Good-bye, Elica."

"But Anna, do you remember we made a pact? We said we would be friends forever. No matter what."

"I remember." Anna looked down at the floor, then brought her eyes to meet Elica's. "But this is where forever ends." Anna then turned and walked out of the house.

When Anna returned to the hotel, she sat down and wrote a letter to Viola at the orphanage, asking if she had any news about Bernie. She sent it that afternoon. But whether the letter ever reached Viola, Anna didn't know because the letter went unanswered.

CHAPTER SIXTY-NINE

1956

I t took eight years from the day those Russian soldiers came to the farm to tell them the war was over for Iwan to make all the arrangements to leave Slovakia and move his family to Israel. However, by the summer of 1956, with the help of several Jewish organizations, they were ready to go. And although Anna had cried when they sold the farm to a young couple, she assured her husband that this was what she wanted. And so, very early on a sweltering morning in mid-July, Anna and her family lined up at the dock. Iwan held Michael's hand, and Anna held Leah's as they waited to board an old ship that would carry them, as well as a handful of Holocaust survivors, away from the horrors they had endured to their new lives in the promised land.

Plans had been made for Iwan and the family to live on a *kibbutz*, a communal farm where everyone worked and lived together. Anna looked around her as they boarded the ship. They were surrounded by a ragged group of people, mostly poor, some maimed, and others psychologically damaged from the torture they endured. But all of them were strong because these were the survivors. Even though the Nazis had employed every possible method they could conjure up to kill them, they were still alive against all odds. They were here and had found the courage to board this ship, headed for an unknown land, and to begin again. The ship's accommodations were poor. People had no beds. They were forced to sleep on the deck and eat whatever was available. But everyone on board was excited. They were all on their way home.

EPILOGUE

1958 Austria, Summer

Elica had just finished hanging several sheets to dry for one of her customers. It was a blistering white-hot day, and her face was covered in sweat. She sat on a chair that she kept outside when she worked because her back had begun to ache lately. She looked down at the skin on her hands. It was peeling again. Perhaps she would be able to find a little extra money for some hand lotion this month. Sighing, she closed her eyes and longed for a glass of something cool to drink. *It has been such a hot July this year.*

"Excuse me," a young man with golden hair had entered her backyard, and now he stood before her, "I'm here looking for a woman by the name of Elica Frey."

"I am Elica Frey," she said, and at first, she was uncomfortable. *Who is this man, and what is he doing here?* Over the past few years, she'd stopped going out of the house. She no longer wanted to face anyone. It was just easier this way. Her mother did the shopping, and all Elica did was stay home, work, and cook. She was flustered by this stranger who had dared to come into her yard. She stood and tried to turn so he could not see her scar. But then... she looked at him. His resemblance to her was uncanny. She was mesmerized by how much he looked like her. For a moment, she forgot herself and turned to get a better look at him. That was when he saw her entire face. It was as if she were struck by a blow when she saw the horror in his eyes. Immediately, he tried to cover his expression with a quick, nervous smile. But it was too late. She'd already seen it.

"I am Enzo Leoni. But you will know me by my other name..." he cleared his throat. "I think you called me Theo."

Elica's hands flew to her face. She felt the tears begin to form behind her eyes. "Theo," she repeated. "Theo. How did you find me?"

"Can we sit down somewhere and talk?" he asked.

"Yes, yes, let's do that. Please, come inside," Elica said.

The house was very sparsely furnished with old used furniture that had been in the family Elica's entire life.

"Please, won't you sit down?" she indicated a chair. "Let me make some tea."

Elica put a pot of water on the stove to boil for tea. Then she sat down across from him and looked at him. He was so handsome that it made her heart ache to look at him. *Once, long ago, I was beautiful like that. My Theo, he grew up to look just like me.*

"So, you wanted to know how I found you?"

"Yes, yes, please. Tell me."

"Well, it's a very long story. But I lived in Switzerland with my adopted mother when a woman came looking for me."

"Switzerland?"

"Yes, Switzerland. My mother took me across the Alps when I was very young. I don't remember it, but she said it was a treacherous journey."

"My goodness," Elica whispered.

"The woman who came looking for me was called Moriah. She asked me if my name was Theo. My mother responded. She said, yes, that you, my birthmother, had called me that."

"Your mother told you that you were adopted?"

"Yes, I have known for as long as I can remember. My mother told me when I was very young. She said she and my father couldn't have children, so they went to the orphanage to adopt a child. They chose me, and because they chose me, it made me even more special."

"Your parents were good to you?"

"Oh yes. I don't remember my father. He died when I was still very young. But my mother has been wonderful. And yes, I have had a good life."

"This woman, Moriah, who was she?"

"She said she was friends with a girl named Bernie. And that Bernie knew you, my birth mother. Before she died, Bernie told Moriah that you lived in Vienna. And your name was Elica Frey."

"Poor Bernie," Elica sighed, and the old guilt came over her again. She could not look directly at Enzo, but continued, "She was a dear friend to me."

"I'm sorry to be the one to tell you. I thought you might already know."

"You mean about Bernie being dead?"

"Yes." Enzo looked down at his feet.

"I didn't know. She was my blood sister," Elica said. There were tears in her eyes.

"Blood sister."

"Yes, just something we did as children. Never mind about it." Then, smiling through her tears, she added, "I'm glad you came to see me. When I look at you, I can see that you are my son. It's written all over your face. I am your birth mother." Tears flowed down her cheeks.

"Do you want to know what happened to Bernie? Do you want to know how she died?"

Elica sucked in her breath. She was dizzy, but she couldn't say no. "Yes, I want to know."

"Moriah told me that Bernie died in the concentration camp. That was where they knew each other. Before Bernie died, she asked Moriah to find me and tell me about you. It was her dying wish."

"Dear God," Elica said. "I wish I could talk to Bernie. I have so many things I wish I could say."

"Bernie told Moriah to go to the orphanage where my parents had adopted me and to ask for a woman named Viola. My mother talks to Viola often. Viola was a nun. She helped my mother escape from Italy and cross the border to Switzerland after my father was hung in the square with Mussolini."

"Mussolini?"

"Yes, my father worked with Mussolini. I have heard that Mussolini was not a good leader. But, like I said, I never knew my father. However, my mother loved him, and although she said nothing, good or bad, about Mussolini, she always told me that my father was a good man. She said he was very kind to his family, anyway. Maybe he was not so good otherwise. I don't know, really. What I do know is that he was a fascist, and he worked for Mussolini. However, Mother has never been political. But, when the country turned against Mussolini, my father was in trouble. And that meant my mother and I were in trouble, too. After my father's death, my mother needed to get out of Italy. That's when she went back to the orphanage to ask for help. And Viola helped her. My mother said Viola told her she had always felt responsible for my well-being because Bernie had left me in her care. When Moriah got out of the camp, she went to Italy to see Viola to fulfill her promise to Bernie. Moriah told Viola everything I just told you. After she finished, Viola brought Moriah to Switzerland to meet me and my mother. That's when I learned that you, my birthmother, might still be alive. That's how I learned where you might be living and how I might find you."

"So you came here not knowing whether you would find me here or even if I would be alive or not?"

"Yes, I did because I wanted to meet you if you were alive."

"How did your adopted mother feel about that?"

"She knows I love her and she will always be my true mother. She raised me. She stood by me through everything. And as you can see, we have been through a lot together. But she understood that I needed to meet you. It was important to me.

"So, tell me, Elica Frey. I know you are my birth mother. But I know little else about you. Who are you? Were you involved with the Nazis? Was my father a Nazi?"

"Oh no. No, Theo, I'm sorry. I mean Enzo. I was married to your father. He was a wonderful Jewish man. Your father. His name was Daniel."

"He was Jewish? I had no idea. Tell me about him, please. Tell me why you gave me up? I need to know that."

As calmly as she could, Elica told her son about his father. She told him how they had been happily married before Daniel had been taken by the Nazis. She explained that she had to go and see if she could help Daniel, so she'd left her son with her friend Bernie. "I planned to return. I never wanted to lose you. But by the time the Gestapo let me go, you and Bernie were gone. You were on your way to an orphanage somewhere in Italy."

"Why didn't you go and look for me?"

"I had no money. Besides, my face was so scared. I was so traumatized. I had nothing to offer you. And I was afraid you'd look at me and think I looked like a freak. Forgive me, please."

He nodded. And finally, after all of these years, he knew why he'd been sent to the orphanage in the first place. It wasn't because his birth parents didn't love him. Elica had left him with her friend to protect him because she knew she was going into the spider's den when she entered the Gestapo headquarters. And she didn't dare risk taking him with her.

"You should have come looking for me. Maybe not right away, but later. Once I was grown up," Enzo said softly. "I would have accepted you no matter what."

Elica quickly wiped a tear that had fallen on her cheek. "I couldn't. I couldn't bear you seeing me the way I am." She indicated her face. "Besides that, I am poor. I had nothing to give you. So, I stayed away, hoping you had a good life, a life I could never give you." She sighed. "But there is something you should know. Not one single year passed when I forgot your birthday. I thought of you all the time. Please, Enzo, I have suffered so much. Please, I am begging you to forgive me."

"Of course I do. You see, the truth is I've had a good life. I was fortunate," he said, smiling. Then he walked over and hugged her tightly. Elica wept in his arms.

He stayed, and they drank tea and talked for several hours. It was getting late, and the sun had begun to set. "I am glad I came to meet you, but I must go now," Theo said.

"Can't you stay for dinner?" Elica wanted to beg him. She'd been so lonely for so long. After he left, she would only have the memory of this day to hold on to.

"I can't. I wish I could, but I have a train to catch. My wife and son are expecting me back home tomorrow. Besides, I've got to get back to work."

"You're married, and you have a child?"

He nodded, "Yes, I am. So that makes you a grandmother."

She wiped her tears with the back of her skirt. "Thank you for coming to see me," she said. "It meant more to me than I can ever say."

"I was wondering if perhaps you would like for me to come again with my wife and child. For Christmas, perhaps?"

"Oh yes, yes I would."

"Good, I'll get the time off from work, and we'll come. Then perhaps we can plan to see each other a couple of times a year. Maybe you can come to Switzerland. I think you would enjoy meeting my mother," he said. Then he smiled as he corrected himself, "My other mother, I mean."

Elica smiled.

After he left, Elica went to the kitchen table and took out a pencil and paper. She wrote to Anna at the *kibbutz*, telling her all that had happened that day.

Dear Anna,

I am grateful for your forgiveness. But that was always your way. You never held a grudge, even when we were young. I suppose you know I have paid dearly for all I've done and never forgiven myself for what I did to you. I know it doesn't matter, but at the time, I was desperate. I saw no other way out. I was weak, young, and stupid. It cost you your family. And then it cost me your friendship. I will never forgive myself for what I did.

But I do have some good news that I will share with you. My son, Theo, came here to Austria to see me today. And even though I never wanted to find him, he finally found me. I know I don't deserve it, but he has graciously forgiven me. However, I am very sad to say that he also shared some terrible information that he received. He met with a woman who knew our friend Bernie. She'd been Bernie's roommate at a place called Ravensbrück. My son said Bernie died there. I thought you might be searching for her, so I wanted to let you know this sad and terrible news so you wouldn't continue searching in vain. Bernie's death is another sin for which I will never forgive myself.

I hope your life is good in Israel. It's so far away, I can't imagine what it's like there. Sometimes I read articles in the newspaper about it. It seems so foreign. A desert. But I am not surprised that you made the move. Anna, you have always had the courage to do the things you felt were right. And I wish you happiness, or at least as much happiness as possible after what we went through. I want you to know that I think of you often as I am terribly lonely. My mother passed away a few months ago. I never thought I would miss her so much. But in the end, she was all I had left. Sometimes, I have dreams at night that transport me back to when we were just children, hopeful and full of aspirations. Who knew what would become of us? We had no idea where our lives would take us. And how all of this might end. Well, I know there is a good possibility that you will not answer this letter. I don't expect it, and I don't blame you. I am sure you want to leave me and everything about me behind. But I just want you to know I am still bound to our promise to be friends forever. So, even with all the mistakes I have made, and believe me, I am so very sorry; I am still left behind living in the past.

Love forever, Elica

Elica sent the letter hoping she would receive an answer, but she was doubtful she would.

———————

Meanwhile, in a country far across the sea, young and full of life, the three young girls sat under a tree. Together, they made a pact while their mothers prepared the afternoon meal in the *kibbutz* Kitchen. This was the country known by the name of Israel. A land where Jews could walk the streets without fear of being persecuted for their religion. A land where they could bear children and not worry that the Gestapo would come for them and arrest them during the night. This was the tiny slice of the world where Anna and her husband, Iwan, finally found peace.

"All right. We are friends forever, right?" Leah, Anna's daughter, said to her two friends.

"Yes, we are friends forever. Forever and ever." Both of her girl-friends answered in unison.

"Then, to ensure we will always be as close as family, here is what we must do. We must make a pact to always be friends and never to let anyone or anything come between us. And once we have sworn on this pact, we must seal it in blood," Leah said.

"Eww, blood. Why do we have to use blood? I hate blood," Elkie said.

"Me too, Elkie. And I hate to cut myself," Miriam, the other friend, said.

"I know, I hate it too. Do you think I like it? But we have to do it. It's the only way the pact will be sealed forever." Leah's voice was filled with logic, as if she were older and wiser than the others.

"All right, Leah. You win. I guess I'll go first," Elkie murmured. "Give me the knife."

But before they could cut themselves, one of the women who worked in the kitchen called out to the girls, "Come on in now, girls. It's time to eat."

"We'll be there in a minute," Leah said.

"Well, you'd better hurry. You don't have time to waste. School is back in session today, and your afternoon classes will start in less than an hour. I want to be sure that the three of you have something to eat before you go to school."

"Yes, Mother," Elkie said. Then she turned to her friends, "We'll have to wait. We'll meet here later tonight. All right? After everyone is asleep."

"All right," the other two answered.

"Blood sister's forever?" Leah said.

"Forever!" the other two answered.

That very same day, Anna received the letter from Elica at the *kibbutz* where she and her family lived. When she saw the return address, her hands shook, and she almost tore up the envelope. But she couldn't. It was time for lunch, but she couldn't go to the main dining room. She needed to be alone to read this letter and to see what Elica had written.

Anna walked outside and sat down under the shade of an olive tree. Then she tore open the envelope, and she read.

She wept as she read about Bernie's fate. Then, still holding the letter in her trembling fingers, Anna closed her eyes and remembered them all, Bernie, Elica, herself, and even Dagna, as they had been so long ago. With the back of her hand, she wiped the tears from her cheeks. Anna steadied herself as she lit a match. Then she took the letter and burned it, watching as the paper was consumed by flames. "Goodbye, blood sisters," she whispered. "This is where forever really ends."

After there was nothing left of the letter but ashes, Anna stood up. She shook the grass off of her skirt. Then she straightened her back and, with her head held high, made her way to the dining room without looking back. She sat at the long table where her new friends, husband, and children were waiting for her.

Iwan had learned a great deal of Hebrew and Yiddish over the years, and now he raised a glass of wine and made a toast. *"L'chaim, to life,"* he said.

**New Series by Roberta Kagan Coming in Summer/Fall 2023
Go to www.RobertaKagan.com and Join
My Mailing List for
First Look Cover Reveals, Exclusive Excerpts,
and More...**

AUTHORS NOTE

I always enjoy hearing from my readers, and your thoughts about my work are very important to me. If you enjoyed my novel, please consider telling your friends and posting a short review on Amazon. Word of mouth is an author's best friend.

Also, it would be my honor to have you join my mailing list. As my gift to you for joining, you will receive 3 **free** short stories and my USA Today award-winning novella complimentary in your email! To sign up, just go to my website at www.RobertaKagan.com

I send blessings to each and every one of you,

Roberta

Email: roberta@robertakagan.com

ABOUT THE AUTHOR

I wanted to take a moment to introduce myself. My name is Roberta, and I am an author of Historical Fiction, mainly based on World War 2 and the Holocaust. While I never discount the horrors of the Holocaust and the Nazis, my novels are constantly inspired by love, kindness, and the small special moments that make life worth living.

I always knew I wanted to reach people through art when I was younger. I just always thought I would be an actress. That dream died in my late 20's, after many attempts and failures. For the next several years, I tried so many different professions. I worked as a hairstylist and a wedding coordinator, amongst many other jobs. But I was never satisfied. Finally, in my 50's, I worked for a hospital on the PBX board. Every day I would drive to work, I would dread clocking in. I would count the hours until I clocked out. And, the next day, I would do it all over again. I couldn't see a way out, but I prayed, and I prayed, and then I prayed some more. Until one morning at 4 am, I woke up with a voice in my head, and you might know that voice as Detrick. He told me to write his story, and together we sat at the computer; we wrote the novel that is now known as All My Love, Detrick. I now have over 30 books published, and I have had the honor of being a USA Today Best-Selling Author. I have met such incredible people in this industry, and I am so blessed to be meeting you.

I tell this story a lot. And a lot of people think I am crazy, but it is true. I always found solace in books growing up but didn't start writing until I was in my late 50s. I try to tell this story to as many people as possible to inspire them. No matter where you are in your life, remember there is always a flicker of light no matter how dark it seems.

I send you many blessings, and I hope you enjoy my novels. They are all written with love.

Roberta

MORE BOOKS BY ROBERTA KAGAN
AVAILABLE ON AMAZON

The Blood Sisters Series

The Pact

My Sister's Betrayal

When Forever Ends

The Auschwitz Twins Series

The Children's Dream

Mengele's Apprentice

The Auschwitz Twins

Jews, The Third Reich, and a Web of Secrets

My Son's Secret

The Stolen Child

A Web of Secrets

A Jewish Family Saga

Not In America

They Never Saw It Coming

When The Dust Settled

The Syndrome That Saved Us

A Holocaust Story Series

The Smallest Crack

The Darkest Canyon

Millions Of Pebbles

Sarah and Solomon

All My Love, Detrick Series

All My Love, Detrick

You Are My Sunshine

The Promised Land

To Be An Israeli

Forever My Homeland

Michal's Destiny Series

Michal's Destiny

A Family Shattered

Watch Over My Child

Another Breath, Another Sunrise

Eidel's Story Series

And . . . Who Is The Real Mother?

Secrets Revealed

New Life, New Land

Another Generation

The Wrath of Eden Series

The Wrath Of Eden

The Angels Song

Stand Alone Novels

One Last Hope

A Flicker Of Light

The Heart Of A Gypsy

Printed in Great Britain
by Amazon

27368013R00172